ALSO BY WILLIAM MALMBORG

DADDY'S LITTLE GIRL

WILLIAM MALMBORG

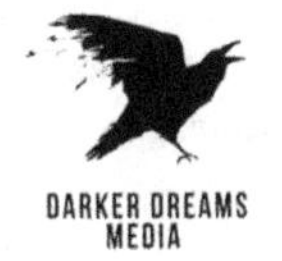

DARKER DREAMS
MEDIA

Darker Dreams Media

Publishers Note: This is a work of fiction. Names, characters, places, and
incidents either are the product of the author's imagination or are used
fictitiously. Any resemblance to actual persons, living or dead, events, or
locales is entirely coincidental.

ISBN-13: 978-0-9962831-8-2

DADDY'S LITTLE GIRL

HEADLINES

From the *East River Times*, April 2, 2002

Local Teen Disappears While Walking Home from School

From the *East River Times*, April 16, 2002

St. Mary's to Hold Candlelight Vigil for Missing Student

From the *Springfield Chronicle*, April 22, 2002

Boyfriend Questioned in Disappearance of Local Teen

From the *East River Times*, April 28, 2002

Family of Missing Teen Offers Reward for Information

From the *Springfield Chronicle*, March 16, 2008

Dateline to Feature Special on Local Teen Who Vanished in 2002

From the *Springfield Chronicle*, April 30, 2008

Ex-Boyfriend of Missing Teen Claims Dateline Portrayal of Him Biased

From the *East River Times*, May 3, 2008

Remains Found in Bell Woods Not Those of 2002 Missing Teen

SPRING 2008

"Honey, wake up."

Misty opened her eyes, confused.

"We have to go," Mommy said, right hand gripping her shoulder.

"What?" Misty asked, blinking away the sleep, her own hand reaching up to help rub the residue away.

She was on the couch in the family room, sunlight gleaming through the tall windows.

"Come on," Mommy urged, giving her an upward tug. "We have to go!"

Something fell to the floor.

What the—?

Harry Potter!

She had been reading the third book on the couch, the words her mommy had taught her during the last several months getting easier and easier to the point where she had secretly gone ahead, her mind having learned something about Harry's uncle that she couldn't believe. Something her mommy didn't know about yet. Something that she couldn't wait for her to uncover during their quiet time before bed.

Something she had planned on acting surprised about so they could share the moment together.

But now Mommy would know that she had gone ahead, that she could read on her own and didn't need her to say the words. And once Daddy found out—

Daddy!

Was he home?

It seemed too early.

"Is Daddy home?" Misty asked, a final blink bringing everything into focus.

"No, not yet. Come on. We have to go. Now!"

Misty frowned. "What are you doing up—"

Blood.

It was on her mommy's blouse, the crimson color impossible to miss against the white fabric, dots of it splattered across her front, getting larger and larger until—

"Mommy? What happened?"

The front left shirttail had been pulled free of her skirt and wrapped around her left hand, the blood from whatever wound was present seeping through.

Rather than answer, her mommy simply gave her another tug, the panic now visible upon her face.

Daddy was going to be mad.

Mommy wasn't allowed upstairs.

She was supposed to stay in the cellar.

And to make sure of that, Daddy had the chains that connected her to the wall. Lots of chains with lots of different cuff links, some high up if she had been naughty so that she had to stay standing all day, others low so she could sit or lie down.

Today had been a low one, her left wrist simply connected to the wall next to her rocking chair, but yesterday, and many of the days before that, had been high ones so that she was on her toes the entire time, Mommy having made Daddy angry several nights earlier. Misty had heard the shouting during their bedroom time, shouting that was so loud that the head-phones and music Daddy told her to listen to wouldn't have kept it out even if she had been wearing them rather than standing by the door, listening.

Misty didn't like it when Daddy left Mommy in the high ones for several days, because then Mommy couldn't use the bucket and made messes on the floor that she had to clean up, which wasn't fun. Cleaning out the bucket wasn't either, but was easier, her fingers able to pinch her nose shut while she carried it to the bathroom to flush down the potty. With the floor, she had to get Daddy's butt gloves, paper towels, and soap, and couldn't pinch her nose shut with her fingers. Even putting a wooden clothespin on her nose didn't keep the stinky from getting through.

"Did you hurt yourself?" Misty asked.

"Honey, come on," Mommy demanded and then gave a good solid yank that pulled her straight off the couch. "We're leaving."

"But Daddy will—"

"Stop calling him that!" Mommy screamed.

Startled, Misty pulled away from her grip, lip quivering, tears appearing.

"Honey, I'm sorry," Mommy said. "Please, come on. We need to leave before he comes back."

A wince followed.

Mommy was in pain.

That's why she was acting like this.

She had hurt herself and now was confused.

So confused that she was trying to leave.

Trying to leave!

No.

Daddy had warned her this might happen, that Mommy might get crazy and try to take her away. He had warned her, and then showed her what she needed to do. Several times.

"I need my shoes," Misty said.

"Where are they?" Mommy asked.

"This way," Misty said, taking her mommy's hand and leading the way to the front door.

Her shoes were really by the back door, for when she went out to the playhouse Daddy had built for her, but Mommy wouldn't know that. Couldn't know that. Not when she was only allowed upstairs when Daddy wanted to spend bedroom time with her.

Mommy also didn't know about the zappy thingy.

Unlike her shoes, the zappy thingy was by the front door, in a slot that Daddy had shown her, and he'd had her practice retrieving it and using it for hours and hours.

The practice had made her good at grabbing it and zapping with it.

So good that Daddy had bought her a Happy Meal from McDonald's, one that had a toy inside. He had also promised that if she ever had to use the zappy thingy on Mommy, he would buy her more Happy Meals and more toys. Better ones than what came with the Happy Meals. Maybe even a doll.

"Daddy! Daddy! Daddy!"

"Whoa, honey, remember what I said about when I first come home."

"I know, I know, I know, but I had to use the zappy thingy!"

Daddy's face changed. "What?"

She took him by the hand and hurried him into the family room, the journey this time around much easier than it had been with Mommy since he could walk. With Mommy, she'd had to drag her by the foot, and though Mommy was skinny, it had still been hard.

"I couldn't get her all the way back downstairs," Misty said as they came upon the stairway banister. "So I put her here and used the handcuffs just like you showed me, only I had to do just one hand because her other hand was hurt."

"Oh my God," he said, his eyes looking down at the thumbless left hand.

"I think Mommy bit herself, because when she woke up again after I zapped her, she started trying to chew on her other thumb. And she kept screaming at me—"

"No, no, no," Daddy said, dropping to his knees in front of Mommy.

"—so I taped her mouth shut, but she kept pulling it off, so I zapped her again and then used lots of tape so she couldn't peel it away." Around and around she had gone with it, using up nearly half the roll, covering everything but Mommy's eyes.

Daddy started peeling the tape away, his voice mumbling things as he worked at it, Mommy's head bouncing around with the frantic pulls as the tape unwound.

During all of this, Mommy stayed sleeping.

It was kind of crazy.

Misty would not have been able to sleep through such a thing. Never. But then Mommy was able to sleep through all kinds of things that would have kept Misty awake, especially those times when she was standing in the chains. Standing like that hurt, Misty having decided to try it once to see what it was like and then having gotten stuck until Daddy came home. He had been so mad at her that he left her like that all night as a punishment for messing around in the cellar, her toes just barely on the ground, the cuffs digging into her wrists, her skirt eventually getting soaked when she could no longer hold her urge to use the bathroom, her screams for him to free her going unheard since sound couldn't leave the cellar. Making that night worse, he had taken Mommy to his bedroom, leaving her all alone.

She had not been able to sleep that night, and now, if she

was the one with her head bouncing back and forth as the tape was unwound, she knew she would not have been able to stay asleep. But Mommy could. Even once the tape was fully gone and Daddy slapped her cheeks several times while shouting at her to wake up, she didn't.

SPRING 2017

ONE

"Cow."

"What?" Ramsey asked, eyes momentarily shifting from the empty road to the passenger seat.

"Another cow," Tess said.

"What are you talking—" Ramsey started, but then, realizing what she was doing, shook his head and looked back at the road, the pavement and the fields it cut through stretching as far as the eye could see. Anger appeared, and for a moment he was going to say something but then decided against it and remained silent.

Tess looked at him, waiting, and then said, "Sorry."

Ramsey didn't reply.

"Sorry!" Tess repeated.

"All my life," Ramsey snapped.

"What?"

"You and Mom, you always tease me about everything I'm passionate about."

"No we don't."

"Yes! You do."

Tess didn't reply to that.

Ramsey took a breath, trying to push the anger back down. It didn't work.

"I'm sorry," Tess said.

This time it sounded sincere.

Ramsey hesitated. He didn't want to say it was okay because it wasn't. He was pissed. Had been for a long time. But he also didn't want the tension to remain, not when they would be in the car together all day. He had to say something. "Thanks." It was all he could think of.

Tess turned and looked at him.

He kept his eyes on the road.

After several seconds, she turned her eyes back to her window and looked out at the field.

"That doesn't really happen, does it?" Tess asked a few minutes later.

"Does what not really happen?"

"Cows flying by the car. We're not going to see anything like that, are we?"

"I don't know. I never have, but it can happen, so..."

Tess shivered.

"Chances are we won't. Not much cattle down here. It's mostly crops. Corn, soybeans, and whatnot."

"Good, because I don't think I could handle seeing that. Poor things."

"Be thankful we're not in Texas. Down there, after a storm, they spend weeks pulling mutilated bodies out of trees, the stench from the rotting parts cooking in the hot sun making it nearly impossible to go outside."

"What?"

"And if the winds within the vortex are strong enough, they'll pull the flesh right off the bone—"

"Stop!" Tess urged. "You're gonna make me sick."

"Speaking of cows, we should find a place to eat soon

before the storms blow up, because once they do—"

"Ramsey, don't."

"Don't what?" he asked.

"Force me into a steak place."

"Tess, I'm not—"

"I will call it quits."

"Quits?" Ramsey asked. "And then what, walk home? We're four hours away."

"You won't leave me behind."

"No?"

"I'll call Mom. She'll come pick me up."

"You'd make her drive four hours just to make a point?"

"What point? I'm just saying, if you try to force me into a steak place, I'm calling it quits and then Mom will be pissed that she had to leave work, and you'll have no one to help you film your stupid twisters."

Ramsey shook his head.

Tess went silent as well.

"You know," Ramsey started, but then stopped.

"What?"

"Nothing."

"What were you going to say?"

"Just that I don't think we're going to be seeing any steak places, and even if we did, I wouldn't drag you into one."

She stared at him.

He turned and stared back.

Suspicion was present in her eyes.

He looked back at the road.

A sign for St. Louis appeared.

With it came a craving for a pork sandwich from Bandana's, which was a BBQ joint he and Courtney used to always stop at while heading west. The two had been best friends in college, their spring and early summer months often spent on the road following the storm systems, video cameras ready to capture the footage that would propel them into the big leagues of the chasing community.

Tess would not approve of a BBQ place.

Shit, she wouldn't approve of anything that focused on meat.

She wasn't a militant vegan, but she was far from being a passive vegetarian. Instead, she had found herself a spot in the middle, one that would allow for those around her to eat the flesh of animals, but only if they accepted her unrelenting scorn as well as the occasional descriptive statement or two detailing how abusive the factory farm industry was.

"How about Cheddar's?" Ramsey asked, a tall sign hovering over a patch of trees in the distance.

"What's Cheddar's?" Tess asked.

"It's like diner food, mom-and-pop style, yet also a chain."

"Hmm…"

The exit was drawing near.

"We need a decision."

"Are we near that place that throws rolls to you?" she asked.

Momentarily confused, it took a second for Ramsey to understand what she was asking, and he eventually said, "Oh, no, that's in Missouri. Like two hours from here."

"Okay, then Cheddar's will do."

"Great." He signaled for the exit and soon found himself keeping the wheel twisted at a hard angle as they looped around a giant curve that backtracked around to the food area. Several other establishments were present as well, though none of them would have met with Tess's approval, so he didn't even offer up the suggestion of trying one of them instead.

"You know, that place got sued," Tess said.

"What place?" Ramsey asked, his eyes shifting around

and absorbing the looks of all those that were staring at them —at Tess—her jet-black hair, leather pants, skintight T-shirt, and leather coat having drawn quite a bit of attention as they walked in and were led to a table.

"The one that throws rolls."

"Oh." He turned his attention away from the looks, not wanting Tess to see that they were getting to him. "Really?"

"Yeah, someone got hit in the face with a roll and the next thing you know, lawsuit." She sipped her water.

"Wow, throwing rolls is their thing. It's what put them on the map."

Tess nodded but didn't say anything else on the subject.

Ramsey sipped his Coke.

"Do you really think we'll see a tornado?" Tess asked.

"For sure. The conditions are perfect. Best I've seen in years. Two to three hours from now, this entire area is going to be pitch-black and sirens are going to be echoing. There'll be an outbreak and it will be record-breaking."

Tess shivered. "Remember when we were kids and that storm came in while we were at the pool and we had to hurry home and then the sirens started going off?"

"Like it was yesterday."

"I've never been so scared in my life."

"Me either."

"We're not going to get that close, are we?"

"No, no, no." He shook his head. "We'll be miles away from the storms, on the front side. That way we can see the tornado as it touches down without any rain blocking our view."

"A couple years ago those storm chasers were killed. They had a Discovery Channel show."

"I know, I remember." He and Courtney had not been out that week, mostly because they hadn't been able to get their shit together in time to head all the way out to the Oklahoma area. That was the one downside of being a storm chaser who lived in Chicago. Getting to Tornado Alley at the last minute could prove difficult. Fortunately, Illinois, Iowa, and Missouri all had dozens of tornadoes every year as well, and those storms were easy to go after with only a day's notice.

"I looked them up the other day after Mom made you ask me to come with," Tess said. "They were experts. Scientists. Not thrill seekers like all those others that go out."

Ramsey nodded. "The storm that hit them was an odd one. A wobbler. And it made a turn that no one expected. Several people died that day and many chasers were injured, but things like that are very rare."

Though he didn't know if it played a part, storm chasing had become so popular in recent years that chasers would often find themselves caught in large back-road traffic jams as all the chasers went after the same storm. Being caught in bumper-to-bumper traffic on an unpaved farm road with nowhere to go for shelter would be a disaster and was one of the new dangers that storm chasers faced. Fortunately, such traffic jams were unlikely to happen with the storms they were chasing. They might see a couple other amateur chasers, but they would be few and far between. "We'll be fine. Nothing to worry about."

With that, their food arrived, both their plates being meatless. Grilled cheese for him, a pasta dish for her.

"I bet this eats up tons of data," Tess said while looking at the iPad screen. "Is this all on the family plan?"

"Yeah, but I pay Mom whenever it goes over," Ramsey said, memories of the first time he had used his phone as a hot spot so that he could have a radar going on his old laptop returning. That bill had been quite the shock. Things were better now, the new plan his mother had gotten for the three of them providing more data than they'd had back when he first chased. Plus, he didn't chase as often as he once had, the ugliness that had unfolded with Courtney having ruined things for quite some time.

Courtney.

He gave a mental sigh and pushed her from his mind.

"See anything yet?" he asked.

"There's a storm southwest of us. I don't see any hook though."

Ramsey could see the storm on the horizon, the cones looking like distant mountains one could spend years climbing. Every now and then a bolt of lightning would dance through the upper layers, eventually making its way down to the earth. No rumbles would follow, the distance too great for them to hear.

"The hook will only appear just as a tornado starts to develop," Ramsey said. "This one is firing, but it may not actually produce a tornado until it's further north—if it does at all. We'll watch it, but I think the ones that are just getting started in Missouri will be better."

"They have a warning on it."

"Tornado?"

"Um…no, just a severe thunderstorm. Hail and high winds."

"I'm not surprised. It's a monster, but not a supercell. Still, you wouldn't want to get caught outside in it."

With that, he pulled over to the side of the road.

"What're we doing?" Tess asked.

"Let's watch it for a bit," he said. "We're in a good position to skirt north and then west once it passes and catch the ones that are crossing over from Missouri."

"Oh, okay."

"Oh my God!" Tess said. "Is that a tornado?"

Ramsey risked a glance in the direction she was pointing, his foot having brought the Kia to eighty miles an hour as they raced to get ahead of a storm that had just had a tornado warning issued on it, one that they were in danger of missing given a detour they had to make thanks to a farm road that had been closed.

Sure enough, he saw a funnel reaching for the ground.

"It is," he said and quickly slowed the car so that they could pull over and film it.

They weren't in the best position, and they had missed the touchdown, which would lower the asking price on the footage if he did try to market it, but it was still a tornado, and if they caught it destroying a structure like a house or a barn, the footage would sell.

"You got the camera?" he asked as they stopped on the shoulder.

"Y-yeah," she said, reaching behind the passenger seat to grab it.

They exited the Kia.

"It's so calm," Tess said, hands getting the camera ready to record.

Ramsey didn't reply, his hand holding his cell phone sideways, filming the storm.

"Eerie even," she added, tracking the tornado with the bigger, professional camera.

Ramsey wanted to remind her to stay quiet while filming. Background commentary made the footage less appealing to the networks. But then he decided against it. This tornado, while classic looking, wasn't going to be marketable. Local news agencies would use it if offered, and it might even make it into a broadcast about the storms in St. Louis or Chicago if no other footage was produced, but the most they could hope to achieve as far as it being valuable would be having their name credit beneath the clip.

Someone honked at them while driving by.

Ramsey shook his head and thought about all the expletives Courtney would have used about the honker once they were back in the car.

Why people felt the need to lay on the horn like that always puzzled him.

It made no sense.

Worse, it could startle one to the point of dropping the camera. Such had never happened to him and Courtney, but they had known chasers who had lost cameras because of it, ones who sometimes had to call it quits for the day because they didn't have a backup, or because they were so distraught about the cost they couldn't focus on the chase.

Fifteen minutes later, the two were heading north, Ramsey having pinpointed what he felt would be a great position for the storms that had developed in Missouri and were now bearing down on the central Illinois area.

"It didn't sound like a freight train," Tess said, eyes on the fold-down mirror, fixing her hair.

"What?" he asked.

"The tornado. Everyone always says it will sound like a freight train, but it was completely silent."

"Well, we were a couple miles away. When it's bearing down on you, things are different."

Tess didn't reply to this right away and when she did, it was with a statement about how she wondered if the storm chasers who were killed had noticed the freight train sound.

Ramsey considered this. "They probably were too terrified to really think about anything other than getting away as it shifted toward them."

"Did you know when Mount St. Helens blew, people in town didn't hear it because the blast was so powerful it actually knocked the sound waves up into the atmosphere rather than directing them at the town."

"Where'd you hear that?" he asked, risking a glance over to her.

"My science course."

"Seriously?"

"You know," she said, slapping the visor mirror closed, "despite what you and Mom think, I do actually pay attention during my classes."

"I didn't say anything."

"You had a tone."

"I didn't."

"You did."

"Okay, if I did, I'm sorry. It was not intended."

"Bullshit."

"Tess, I'm serious—fuck!"

A car was racing up upon them, the lights on top of it flashing.

"Did you know, despite all the media hype on the shootings of police officers, the most dangerous part of the job of a law enforcement officer is the traffic stop?" Tess noted.

"Which class was that one?" he asked.

She gave him a look, arms folded. "I'm just saying, it's pretty dangerous for them to be walking around on the road like that."

"Then maybe they should stop pulling people over," Ramsey said, bitterness present. He had gotten a speeding ticket. His first ever. Even worse, he didn't think they were going to catch the storm that was bearing down on an area north of them, one that had several warnings issued on it given how dangerous it was looking on radar.

"Tickets are an important part of the revenue for the various jurisdictions. People would also get upset if there were no stops, though they don't like being stopped themselves, because everyone feels it makes things safer. Statistically, it doesn't, but the implication that it does is all that people care about."

Ramsey didn't reply to that.

"And you were lucky," she added.

"How so?"

"At the speed you were going, she could have added reckless driving to the ticket, and then you would have had to appear in court. And I'm not certain, but you might not have been allowed to drive after that, which wouldn't be good, since, well..."

Ramsey hadn't considered it, but now that Tess had brought it up, he realized that such a situation would have been a disaster since Tess didn't have her driver's license, their mother having taken it away several days earlier after she had been at a party where booze had been consumed by several underage participants. Not by Tess though. In fact, she had taken keys and driven her drunk friends home, but angry mothers had conferenced about the situation and extracted statements from their own daughters that implicated Tess as having been drinking the most of anyone, and the next thing she knew, their mother had confiscated her driver's license and car keys.

Tess was also grounded, which, in her words, *was total bullshit!*

But such was life.

"I don't think we're going to catch this storm," she said, her focus back on their task.

"We're almost there."

"You said that it's best to be in front of it."

He didn't reply.

"With the speed it's moving at and the distance we still need to go, we will reach the area just as it reaches it too, and that could be dangerous."

"I think we'll be okay," he said.

Tess didn't reply.

They weren't going to make it.

He knew she was right.

Even so, he was going to try, mostly because the storm was bearing down on a small farming town, and if they couldn't get footage of the tornadoes, maybe they could get footage of the destruction. Such footage was marketable, though not in the same way that tornadoes were, and while the storm-chasing community frowned upon marketing such footage, he would do it anyway.

Memories of Courtney unfolded and the fight that had ended their friendship.

He had gotten footage of a body, a teenager, her legs sticking out from the rubble of a house that had been destroyed.

It had looked nothing like the scene from *The Wizard of Oz*, part of the right leg having been ripped open, bone exposed, but he had made a comment about ruby slippers anyway, and then, despite her telling him not to, had uploaded the footage online knowing it would bring attention to their site.

Bring attention it did, but not in a good way.

They were ousted from the storm-chasing community, which then led to him being ousted from Courtney's life.

Oops.

"You have the camera ready?" he asked a few minutes later, the storm looming to the left as they neared the town.

"Yes," Tess said.

"Good, because we are going to be cutting it close."

"Too close," Tess said.

Ramsey didn't reply.

A hailstone hit the windshield with a cracking sound that caused Tess to shout.

Ramsey was startled as well, but kept his foot on the gas.

Another stone hit, causing the passenger side of the glass to spiderweb.

"Fuck!" he snapped.

"The bridge," Tess shouted.

He saw it.

It was about a mile ahead of them.

More hail was falling, and while he couldn't tell exactly how big the stones were, he knew they were large enough to cause serious injury should someone be caught out in them. He also knew the car was going to be a mess.

Another stone hit the windshield, causing a second spiderweb before they made it to the overpass.

Shortly after that, they heard tornado sirens echoing from the town up ahead, one that was about two miles from them if the big blue sign beyond the overpass was correct.

"Are we safe here," Tess asked.

"Yes," he lied.

Despite what many people thought, being under a bridge was not a safe place to be if a tornado came down upon them because it would act as a funnel for all the debris the tornado would be throwing around. Instead, finding a drainage tunnel that went beneath the sides of the bridge would be ideal, just as long as they weren't flooded. Failing that, dropping into the drainage ditch itself would be the best option.

Beyond the bridge, hail bombarded the land.

Ramsey opened his car door.

"Are we filming this?" Tess asked.

"Nah, I just want to get a better look."

Tess did not reply to that and stayed in the car while he approached the edge of the underpass, the sound of the hailstones crashing down echoing within the concrete structure. It was so loud he could barely hear the sirens in the distance.

A stone bounced toward him, settling near his foot.

It was the size of a Ping-Pong ball.

He picked it up and snapped a picture with his cell phone.

"Ramsey!"

He turned.

Tess was halfway between him and the car, shouting his name.

Behind him the hail started to slow.

"Yeah?" he asked.

"I saw a hook," she said, concern present.

"A hook?" he asked, momentarily confused. Then he understood. "I'm not surprised. The sirens are going off in the town."

"No, just now, a new hook."

The hail stopped.

"Where?" he asked and then, sensing something, "Oh shit!"

On cue, a heavy rumble filled the air.

Freight train!

Beyond the bridge, the wind started to pick up, grass, crops, and other pieces of debris flying by.

"What do we do?" Tess shouted, voice barely audible.

Ramsey looked up at the concrete girders near the top angle of the bridge structure, memories of watching footage from the nineties of a TV news crew and a family that sought shelter behind such structures appearing within his head. As a kid, while watching the clip over and over again on his VHS tornado tape, he had desired to experience such a thing. Now he wanted to be anywhere but where they were.

"Ramsey!" Tess screamed.

"Come on!" he shouted and grabbed her hand.

As expected, there was a ditch alongside the road, one that had a tunnel that passed beneath the bridge.

He guided her toward it, Tess screaming something that he couldn't understand given the wind.

"Get in!"

She did, though most likely it wasn't due to his words, but simple common sense when she saw the opening.

He followed.

Inch by inch, foot by foot, Tess worked her way to the center of the tunnel, Ramsey right behind her.

It felt very confining, the sensation made worse for him given that Tess's body was blocking the light at the end.

Panic started to work its way into his system.

He took a deep breath.

Beyond the tunnel the roar of the tornado became deafening, yet amazingly, Ramsey couldn't feel any wind. Not even a trickle. They were safe. And as long as nothing ended up blocking both tunnel ends, they would be fine.

"It's not so bad," Tess said.

Ramsey looked from the car to her and then back to the car.

"I mean, it's still going to be drivable, right?" she added.

Ramsey didn't reply. Couldn't reply. All he could do was stare at the car, one that he had bought brand new last year. One that only had ten thousand miles on it. The windshield was completely gone, as was a wiper. It had also lost its passenger-side window and mirror, and the back windshield had a hole through it.

He opened the driver-side door.

Glass spilled out onto the pavement.

"I bet it was a fence post," Tess said.

"What?"

"That went through the windshield." She hesitated, studying the car. "Actually, it probably went through the back window first and came out the front."

Ramsey simply nodded.

"Whoa!" Tess shouted. "Look."

Ramsey followed her finger.

The large blue sign that announced the exit ahead was mangled, the metal having been twisted around and crushed in such a way that some might view as artwork, had a famous sculptor designed it. Ramsey did not. He viewed it as a testament to how lucky they had been.

Get a picture.

He did, the storm-chaser side of him kicking into gear, his phone documenting the aftermath of the twister.

And then Tess was at his side, video camera in hand.

"It still works?" he asked.

"Yeah," she said. "And there isn't a scratch on it."

"Holy shit."

"You were right."

"About what?"

"About how crazy tornadoes can be. Didn't you say you've heard stories about how houses would be destroyed, but then they would find a carton of unbroken eggs from the same house a mile away? Or that people have been pulled from houses and set down in fields without a scratch on them."

"Yeah, there are stories like that."

"Well, this camera can now be a part of all that."

Ramsey nodded, though honestly, he didn't think that a camera surviving inside a car that had something fly through the windshield was as remarkable as a carton of eggs being carried a mile and set down unbroken. Had the car been picked up and thrown a mile with the camera going unscratched, then that would be something.

"Shit."

"Is it live?" Tess asked.

"Only one way to find out, go touch it."

Tess glared at him.

"We'll have to find another way into town."

"There was a road back there," Tess said.

"Yeah?" Ramsey questioned, head twisted back toward

the rear window, eyes looking straight through the hole as he made a three-point turn. "Well, let's try that and see where it goes."

The road no longer had a street sign and only went south, but it seemed to be their only option, and since it was paved, Ramsey decided it was worth a shot.

Half a mile later, another road connected with it, making a T. Once again, no signpost was visible.

"Is it on the map?" Ramsey asked.

Tess didn't reply right away, her finger tracing their route from the interstate to the exit they had taken, toward the road they were currently staring at. "I think this is it," she said, looking up for a moment and then back at her phone, eyes squinting.

The iPad had not survived.

From where he sat, Ramsey could just make out what appeared to be a town near her finger, one that he guessed was the same town the exit sign had promised: Smallwood.

"Yep, this is it," Tess confirmed. "And it runs parallel to the town, so we should be able to cut over after about two miles or so."

"Okay, great," he said, hands guiding the vehicle into the turn.

"This town is not going to have any power," Tess said four minutes later, the two having been blocked by more downed power lines.

"Yeah, and how long do you think it will take for ComEd or whoever services it to get all the way out here?" Ramsey asked, trying to mask his frustration.

Tess started thinking about this, finger in the air as she pretended to calculate the time within her mind.

"It was rhetorical," Ramsey said while making another three-point turn, this one much more difficult than the previous one given how narrow the road was. "Why don't you find us a new route into town?"

"There was a road about a quarter mile behind us. It goes to the south. If we take that, we will be parallel again to the town, just further away from it, and then can cut across.

"Okay."

"That was a house, wasn't it," Tess said.

"Yeah," Ramsey confirmed.

It had stood in the center of a field, one that was now scattered with debris that had once been the house and barn, nothing but the foundation and part of the first-floor wall standing.

"Should we head over there and see if anyone needs help?" Tess said.

"Do you see anyone moving around?"

"No."

Ramsey hesitated, debating whether or not they should stop. Eventually he decided against it, the lack of movement around the house making him think that if there were survivors, they were trapped somewhere and that the best option was getting emergency personnel to them because they would need equipment and expertise to rescue them.

"The best help we can get anyone out here is getting to town and letting them know where exactly the tornado hit," he said. "They'll know who was home and who wasn't and how to account for those that are missing and whatnot."

"Okay."

They continued onward, heading south on the road that Tess had directed them toward to get around the power lines, eyes peeled for the road that would take them west again.

A few minutes later, they found one and turned onto it, their eyes spotting another house that had been leveled.

Once again, no one was moving near it.

"I hope they got into a storm shelter," Tess said as they passed by.

"Me too," Ramsey said.

"Do you think this was the same tornado that passed over us at the bridge?"

"I think ours was too far south to have been the one to hit these farms," Ramsey said. "Unless…"

"Unless what?" she asked.

"It takes a very strong tornado to level houses this completely. F-four or F-five. Maybe a strong F-three, but…I'm thinking it was a four. What got us might have been the edge of the tornado if it was a four or five. That's probably why the car survived as well as it did. Had a four or five passed directly over us, it would have taken the car right out from under the bridge or smashed it up against the girders."

"But what about the sign? It was pretty mangled."

"The edge of a tornado could do that. Those signs are tough but don't stand a chance against a tornado. An F-two would do that."

"Hmm."

The more he thought about it, the more he felt that a separate, smaller tornado had been at the bridge, maybe one that had spun off from this larger one. All that, however, was something the experts would decide based on what the radar had shown and what eyewitnesses had seen and measured damage paths. Right now, for them, all that mattered was getting into town so that they could get the car looked at and, hopefully, find a place to stay while it was assessed.

Another farmhouse appeared south of them, this one only partially damaged.

Around it a family was moving about surveying the damage.

Their movements were exploratory rather than frantic, which meant they were likely all okay. When a member was injured, the rest of the family wouldn't be taking a stroll around the house looking at the damage; they would be taking the injured member to the hospital.

The next house hadn't been so lucky and like the others they had seen, it was leveled.

"You know what the one positive thing about this is?" Ramsey said.

"What?" Tess asked.

"This was farmland and everything is spaced out. Can you imagine if this tornado had gone through a suburb area, or even the downtown area where houses are side by side?"

"Oh."

Nothing else followed.

They continued down the road, moving at a crawl given the lack of a windshield, both looking around at the destruction the storm had wrought, eyes peeled for situations that might require their immediate help.

"Turn up here," Tess said after several minutes of nothingness.

Ramsey did and nearly cried out as a figure emerged from the field, the white from her dress the first thing he saw as she came at the hood of the Kia, a hand held up to stop them.

Had they been going faster, Ramsey might not have been able to brake in time, but given the gentle speed, the Kia came to an easy halt.

"Help," the girl muttered, a hand to her head.

Blood was present, most of it on the side of her face, but some standing out on the dress she wore.

And then she fell, her legs simply giving out, body crumpling onto the hood of the car and then down the side near the passenger tire.

Ramsey and Tess both jumped from the vehicle, Tess getting to her first given that they were on the same side.

The girl wasn't unconscious, but she was delirious, likely from whatever had struck her in the head.

"It's okay," Tess cooed, one hand holding the girl's left hand while the other was against her back, steadying her. "You're okay."

Ramsey knelt down beside her.

She stared at him with wide eyes, ones that took a moment to focus.

"Can I see?" he asked, hand motioning to her head.

It took a second for her to comprehend what he was asking. Once she did, she gave a slight nod and removed her hand.

A huge swollen bump was present, blood marking where the scalp had torn.

"Are you hurt anywhere else?" Ramsey asked.

Once again, it took a moment for her to comprehend and then she said, "No."

"Okay, that's good," he said and then looked her up and down just in case she was unaware of any injuries that her body was masking.

Nothing beyond the head wound seemed to be present, and all the blood on her dress was likely from that given how much the head would bleed when the scalp was broken.

"Can you tell me your name?" he asked.

"I-I-" She blinked several times and shook her head, hand going back up to touch her wound.

"Ramsey," Tess said, eyes motioning toward the girl's wrist, the sleeve of her dress having come undone and fallen to her forearm.

A nasty-looking rope mark encircled the flesh.

Ramsey reached for her other wrist, the girl watching him as he carefully unbuttoned the cuff and rolled back the sleeve.

A rope mark encircled the flesh around that wrist as well.

Seeing this, Tess looked at him, concern present.

Ramsey looked around to see if anyone else was near.

No one seemed to be.

Rain began to fall.

"Let's get you into the car," Ramsey said.

The girl didn't resist or protest, her hands simply reaching out for their arms as they helped her up.

"I got her," Ramsey said once they were at the back door of the Kia. "Why don't you open it and make sure we got all the glass out?"

Tess nodded.

A few seconds later, she gave the all clear and together they helped the girl into the back seat.

TWO

"*I don't know how many twisters,*" her father's voice echoed, "*but right now it looks like the worst of it was west and south of town. I've counted at least twenty houses that were completely destroyed, others that are still standing but will probably have to be torn down, countless mangled vehicles that were thrown from God knows where, and at least*" —he paused—"*Lindsey, if you're listening, I want you to turn it off right now.*"

Lindsey felt a chill and started to reach for the switch on the scanner, but then realized that there was no way her father would know whether or not she complied with his instruction, not unless she told him later, and she let her hand fall back to her side.

"*I've counted four dead bodies so far. Two of them I've identified as locals. The others were in cars that may have been picked up from the interstate or some other road and tossed into the fields. There are also tons of power lines down. I've flared three areas where road-ways are compromised, but I'm guessing there are several more that need to be marked.*"

Nothing else followed for several seconds.

Lindsey had thought her father was going to mention a name she would recognize. Maybe he had been planning on it but then, realizing she would likely have ignored his instruction to turn off the scanner, decided against it.

Oscar?

He had been planning on driving over after school, the two having agreed to spend the afternoon together since her father was working the three to eleven shift.

Had he gotten caught in the storm? Was his one of the vehicles her father had spoken of?

Mentally, she urged her father to confirm or deny it, but all that followed on the scanner were reports from other officers about more power line situations and vehicles they had found that were crushed like tin cans.

One also advised that one of the goalposts on the south side of the football field had been mangled, but that the school itself seemed okay and could serve as a shelter for those who were now homeless or without power.

Five minutes drifted away, and then ten.

Reports of more dead bodies came in, but none of them were named.

Nothing about Oscar echoed.

She looked down at her phone.

The battery was at five percent.

Past experience told her that if she tried to make a call, the phone would die, and plugging it in was not an option since the power was out.

On my way, his last text had read.

She had followed it with a *Yay!* And then, as the sky darkened, *Hurry!*

A "Read at 3:16" note sat beneath the text bubble.

She typed, *You OK?* And hit Send, eyes watching as it was delivered, waiting for a "Read" note to appear.

None did.

Could he still be driving?

If so, he could at least pull over and send a message letting her know he was okay.

Or ask if I'm okay!

Anger appeared but then was replaced by dread.

Oscar had not asked if she was okay, and he would have following the storm. He was a good guy, and even if his motivation for coming over was because she had promised to give him a squeaky, she knew that he cared about her deeply and those feelings toward her and his desire to spend time with her were a foundation that everything else was being built upon.

What if his body is right outside?

What if he was pounding on the door to be let in while you were in the basement curled up in the corner?

Once the thought was planted, she had no choice but to check and stepped out the front door.

Holy shit!

Tree branches were everywhere, as were pieces of debris, the street and yards littered with chunks of what had once been walls and floors and roofs. Even a toilet had been ripped free and thrown, sod torn up where it had skidded to a halt fifteen feet from the front door.

Fortunately, all the houses on her block were standing, though most were missing shingles.

Siding had been peeled away as well.

And the trees had all been shorn, the spring blossoms completely gone, along with many branches, each one looking as if it had gone back in time by a month.

"Crazy, isn't it?" a voice said, causing her to jump.

Dennis, a boy she had grown up with and had been friends with during grade school, was standing by the front porch.

"Yeah," she replied.

"I guess it was coming right for us and then just fizzled out over by the school." He smiled. "Must have known I have a math test tomorrow."

"Must have," she said, eyes still taking in all the debris.

"Can you imagine? It was so powerful that it sucked up all this stuff and then threw it all over the neighborhood as it spun itself out." He pointed. "I mean, look, you've got a freaking toilet in your yard. Chances are someone was shitting in it this morning, and now it is in your yard."

Lindsey turned and gave him a look.

"And soon the looters will come out," he added.

"Looters?" she asked, shaking her head. "No one is going to be looting anything."

"Just wait," he said.

She felt a buzz from her phone and looked down.

You OK? the text read.

It wasn't from Oscar, but from her friend Gloria.

Yeah, she typed and hit Send.

"That him?" Dennis asked.

"Him?"

"Oscar," he said. "Bet he's bummed."

"Bummed?"

"He was coming over, wasn't he?"

"What?"

"Wait, he wasn't coming over?"

"What are you talking about?" she demanded. Then, remembering that the two had gym class together in the afternoon, asked, "Did he say something to you about coming over?"

"To me, no. But I overheard him talking with Tony and Mike."

"And?"

"And what?" Dennis asked.

"And what was he saying?" she urged.

"Just that he was going to your place after school and that your dad wouldn't be there."

Lindsey stared at him, horrified that Oscar had been so vocal about a get-together that needed to stay a secret because her dad would kill them if he found out.

"Oh, and something about how Tony better not have poked any holes in it."

Lindsey's eyes went wide. "Holes in what?"

"I don't know, they were on the other side of the lockers."

Lindsey couldn't find any words.

"Anyway, glad you're okay. Seems we got lucky."

"Yeah," she muttered, eyes going back to the debris.

More people were out and about now, looking around their homes, studying the damage.

Twenty-five minutes earlier, they had all been huddled in basements, awaiting destruction as the roar of the storm descended upon them. She had been one of those people, knees pulled up to her chest, arms around them, tears gushing. Death had been lurking, waiting, and now it wasn't. She should have been overcome with happiness at having been spared, the volume of debris all over the place evidence of how powerful the tornado had been, yet the only thing she could think about was Oscar and how he might have been telling everyone they were going to be having sex.

Were we?

She had promised to touch him, to reach into his pants and explore his manhood.

They had talked about it at lunch, while in his car, their hands having already done some on-top-of-the-clothes stuff, which she had liked. His fingers on her breasts, gently rubbing her nipples through the tight shirt and bra she had been wearing, a sensation of them trying to poke free of the material appearing. And she had felt him through his pants, her fingers reaching beyond the bump to cup the underside of his testicles, Liz having told her guys really liked that.

Afterward, walking back to class had been difficult, especially for him given his obvious arousal.

At no point had she said they would do anything that would require the use of a condom, yet from what Dennis had heard, Oscar obviously had gotten one from his friends, which meant he was expecting them to have sex.

She shook her head.

That would have been too much.

Touching each other she was fine with.

Her hands on him while his fingers were inside her—it was something she had actually been looking forward to. She had even considered using her mouth on him, though wasn't fully sure that she would go that far. Questions on what such an act was like had been voiced to Liz, her boasting about having swallowed her boyfriend while at a party having intrigued Lindsey and Gloria, but how exactly such an act was pleasurable to the giver was still a mystery.

"Does it taste like pee?" Gloria had asked.

"No, gross!" Liz had replied.

"Well, then what?"

Liz struggled for an answer and finally said, "You just have to experience it to understand what it's like."

Gloria had grimaced and said, "I don't know."

Lindsey, however, had been intrigued, though she didn't dare voice that.

Liz had then reminded them to make sure their boyfriends reciprocated. "Teach him how to use his tongue early on so that you're not the only one going down."

Thoughts on that and what it would feel like had dominated her mind for days, and it was something she really wanted to experience. Something she had been hoping would unfold that afternoon.

An odd laugh escaped her lips at the thought.

Nothing like that would happen today or at any point in the near future. Of this she was certain.

She looked down at her phone.

Still nothing from Oscar, not even a "Read at" note beneath the most recent text she had sent him.

He's dead.

She wasn't sure how she knew this, but the certainty of it was impossible to dismiss.

Her phone buzzed.

She looked down.

It was her dad.

"Hey, honey, sorry I didn't call earlier," Norman said, his eyes watching for washouts and mud patches that could lock up his tires on the old gravel road as he navigated himself farther into the southern outskirts of town. "I was pretty busy with—"

"Dad!" Lindsey said, cutting him off. "My phone is about to die and we have no power for me to charge it."

"Just plug it into the car."

The silence that followed put a smile on his face, mostly because it was becoming a rare thing to be able to suggest something to his daughter that she hadn't already figured out for herself. Such moments were to be cherished.

"Oh my God, I feel so stupid," Lindsey said, the sound of the car starting echoing in the background.

He considered making a joke about how he never would have thought about plugging a phone into the car outlet when he was her age, but then decided against it as his eyes caught sight of a vehicle in a field.

Van?

It was about fifty yards from the road, on its driver side, and while it did not appear to be mangled like some of the other vehicles he had seen, the fact that it had ended up so far from the road meant it had probably been bounced around pretty hard.

"Honey, I need to check something out," he said, trying to keep the horror of what he might discover from his voice.

"What is it?" she asked.

"Looks like a van." He spotted a VW logo on the front. "Shit, it's an old Volkswagen."

"Anyone we know?"

"Not with one like this. It looks like it was driven straight out of the sixties."

"What do you mean, like tie-dyed and peace signs?"

"No, just green, but the model. I haven't seen one like this since college." He shook his head. "I need to go check and make sure no one's hurt. I'll call you back in a bit."

"Okay," Lindsey said.

"And if you need anything, don't hesitate to call Judy."

He heard a grimace on her end.

Lindsey was not fond of Judy, and though Judy tried to pretend she enjoyed the company of Lindsey, Norman knew it was a front. The two hated each other, and there was nothing he could do to change it.

"I think I'll be fine," Lindsey said.

"Oh, I'm sure you will be," Norman said, eyes still on the vehicle, looking for movement. He did not want to see another mangled body. "And the weather people are saying the worst of the storms are finished for our area, so all should be good from here on out."

"Yeah," she said.

"Anyway, I have to go. I'm not sure when I'll be back in, but I'll keep you posted on what's going on."

"Okay."

"Love you."

"Love you too."

The call ended.

Norman tucked the phone into the cubby by the cup holders and stepped from his cruiser, feet taking him toward the vehicle, eyes still on the lookout for movement or any other sign of life.

Nothing.

If anyone was still inside, they were probably dead.

Bracing himself for such a discovery, he crouched down to peer through the broken windshield.

No one was in the two front seats.

Blood was present on the driver seat and window, which was cracked.

He looked up at the passenger door and then beyond it to the side door.

A bloody handprint was present.

It looked like someone had climbed up through the door and then sat atop the vehicle for a moment, bloody hand on the surface, before jumping down.

An impact point in the mud marked the landing point.

But where had they gone?

Tracks went around the van and headed off toward an old farmhouse in the distance, one that looked to have been spared by the tornado.

He had no idea who—if anyone—lived there.

No one was out and about, which was kind of odd given that the typical homeowner would want to check to see if there was any damage following a storm. And if an occupant from the van had gone there for help, it would seem like there would be some sort of commotion.

Unless the person that had started toward the house didn't make it.

For all he knew, the homeowners could be inside, oblivious to an injured person that had collapsed while walking toward them for help.

He started toward the house, his foot crunching upon something with his first step.

Keys.

He reached down and pulled them free from the mud.

Surprise appeared.

Two of the keys were typical and looked to belong to the van and the front door of a house or apartment. The third wasn't typical, not unless the owner was a member of law enforcement, since it was a universal handcuff key.

Now that she knew her phone wasn't in danger of dying, Lindsey tried calling Oscar while sitting in the garage, vehicle running, phone plugged into the lighter.

The call went straight to voicemail.

She left a message asking if he was okay and begging him to call her as soon as he got the message.

Following that, she went online to check his Facebook and Instagram pages, but nothing new had been added to either.

Will Facebook do one of those "check in" things? she wondered.

With terrorist attacks they did, and for hurricanes, but those incidents seemed to be large scale, whereas a tornado going through a small Illinois town wasn't. Then again, the tornadoes were hitting all over the place throughout Missouri and Illinois, so maybe that would trigger some sort of regional check-in.

If so, nothing had been started yet.

Her phone buzzed.

She looked at it.

Gloria again.

Liz lost her house, the text read.

What? Lindsey asked back.

Call me.

Lindsey did.

"Lindsey," Gloria answered.

"Yeah," Lindsey said. "What do you mean she lost her house?"

"It's gone. Completely."

"Fuck, is she okay?"

"Yeah, she's fine. Shaken, but fine. They have a storm

shelter out there. Like away from the house or something. They were in it."

"That's good."

"Yeah, but she can't find Gizmo."

"Oh no."

Gizmo was Liz's cat, a large orange tom that roamed her family's farm taking care of mice, birds, and snakes, the sight of him once coming in from the field with a dead corn snake in his mouth something that Lindsey would never forget. Though vicious while on the hunt, Gizmo also had a gentle side that saw him curling up in laps where he would purr for hours. He also apparently slept with Liz, often joining her during the first part of the night, then leaving to head out through the kitchen cat door to hunt, and then coming back during the wee morning hours.

"She's pretty upset," Gloria said. "I told her he probably found a place to hide during the storm and is just spooked right now, but that didn't seem to help her calm down. Anyway, she wants to know if we can come out and help her look for him."

"Right now?"

"Yeah, she's worried that if she doesn't find him before it gets dark and if he comes back and finds the house gone, he will think they've abandoned him and he'll leave." Gloria sighed. "She's a complete wreck right now."

"I don't think driving around is a good idea," Lindsey said. "My dad says there are power lines down all over the place and debris everywhere. We might not even be able to get to her place, especially if that is where the tornado hit."

"Come on, Lindsey, we have to at least try."

Lindsey didn't reply.

"She would help us if it was the other way around," Gloria added.

"I know, you're right. It's just…I don't know."

"Come on, what else are you going to do? Sit around in the dark for the rest of the day?"

She has a point, Lindsey said to herself.

Gloria also needed Lindsey to drive since she didn't have a license yet.

But what about Oscar?

Something was wrong. He was either hurt or worse, and his phone was either off or had been destroyed.

Whatever the situation was, sitting around her house in the dark wasn't going to help him. Instead, she would simply focus on the conversation he'd had in the locker room that Dennis had overheard and what it all meant.

"Lindsey?" Gloria asked.

"Yeah, I'm here, was just thinking."

"Well?"

"Okay, I'll help."

"Great. I'll be over in a second."

"Okay."

Gloria was one street over.

Lindsey reached up and hit the garage clicker and then shifted to back up.

The garage door did not open.

Puzzled, she hit it again, only then realizing that with the power out, she would have to open it by hand.

Idiot, an inner voice said as she stepped out.

A cloud of exhaust enveloped her.

Oh fuck!

Lips squeezed shut, she hurried over to the door and tried lifting it, but it would not budge.

How the…

And then she remembered, her right hand quickly twisting the handle on the inner part of the door over to manual and then shoving it upward.

Air rushed in as the exhaust rushed out, Gloria appearing

at the end of the driveway as Lindsey hurried from the dark garage, taking a deep breath.

"Whoa! You okay?" Gloria asked.

"Fucking almost killed myself."

"What?"

Lindsey explained about her phone being almost dead and charging it up while in the car.

"And you sat in there the entire time?" Gloria said. "Smart move."

"I was talking to my dad," Lindsey said. "And then you."

She didn't say anything about Oscar, mostly because she didn't want to think about the possibility of him being dead. Or dwell upon the fact that he had been bringing over a condom.

Gloria waved her words away and said, "Do you think we should bring water or something?"

"That's not a bad idea."

They headed inside and into the kitchen.

Cool air billowed out from the dark fridge, Lindsey quickly grabbing bottles of water and soda, which she handed over to Gloria, who put them on the counter.

"Such a waste," she said as the fridge door closed.

"What?" Gloria asked.

"All the stuff in the fridge. We went shopping last night, me and my dad since it was his day off, and now all of it is going to spoil."

"Maybe they'll get the power back on in time."

"Maybe," Lindsey said, though she knew they wouldn't. Last time a storm had knocked out power, it had taken two days for it to come back on, and there hadn't been any tornadoes with that one. This time around, entire areas of the town had been destroyed, as well as other towns all across the state. They would be lucky to have power on by the weekend. She looked at the water and soda. "Anything else you can think of?"

"Have a cat whistle?"

"Ha, I wish." She hesitated and then, "Do you really think this is a good idea?"

"Honestly, no," Gloria said. "But…"

"But…"

"I think it will help Liz. Even if we don't find him, which we probably won't, it will keep her mind off the fact that she lost her house and make her feel like she is doing something productive and isn't helpless."

"Yeah."

"And afterward we can all come back here and hang out or something while her parents go…shit, where does someone go after their house has been destroyed?"

"A motel?" Lindsey suggested. "That one north of town?"

"That'll help what, twelve families?"

"Isn't there one north of here at the exit? The big exit with the McDonald's."

"Yeah, there's that.

"And there's one over in Smith's Grove."

"Okay, I guess they'll all go to those ones, if they can find transportation." Gloria looked around. "You have a bag or something that we can put all this in?"

"Yeah." Lindsey opened up a cabinet and pulled out a brown paper bag that the groceries had come in and handed it over.

Gloria filled the bag and then asked, "Should we bring any food? Snack items, things that might go bad."

Lindsey thought about it for a moment and then shook her head. "This stuff is fine. We won't be out there very long."

"Yeah, you're right."

"Let's go."

It took Norman eight minutes to walk to the old farmhouse.

No bodies were present during the journey.

He was also surprised by the lack of debris, though figured that was likely due to how spaced out the homes were in the farm areas. Back in town, things were different, Judy having called him to advise that while his street had been spared, many of the neighborhoods around it hadn't been, and debris was everywhere.

"*Aside from needing some new shingles, your place looks pretty much untouched,*" Judy had said. She had then offered to go get Lindsey if he liked, but he had told her that wasn't necessary and that he was going to call her in a second.

That second had turned into ten minutes given that he had come upon a car with a body inside, one that looked like it had gone through a crusher in a junkyard.

Cars and houses.

Two hours earlier, they had all been fine. Now...

He shook his head.

It was amazing how quickly things could change.

He spotted the doorbell and pressed it.

No one answered.

He pressed it again and then knocked several times.

Still nothing.

He stepped back and studied the house, wondering if it was one of the many that had been abandoned during the last several years. If so, it had done well thus far given that the front door and all the windows he could see were still intact.

A noise echoed from beyond the house.

It sounded like a crash or slamming of some kind.

He walked along the front porch until he came to the side of the house. "Hello?"

Nothing.

Steps led down to the gravel of the driveway, which he followed to the rear of the house where a large round area for parking and turning around was present. Beyond it, the gravel continued and led to a barn.

The door to it was halfway open and moving with the wind.

Could it have been what slammed?

At home, they had a back door with a screen that occasionally would come unlatched, and when the wind caught it and threw it into the frame, it sounded like the entire house was about to come down.

The entire house almost did come down.

If the tornado had continued eastward through the school and beyond...

He shook the thought away and called out once again.

All was still for several seconds, his feet about to turn himself around so that he could head back to the patrol vehicle and radio in to see if maybe the county itself had helped at the van but failed to mark it, when a young lady stepped through the partially opened door, a shovel in hand.

She stopped when she saw him, startled.

"Hi," Norman said, eyes instantly spotting a look of terror on the girl's pale face, one that she was trying, but failing, to mask. "Everything okay?"

"Y-yes," she said and forced a smile, hand leaning the shovel against the barn wall. "It missed us."

"You were lucky," he said and took a step closer. "Are your parents here?"

"Yes," she said, a hand smoothing her hair. "We're all okay."

Something was off, but he couldn't put his finger on it.

"You know, there's an overturned van in your field." He took another step. "Did anyone come by asking for help?"

"Help? N-no." She shifted her eyes toward where the van would be, the house blocking the view, and then back at him, all while her body trembled. He then noticed something running down her leg where it emerged from her skirt.

Jesus, she just pissed herself.

"Are your parents in the barn?" he asked and started toward it.

"Um…no, they—"

"Mind if I take a look?" he asked.

"Um…go ahead," she said, hand motioning him toward the door.

Norman gave her a nod and then started toward the door, the darkness within heavy despite the fact that the afternoon sun was out and once again shining upon the land.

He stepped through the doorway.

A muffled moan echoed.

He squinted, his eyes taking a moment to adjust. Once they did, he saw a teenage girl on the floor, wrists behind her back, knees and ankles bound, mouth gagged.

Shit!

He spun just as something came at his head, the object catching him square in the face, the crack of his nose and a spurt of blood registering within his mind.

Another shovel blow landed.

Sparks flashed.

He staggered several feet, his eyes momentarily clearing before everything went dark again.

THREE

"No, Mom…no…I wasn't being reckless. No. We got caught in a hailstorm and took shelter under a bridge and then a tornado hit the bridge. It wasn't—" Ramsey went silent. "No, we're going to have to stay here tonight. At the local high school. The police are setting up cots and stuff for everyone that lost their homes." He listened some more. "Mom, I know, but it would take forever and the entire town is a mess with power lines down all over the place and it's going to be dark soon." More listening. "It will be better to wait until tomorrow."

Tess watched without comment, a plastic cup of water in her hand.

"Yeah, we'll call you tomorrow once we have more information," Ramsey said. "Love you too. Bye."

"Mom's mad," Tess said.

Ramsey gave a "so so" wave and said, "I think she's more concerned than mad. And confused. She wants us to call the roadside help number on the insurance card. I told her it wouldn't do much good, but she doesn't seem to get it. I mean, what are they going to do, bring us a windshield tonight, in the dark, and install it on the car so we can then drive home?"

"How are we going to get home?" She didn't like the idea of staying in the high school. Not when they would be surrounded by tons of people they didn't know, all of whom were probably friends with each other and would have all their own little groups.

"I don't know," Ramsey said with a sigh. "Most likely we'll have to have it towed somewhere. I'll call the roadside line on the insurance card tomorrow and see what they say. If worse comes to worse, we'll have to simply drive it home the way it is."

"We can't do that," Tess said.

Ramsey didn't reply.

"You've seen what a tiny rock will do to a windshield when kicked up on the highway. Now imagine that is your face."

"Yeah, you're right."

"And you have no mirror."

Ramsey nodded.

She took a sip of her water and once again thought about the high school and cots. Would everything be sterile, or had the cots, blankets, and pillows been used before and then just tossed into a storage area?

She shivered.

"You okay?" Ramsey asked.

"I just want to go home," she said.

"Yeah, me too."

"I told you not to try and catch the storm."

Ramsey looked away.

"You told Mom you weren't being reckless, but you were. You were driving over eighty miles an hour and you tried to catch a storm as it hit the area, which you've said is the most dangerous thing a storm chaser can do."

He did not reply.

"And you didn't even tell her about finding the girl or that the police are now—"

The door to the room opened, a uniformed woman stepping inside.

Silence followed.

"My name is Lieutenant Bell," she said after studying them for a moment, her gaze lingering on Tess's outfit longer than was necessary. "I understand you two are the storm chasers that found the girl?"

"Yes," Ramsey said with a nod.

"Though given the damage to your car, it looks like the storm chased you this time around."

"He tried to catch it even though he knew it was too far for us to get around," Tess said, arms crossed. "He drove right into it."

"Tess."

"We had to seek shelter under a bridge and then in a drainage pipe."

"Tess!"

"What?" Tess demanded. "It's true."

"Yeah, well, you don't have to give everyone we talk to a play-by-play of how I fucked up, okay." He sighed and then turned to the officer. "When can we head over to the high school?"

"In a bit." She paused to grab a chair and took a seat. "Tell me about the girl."

"We already told the first—" he started, but then let out a frustrated sigh. "We were simply driving down a farm road trying to find our way into town when she ran out asking for help."

"And?" Lieutenant Bell asked after several seconds.

"And then we brought her here."

"Ramsey, don't be a dick," Tess said. She turned to the lieutenant. "We thought she had simply been asking for help because of the storm. Like her house had been destroyed or something. But then we saw the marks on her wrists and thought we should get the police because it looked like she had been tied up."

"And was this near a house that had been damaged, one that she might have come from?"

"I don't remember seeing any in that particular area," Ramsey said. "Some further down the road had been destroyed, and there were lots of power lines down, but the houses themselves were so spaced out from each other, and so far from the road, that it was hard to even tell where they would be unless we could see the rubble in the distance or knew where one should be."

"What about a vehicle? Did you see any that she might have been in and crawled from?"

"No, I didn't," Ramsey said. He looked at Tess, who gave a similar answer.

"How far were you from 39? Do you think she could have been in a vehicle that was thrown from it?"

Ramsey shook his head. "It would have gone the other direction, eastward if it was from the highway."

Lieutenant Bell jotted that down on a notepad and then asked, "What happened once she was in the car? Did she say anything that could help explain her situation?"

"Not really," Ramsey said.

"Just asked for help a few times and then got quiet," Tess added.

Lieutenant Bell nodded.

"Is she going to be okay?" Tess asked.

"Physically, there is no reason to think she won't be. Mild concussion, likely from a hailstone."

"What about her wrists? Was she a captive?"

"She says the marks are from a game."

"A game?"

"That's what she says," Lieutenant Bell said.

"What kind of game would leave marks like that?"

Lieutenant Bell shrugged. "You'd be surprised. Kids today are getting into all kinds of mischief, what with the Internet giving all kinds of ideas, and parents exploring weird kinks." She eyed Tess's outfit again. "My guess is that she stumbled upon one of those *Shades of Grey* books that her mother was reading and decided to give it a try with a friend or something."

"Kinky bondage games?" Tess asked, cocking an eyebrow. "She seems a bit young, doesn't she?"

Another shrug. "Those marks were created with a rope, something that isn't that difficult to find around here. A few loops around the wrists and an aggressive pull, and you have rope burns."

"They looked a bit deep for a simple tug on a rope," Tess said.

"You have experience with this type of thing?"

"What? No."

"Well then, we go with what the girl says, that it was part of a game she was playing with her friend."

Ramsey waited to see if Tess would offer a reply.

She didn't.

"Anyway," the officer said, "we're going to keep her here until we can find out who her parents are and make sure they're all right. In the meantime, do you think you would be able to pinpoint the area you found her in for us so we can try to narrow down where her home is? We doubt she walked very far given that she was barefoot."

Ramsey shook his head. "I don't know. We had no idea where we were and kept having to turn around and backtrack because of power lines and trees and whatnot. And then once we found that officer parked by the fallen tree, she led us here."

"Okay, well, if you do think of anything that can help, it would be appreciated."

• • •

Bitsy knew she had made a mistake, and now wasn't sure how to fix it. Or if she could fix it. All she had tried to do was get help, the sight of Misty and the Daddy-man strapped into their seats, both unresponsive and bloody, having caused her to panic. But now here she was, sitting in a plastic chair, in a room that was part of a building filled with people in uniform, people she had come to realize were police officers.

She shuddered and hugged herself.

All her life she had been warned about the police and how they needed to avoid them at all costs. She and Misty were kept away from people in general, the Daddy-man explaining that they were too odd for others to understand, but police were the ones they tried the hardest to steer clear of.

And now here she was, her first time out by herself and she had ended up in one of their interrogation rooms.

Why?

The door to the room opened, a woman in a police uniform stepping in.

Misty?

No.

This was the one from the car.

Even so, memories of games they had played, ones where Misty wore a police uniform while Bitsy was the prisoner that sat handcuffed in a chair waiting to be interviewed about the Daddy-man, unfolded.

Only now she wasn't in handcuffs.

And she had a plastic cup of water to drink.

And they had bandaged her head after gently wiping away the blood.

Still, they were probably going to start asking her about the Daddy-man, and if she didn't answer...

Bitsy hugged herself tighter and started rocking back and forth, wishing she was back in her box. Or in the playroom. Or even hanging in the—

The woman took hold of a chair and pulled it close.

It didn't squeal against the floor while being dragged. Misty would have made it squeal.

Bitsy stopped rocking and looked at the woman, face trying to mask the fear she felt, all while a voice in her head told her to stop being a baby and be strong.

"Hi, do you remember me? My name is Katie Adams. Those two storm chasers brought you to me after finding you wandering around."

Bitsy wasn't sure how to reply to that and simply gave a slight nod to acknowledge the statement.

"I'm probably going to have to head back out soon, but before I did, I wanted to find out your name so that we can help you find your parents."

Don't tell them anything, ever!

The instructions were clear, yet so were the tortures that would be inflicted upon her if she didn't speak. While playing, Misty had always lit one of the Daddy-man's cigarettes prior to asking her questions, which she would press against Bitsy's flesh if she did not answer.

No one in the room was smoking.

They even had a No Smoking sign on the wall.

But she knew that could change. And even if they didn't use cigarettes to make her talk, they might have other items. Misty did. When playing games in the basement playroom, Misty had all kinds of items and devices. Horrible ones. All bought and put together by the Daddy-man. The cigarettes were always only the first step.

She would talk.

Eventually.

She always did.

She always lost the games.

And afterward, as punishment for losing—

A shiver raced through her.

"Honey," Katie said, a hand reaching out to take hold of hers.

Bitsy flinched and pulled her hand back.

"Bitsy," she whispered.

"Bitsy?" Katie asked.

"My name."

Bitsy looked down in shame. With Misty, she typically resisted the first round up until the moment that the cigarette tip was pressed against her nipple, or against the flesh between her legs, her determination to make her playmate proud giving her a resistance that she couldn't seem to find now.

Misty's hurt!

I was going to bring help.

But police help?

No.

She had wanted those people in the red car to help, but instead they had brought her here. Why?

"Your name is Bitsy?" Katie said, almost as if a confirmation.

"Yes," Bitsy said, voice soft.

"Bitsy what?"

"Cole."

"Bitsy Cole."

Bitsy nodded.

"It's very nice to meet you, Ms. Bitsy Cole," Katie said and held out a hand.

Bitsy stared at the hand for a moment and then reached out her own.

"Nice to meet you, Ms....um...Police Officer Adams."

"Please, call me Katie."

Hand released, Bitsy tucked it back up under her armpit, but then, realizing how pitiful such a display was, summoned up the courage to withdraw her hands and fold them in her lap, her back straightening against the chair.

"How is your head feeling?" Katie asked.

"Fine," Bitsy said. It was a bit sore, but unlike the cigarette tips, she could endure it.

"Officer Leland, the young man that looked at the bump and cleaned it up, feels you have a slight concussion. Do you know how it happened? Did you get caught in the tornado?"

Bitsy nodded. The memory of hearing Misty scream about the twister from the front seat beyond the curtain and then feeling the world tumble as the van flipped end over end filled her head. After that, the only sound was that of the loud siren somewhere off in the distance, followed by a thumping from the wooden box along the rear driver side of the van, one that contained the Daddy-man's latest schoolgirl.

The padlock on the box was still in place.

"Were you in a house that was hit, or in a car?" Katie pressed.

Bitsy stifled a shiver that wanted to overtake her, one induced by the pain that was sure to follow now that a question had been asked that she would have to make an effort not to answer.

"Bitsy, it's okay," Katie said. "You can talk to me."

Bitsy gave her a weak smile and then shook her head.

"Earlier you mentioned that we needed to help them. Who were you talking about?"

Bitsy felt torn. They did need help. Being unconscious like that probably wasn't good. Yet bringing the police...

No.

That wasn't helpful and it would upset both Misty and the Daddy-man. So much so that Misty might decide once and for all to get rid of her. "*And no one will ever take you because no one likes a second-rate, hand-me-down toy,*" Misty had said.

No, best not to let the police help.

I don't even know where they are.

While at the red car before she had fallen down, she had known the way to them, but now, even if she decided to let the police help, she wouldn't have been able to guide them there. Not unless they brought her to the creepy cemetery she had wandered through after leaving the field, one that had led her to another field before she had stumbled upon the road with the red car.

And they don't know where I am.

This chilled her to the core.

If someone else helped them and they decided to continue on the journey of finding a new place to live, they might leave her behind simply because they had no idea where she was and couldn't waste time looking for her.

She had to get back!

But how?

Even if she could get out of the police station, she had no idea how to get back to the van.

She had no idea how to get back to Misty.

Tears arrived.

She hadn't thought any would appear until the pain began, but then realized it had begun, only in a way she hadn't anticipated, a way that was worse than any physical type they could inflict upon her once the actual torture began.

Katie was staring at her.

Bitsy wiped at her eyes. "Sorry."

"It's okay," Katie said. "You've been through a lot."

Bitsy nodded.

"And if you don't want to talk to us right now, that's fine. I'm a bit worried though that time is not on our side, and that those you want us to help might not benefit from a delay, but if you're not ready or not able to talk about it just yet, I'll respect that."

Bitsy stared at her in confusion. The games never went this way.

Were they trying to trick her?

Did they know she might have played games where she was interrogated by the police and therefore wanted to throw her off and not have her anticipate what was to come?

Why wouldn't Misty have played like that?

Had she not realized things could go this way?

"That's a nice dress you have on," Katie said, catching her off guard.

"Thank you," Bitsy said, looking down at it. "It's one of Misty's favorites."

"Misty?" Katie asked.

Horror raced through her.

They had tricked her.

Katie had tricked her.

"Who's Misty?" Katie asked.

Bitsy didn't reply. Couldn't reply.

"Is she someone that needs help?" Katie pressed.

Bitsy wanted to cover her mouth with her palms, her panic at not being able to trust herself to answer without revealing something growing. Instead, she gave a slight shake of the head.

"No, Misty doesn't need help?" Katie asked.

"I think they're okay now," Bitsy said. "I was just scared after the van flipped."

"You were in a van?"

Bitsy's eyes went wide and this time she did cover her mouth.

"Was it just you and Misty in the van, or were there others?"

Bitsy kept her hands over her mouth.

They hadn't even started to torture her, and yet she had already revealed three things.

Misty was right: she was a horrible, useless toy.

"Honey," Katie said, her hands reaching out and gently taking hold of Bitsy's wrists so that she could remove her hands from her mouth. "Everything's okay. You have nothing to be scared of here. All we want to do is help you and anyone else that needs help."

Bitsy shook her head again and said, "I can't."

"It's okay," Katie said. She reached up and wiped away some of Bitsy's tears. "I understand. We all do."

Bitsy nodded and then wiped at her face, the dirty sleeve of her dress soaking them up.

"That is such a pretty dress," Katie said once again.

Bitsy smiled.

"Is it okay if I get a picture of you wearing it?"

"A picture?" Bitsy asked.

"Yeah, just a quick one."

Bitsy was confused and a bit wary, her mind thinking this could be another trick.

But how?

No ideas appeared.

"Okay," she said.

"Great." Katie pulled out her phone. "Why don't you stand over by the wall? That way there won't be anything in the background."

Bitsy nodded.

"You know, I could take one for you too if you have a phone."

"I don't have one."

"Really? Was it lost in the storm, or you just don't have one at all."

"Don't have one at all."

"I see. What about Misty?"

"What?" Bitsy asked, caution building.

"Does she have one?"

Though she had no idea how answering this question could impact Misty and the Daddy-man, she bit her tongue and stayed silent.

"Never mind," Katie said. "That's not important." She held up her phone. "Smile."

Bitsy tried.

She always did.

Misty liked it when she smiled for the pictures, though

given the things she liked to take pictures of, Bitsy wasn't always able to produce one. Today was no different, though this time it wasn't pain that was keeping her lips and cheeks from producing a grin. Instead, it was fear.

"Ta-da!" Katie said, lowering the phone. "Would you like to see?"

"Yes," Bitsy said.

"Come take a look."

Bitsy did and frowned. "My dress is really dirty."

"You know, it really is, and I'd hate for the blood and mud stains to set in. How about we bring you some fresh clothes so that we can have the dress cleaned? And mended." She pointed to the sleeve that had torn. "That way it will be good as new once you're ready to wear it again."

Bitsy didn't know how to reply to this.

"Of course, we can't have you putting on clean clothes with your hair and face all muddy, so first things first, I think I should show you where the showers are. How does that sound? Would you like to get all cleaned up and then put on some fresh clothes?"

Bitsy felt her jaw dropping a bit, but then realized this could be a trick.

Play along.

"Yes, I would like that," she said.

"Well then, come with me." Katie held her hand out.

Bitsy reached out her hand so that Katie could take it and lead the way, an awkwardness developing since she wasn't used to being led like this. Normally, Misty would put a leash and collar on her and she would either crawl on all fours or walk with her hands behind her back, bound. Now, with one hand in Katie's grip, she didn't know what to do with her free hand and simply let it hang limply at her side.

From the room they took a left and soon entered a hallway she hadn't been in yet, one that had rows of pictures of people in uniform.

A heavy-looking door loomed.

Would there really be showers beyond it, or was she being taken to a stairway that would lead down into the torture room, one that would likely be even more extensive than the one they had back at the house given the funding places like this received?

Fear returned with the thought, and for a moment Bitsy stiffened.

Katie must have felt this reluctance through her hand, the grip she had tightening, as did the force with which she pulled. It wasn't much, yet was enough for Bitsy to know she would be no match for the woman if she tried to get away.

They stepped through the door.

No stairway loomed.

No chains or torture items were present.

Instead, there was a row of odd cabinet-like structures, each with a narrow door and lock on it.

Is she going to put me inside one?

Even as she thought it, she knew that wasn't going to happen. They were too small. That wasn't to say she had never been forced into a small confined area. Her box was one such item and she stayed in that every night unless Misty wanted to sleep with her, and some of the cages they had at the house were so tiny that she had to stay hunched over while inside, on her knees, unable to turn. Misty would typically lock her hands behind her back while in there, but even if she didn't, Bitsy wouldn't have been able to move.

These cabinets seemed too small for that.

And then she saw the shower area.

Katie hadn't been tricking her.

Unless being able to shower was part of the trick?

"Here you are," Katie said. "You can simply put your clothes on the bench right there, and while you're showering I'll bring you some soap and shampoo. And a towel and some clothes will be waiting when you're finished. After that, maybe we can talk some more."

Bitsy nodded.

"First though, before you take a shower I have to ask you a very important question, okay?"

"Okay."

"Did anyone touch you down there between your legs?"

Bitsy backed up a step, hands covering her private area.

"It's okay, you can tell me if someone touched you," Katie said.

Bitsy didn't reply, hands still covering herself.

"Someone did touch you, didn't they?"

Bitsy nodded.

"Was it a man?" Katie asked.

Bitsy shook her head.

Katie looked momentarily confused. "A woman?"

Bitsy nodded.

"And did she put anything inside of you?" Katie asked, voice soft.

"No." *Not this time. I put things in her.*

"Has anyone ever put anything inside of you?"

The answer was yes, but Bitsy didn't want to tell Katie this. Couldn't tell her this.

"It's okay."

Bitsy shook her head.

Katie stared at her for several seconds and then nodded. "Okay. I'm going to step out so you can shower. If you need anything, I'll be just down the hall."

Bitsy nodded again.

Katie smiled and then left the locker area.

Bitsy waited for several seconds, fearing that Katie might come back in once she was undressed and surprise her.

No one came in.

She was all alone.

She began to undress.

.   .   .

"You can't simply stand all night long," Ramsey said, sitting on the edge of a cot, hands struggling to put a small pillow into a pillowcase.

Tess didn't reply, thoughts on all the microbes that were likely crawling around dominating her mind.

"Earth to Tess," Ramsey said.

"I don't want to stay here," Tess said.

"Yeah, well, we don't really have much of a choice, now do we?"

Tess didn't reply, mostly because she knew he was right. They didn't have a choice. And it was all because of him. She had told him not to try to catch the storm, had told him it would be too dangerous, and yet here they were, car wrecked, stuck in a sweaty school gymnasium with cots that were still being set up as more and more families arrived, the pillows and blankets having apparently been stored in a basement storage area specifically for disasters such as this.

"If you had listened to me, we wouldn't be here right now," she said.

"I know."

"Why doesn't anyone ever listen to me? You, Mom, teachers, that bitch at the police station—"

"Tess, come on."

She crossed her arms.

"Tess, you're being dramatic, and I don't know about you, but I've had enough drama for one day."

Tess thought about that and, after several seconds, let her arms fall back to her sides.

"I'm going to go find a soda machine," Ramsey said. "You want something?"

"Shouldn't they have food and drinks for us?"

"They might, but they're still setting everything up, so…"

"This police department isn't very good."

"What?" he asked, the change of topic throwing him off.

"They should have kept our car."

"Why? It's just the windshield that was busted."

"No, for evidence, just in case we were the kidnappers of that girl."

"Why would we have brought her to the police station?"

Tess shrugged. "Criminals do stupid things sometimes."

He shook his head. "You sure you don't want anything from the soda machine?"

"I'm sure," she said.

With that, he headed toward the doorway of the gymnasium, which was right next to a gaudy mural that had been painted with a weird frontier setting and a man in a fur-skin hat and clothing. It was obviously a silly mascot of some kind for the silly sports collective, but of what exactly she couldn't decide.

The sound of the metal legs of a cot hitting the linoleum surface of the gymnasium floor caught her attention.

She turned and watched a family of five setting everything up about fifteen feet from where she and Ramsey had set up. Other families were farther away, creating their own spaces. Nothing was being organized it seemed. Cots were being handed out as people came in through the main doors of the high school, as well as the blankets and pillows and cases, but that was it. No direction was given. No one was in charge. At the moment, that was okay, but as the place got more and more crowded, it might start to pose a problem.

It took several minutes for Bitsy to get up the courage to step beneath the hot water, not because she was worried about being burned by the heat, but because bathing with hot water without Misty's permission was forbidden to her. Once she did work up the courage, guilt appeared but was quickly displaced by the soothing warmth that encased her body.

Several minutes came and went, Bitsy doing nothing but standing beneath the spray.

She didn't want it to end, ever.

Will Misty find out?

The question caused a shiver to race down her spine, as did thoughts on how Misty would decide to punish her if she did, memories of past experiences plaguing her mind and knocking away any joy she felt from the hot water.

She looked at her wrists.

Hanging by them had not been part of a game like she had told the police, but punishment for acting like a boy, which Bitsy was sure would have lasted longer if the Daddy-man hadn't arrived home when he did and found her dangling in the dungeon, barely conscious, lungs heaving as she struggled for each breath.

He had been upset, though Bitsy had been too delirious to understand why. Whatever the reason, he had told Misty to take her down and put her away.

Into her box she went, Misty not saying a word to her until sometime later when she threw open the box and instructed her to start packing their things, an odd franticness present. Anger was there as well, especially when Bitsy had trouble gripping things with her hands, the time spent hanging from her wrists having instilled a numbness within her fingers that wouldn't fade away.

Bags packed, they had headed out to the van, Bitsy sitting in the back beyond the curtain while Misty and the Daddy-man sat up front, Misty asking questions on where they were going, the Daddy-man answering them. Every now and then there would be a thumping sound as well, from the box that the Daddy-man had his new schoolgirl in, one that Bitsy hadn't seen yet and probably wouldn't until Misty and she crept down into the cellar dungeon while he was working.

They were always so pretty, though not as pretty as Misty.

Bitsy had made a point of telling her this many times, the

most recent being when Misty had put on her new school uniform, one similar to those that the Daddy-man always made his schoolgirls wear, hair done up in pigtails.

"Then why doesn't he want to do this with me?" Misty had asked, hand motioning toward the screen where one of the girls was bent over the edge of the bed, wrists stretched forward toward the headboard frame with rope while her legs were spread wide, the Daddy-man putting his penis into her over and over again.

"Maybe he doesn't think you'll like it," Bitsy had suggested, her own mind having reached this conclusion based on all the tears and muffled screams that the girl was making.

"But I liked it when you put things inside of me."

Bitsy didn't reply.

"And you like it when I put stuff inside of you," Misty added. "Don't you?"

Bitsy forced herself to nod. "But I'm a toy, so maybe it's different, and with you I only used toys. What your daddy is doing is different."

Misty had considered this for several seconds, her eyes going from the TV screen to the mirror and then back to the TV screen. She then looked down at herself, hands touching the white blouse where her boobs pressed against the fabric.

Bitsy watched, jealousy making a brief appearance as she once again wished her chest would fill out like Misty's had.

"Come here," Misty instructed.

Bitsy did.

Misty took her right hand and pressed it against her left breast, and then did the same with her left.

"You like that?" she asked.

Bitsy nodded.

Misty shivered and then put her hands behind her onto the frame at the bottom of the Daddy-man's bed, fingers gripping it so she could arch her back and thrust her chest out.

Bitsy had an idea where this was going, the two having played games like this before, and without being told ran her hands down Misty's body so that she could reach up beneath her skirt and touch the freshly shaven area between her legs.

"No," Misty said, voice somewhat firm.

"Sorry," Bitsy said. "Usually you—"

"I want to do something different this time," Misty said.

Bitsy waited.

Misty hesitated, surprising her, and then said, "I want to try what they're doing," while pointing at the screen.

An unseen tremble raced through Bitsy's body.

"I want to be the schoolgirl and you be the daddy, but like that," Misty added.

"You mean—" Bitsy started

"I need to find out once and for all if I'll like it."

"But I'll have to act like a—"

"I know, and I want you to."

"Honey, you doing okay?" Katie called, startling her.

Bitsy focused her attention back on the present and peeked her head out from beyond the curtain, barely able to see Katie in the steam that had filled the shower area.

"Yes," Bitsy said.

"Okay, just making sure." She held up some folded clothes. "I'm going to leave these on the bench for you."

"Yes, thank you."

"When you're dressed, come on out to the main area again and we'll see about getting something to eat."

Food.

Given everything that had happened, Bitsy had not realized how hungry she was, the last meal she had eaten having been some of the leftover pizza that Misty had ordered for the two of them after the Daddy-man had left on his hunting trip.

Two days.

A piece of pizza, some soda, and then some quiet time in the playroom, looking at picture books while Misty was elsewhere in the house, her mind not knowing that Misty would soon come to her dressed in the school uniform outfit that she had ordered online and bring her into the bedroom to watch the video.

She wished Misty hadn't done that.

She wished Misty hadn't asked her to act like the Daddy-man.

Not because Misty hadn't liked it, she actually had, and not because she herself hadn't liked it, because she had as well—more than she had anticipated. No. She wished Misty hadn't asked because afterward they had gone to bed together, bodies curled tight, and it had been the most magical moment of her life, one that then was ruined hours later when Misty yanked her from the bed, screaming, and dragged her into the cellar dungeon to hang her up by her wrists.

No reason for this had been given, Misty going back to bed after she had finished securing Bitsy.

It had been horrible, not just because of the pain that hanging by her wrists caused, but because she didn't know what she had done and thus couldn't accept that the punishment was right.

An image of Misty belted into the front seat of the van, unconscious, blood on her face, returned to her and made her realize that she might never know what it was that she had done.

And here she was enjoying the hot water of a shower, all while Misty might be hurt or worse.

Bitsy turned off the water and grabbed the towel.

Once dry, she headed over to the clothes that had been left for her.

Hesitation arrived.

Wearing a T-shirt and a sweatshirt was fine, but the sweatpants were a problem because pants were for boys and thus forbidden for her to wear.

Could this be a test?

Why would the police do that?

She didn't know what to do.

"Feeling better?" Katie asked, coming into the room.

"Yes," Bitsy said, quickly turning even though she had the towel around her still, hiding her nakedness.

"We have some pizzas. Frozen ones since we can't order anything with the town power being out—not everyone has a nifty generator like us—but they're still tasty. Should be ready in a few minutes. And we have soda and ice tea and whatnot."

Bitsy smiled even though Katie couldn't see it and then asked, "It's okay if I wear pants?"

"What?"

She's confused, Bitsy realized, which meant the pants likely weren't an issue or a test. "Nothing, it's okay. At home I'm not supposed to wear pants because I'm a girl."

"Oh, well, if anyone says anything, just tell them that I said it was okay. After all, I'm a girl and I'm wearing them."

"That's different," Bitsy said.

"I see. We'll say you're an honorary police cadet trainee, and these clothes are your trainee uniform and you are required to wear them while training."

Bitsy turned a bit and asked, "Like a game?"

"Yes."

"Then it should be okay." She smiled. "Thanks."

"No problem," Katie said, smiling back. "Come out when you're ready."

"I will."

With that, Katie stepped out.

Bitsy waited a second just to make sure she didn't duck back inside and then, when Katie didn't, dropped the towel and put on the clothes that were waiting.

FOUR

Norman felt a wet impact within the darkness and opened his eyes, his thoughts murky and dominated by pain. Face, hands, back, shoulders—the only part of his body that didn't hurt seemed to be his knees.

Blood.

It was in the back of his throat.

Had been for a while, his mind somehow having registered it within the darkness of his unconscious state.

Or had it?

Confusion appeared.

And then he vomited, all over his own lap, the mixture a horrible concoction of blood, snot, and stomach acid.

Following that, he went to wipe off his mouth but couldn't, his wrists having been cuffed behind him to a rough wooden post.

He used his shoulder instead.

Water splashed all over him, the sensation similar to what he had felt in the darkness.

Norman blinked several times and looked up, the girl from outside standing before him, the terror she had tried to mask earlier easily visible upon her face. Anger was there as well.

She held a metal bucket, one that she dropped now that he was awake.

"Well?" she asked.

"What?" he replied, voice ragged.

"Why are you here?"

Blood tickled the back of his throat, and for a moment he didn't dare speak, the sensation that he was about to vomit again overwhelming.

And then it passed.

"Why are you here?" she asked again, voice growing agitated.

"I saw the van in the field and thought someone might need help."

"That's it?" she asked.

He nodded.

"Are others on their way?"

Hesitation arrived.

The answer was no, but he didn't want to reveal that. At the same time, if she feared more officers might be on the way, panic could cause her to do something they would all regret. He had never before been involved in a hostage situation, but from what he understood of them, it was best to keep the captor calm.

"They know the—" Blood ran down his throat, and this time he couldn't stop his body from forcing it back up.

Pain followed, his shattered nose feeling as if it was being ground down by some unseen force.

The girl waited, arms crossed.

He took a deep breath through his mouth and then choked out a final glob of snotty blood.

"Water," he voiced.

"Is anyone else coming?"

"No," he gasped.

"Do they know where you are?"

He gulped down another breath of air and said, "They know the area I'm in." Another breath. "I radioed in damage and downed power lines near here."

She considered this and then grabbed the bucket and walked over to an area of the barn to his right that he could not see without shifting his entire body. The sound of pipes groaning and water hitting metal echoed.

He waited, his eyes scanning as much as they could without making himself sick, trying to spot something that might help his situation.

Nothing.

She had him facing a wall, his back to the rest of the barn.

The sound of water shut off.

She returned, the bucket obviously heavy given the way she strained once she was within his line of sight. Bucket placed, she retrieved a rag that was in it and stepped up to him.

"Lean your head back," she instructed.

"I can't," he said. Doing so would cause more blood to run down his throat.

She sighed and held the rag over his head, squeezing it.

Water rained down on him.

He tilted his head back just a bit, mouth open.

Water landed on his tongue, though it wasn't much, and then, without warning, he was gagging, the slight tilt enough for the blood to run back from his shattered nose.

The girl let out another sigh and tossed the rag into the bucket.

"Do you know who lives here?" she asked.

Deep breath.

Then, "No."

She eyed him for a moment and then asked, "Did you see a young girl in a dress wandering around?"

"Young girl?"

No reply, just an impatient look.

"No," he said.

She sighed, a look of concern appearing.

Who was the young girl she was worried about?

What had been going on in that van?

"Who is she?" he asked, Hollywood having taught him that one should always keep the hostage taker talking. Trying to identify with them was helpful as well, or so he had been led to believe.

She didn't answer.

"Is she your sister?" he pressed.

"No," she said.

"And who are you?"

"What?"

"Who are you? I know most of the young people around here"—he didn't, but she wouldn't know that—"but I don't think we've ever met." He took a breath, the lack of being able to breathe through his nose making it difficult to complete longer sentences without choking. "My name's Norman."

"Misty," she said after several seconds of hesitation.

"And the girl you're asking about?"

"Bitsy."

"Bitsy?" he questioned. It had to be a nickname.

"Well, her name's Elizabeth, but I call her Bitsy."

"And you're worried she might have been hurt when the van flipped?"

"I'm worried that—" Her face changed. "Why are you asking all these questions?"

He gave a slight shrug and said, "I'm just trying to understand why you attacked me." He paused for a mouthful of air. "And why there is a young girl somewhere behind me tied up."

She didn't reply to that.

"What is going on?" he asked.

Nothing.

"You were in the van that was flipped over, right?"

Still nothing.

"Who else was in it?"

Still nothing.

"There was a lot of blood. Whoever was driving was hurt pretty bad."

Her lip quivered, which caught him off guard, and then she started to walk away, disappearing behind him.

"Misty," he said. "I don't know what happened to you, but whatever it is, I can help you."

His head was yanked back by a fist in his hair, the rough wooden edge of the post snagging his ear and tearing the flesh.

Blood ran down his throat, choking him, some of it bubbling to his lips.

"You don't know anything about me or why we're here, and if you don't stop asking questions I'll cut your throat." Spit rained down on him as she spoke. Tears as well. "Understand?"

"Y-y-yes!" he gasped, his voice barely audible amid the gurgle of blood.

She released his hair, his head quickly snapping forward to choke out more bloody mucus. While doing this, he noticed a slight weight in his front pocket, one that seemed to bounce with his movement.

At first, he didn't know what it was, but then he realized it was the keys he had grabbed from the mud.

She had failed to notice them while stripping him of all his equipment.

All he needed to do was get them out and onto the ground near his fingers and he could free himself.

He glanced down at his shirt pocket, which was closed with a button.

Reaching it with his hands would be impossible, and trying to bounce the keys out would be a fruitless endeavor.

He would need to use his teeth.

And he would have to do it while the girl was not in the barn.

Misty was on edge and decided to step out of the muggy barn to try to calm herself. While out there, feet on the gravel of the parking area, she looked up at the sky, which was now blue with a sun that was getting ready to begin its decent toward the horizon.

How could things change so quickly?

Blue sky, to stormy sky, to blue sky, followed by what will likely be a calm starry night.

It was surreal.

Equally surreal was the fact that they'd had to flee their home, which they had set fire to once they had gotten everything they couldn't spare into the van.

It was just like the weather.

One moment she had been in the family room going through the new schoolgirl's backpack while her daddy made smiley-face pancakes, the next he had been in a complete panic, pancakes forgotten, telling her she had ten minutes to pack her things—all because she had gotten excited about finding an Apple Watch in the side pocket of the schoolgirl's backpack and showed it to him, stating how she could now see how many steps she and Bitsy walked when they went exploring in the fields behind the house, her fingers fiddling with the buttons so she could start tracking.

It was crazy.

She had never before seen him freak out like that.

And it didn't seem to go away.

He had tried to mask it once they were on the road, voicing statements on how it was time for a change of scenery anyway and how he had been considering purchasing a summer home for them to head to during his vacations, but beneath the words she could hear the terror.

All because of the Apple Watch.

If she hadn't shown it to him, everything would have been fine, but show him she did, her excitement too much to contain.

It had ruined everything.

And then, as if things hadn't been bad enough, they had gotten caught in the storm, her daddy screaming as he tried to get them away from it, nothing but open farm roads and empty fields stretched out before them, the roar of the storm intense, power lines sparking, tree branches flying, and then they were tumbling, the impacts as the van bounced across the ground jarring her brain until she blacked out. The next thing she knew, she was hanging on her side, seat belt digging into her breasts and stomach, a faint thumping sound from the back of the van echoing.

Daddy was dead.

It was the first thing that registered, his lifeless eyes staring at her from where his body was crumpled against the driver-side door, seat belt unlatched, a stiffening left hand tight against his throat, which she had later discovered had been pierced. By what, exactly, she couldn't tell, but it had opened his throat and caused him to bleed out, his hand unable to stop the flow.

Bitsy?

Would she have killed him while he was stuck?

No.

Bitsy wouldn't hurt a fly, of that she was certain.

But where had she gone?

In her mind, she had a visual of Bitsy shaking her over and over again and then saying something about going to try to find help, but she had no idea if that was real or just something her mind had created following the storm. One thing she did know, Bitsy was not one to act upon her own intuition, so for her to make a decision to go and get help, things must have seemed pretty bad.

They were bad, her mind noted.

Still are.

Daddy was dead, Bitsy was missing, and a police officer had already come to investigate—all because something had happened while Daddy had been hunting, something with the schoolgirl who had been in the box while they were driving, a box that had seemed to protect her better than the seat belt had protected Daddy. It was unreal.

And unfair.

Up until now, her daddy had seemed...

She didn't know, but she had never before considered the possibility of him being dead. It just didn't seem possible. It had to be a dream, needed to be a dream, one that she would wake up from, her body curled around the pillow in her bedroom, the sounds of her daddy coming home with his latest schoolgirl echoing, Bitsy bringing her coffee...

No.

Bitsy wouldn't be able to bring her coffee when she woke up, not after Misty had lifted her off the ground by her wrists in the dungeon as punishment for what she had done the other night, punishment that wasn't really fair given that Misty had demanded such actions from her.

Was that why Bitsy had left?

Was she upset by what had happened?

Had she decided she no longer wanted to be Misty's toy?

Could she decide such a thing?

Misty put a hand to her head, a dull pounding still present from when she had cracked it against the passenger window during one of the tumbles, all the various thoughts and questions not helping.

This wasn't a dream.

She wasn't going to wake up come morning and find her

daddy enjoying himself in the cellar dungeon with a new schoolgirl, his video camera rolling, the electronics within capturing the activities so that he could watch them over and over again once the girl was beneath a peach tree in back, body helping it grow. Or would this one be apple? Or pear?

Misty didn't know.

Never would.

Nor would she get to watch the video while Daddy was at work, her fingers popping the lock on his door so that she could sit on the carpet before the TV, eyes glued to the screen, watching as he dressed the girls up in school uniform outfits and had his way with them, their mouths screaming against the gags as he put himself inside of them, his body thrusting and grunting until he let out a loud moan and then heaved with exhaustion. Sometimes she couldn't help but laugh, his face and the sounds he made tickling her funny bone. Other times she simply watched and studied, questions building, ones that she would sometimes address with him, though only if she could figure out a way of asking without him realizing she had violated his bedroom space.

Most would now go unanswered.

With this realization came the sadness, tears once again welling in her eyes.

First her mother and now him.

Both gone, never to return.

And Bitsy was missing.

She didn't know what to do.

She had never been alone before, and soon it was going to be dark.

A shiver raced through her.

She was scared.

Though he couldn't see her given that his back was to the

barn, Norman could hear the girl struggling against her bonds, the clink of the handcuffs unmistakable.

Several minutes passed, and then, "Hello?" she asked, voice dry and crinkly. "Are you awake?"

"I am," Norman said, somewhat surprised that she had been able to get at the tape given that her hands had been cuffed behind her back. "Who are you?" he asked.

"Abigail Abbott."

He did not recognize the name

"You're a police officer?" she asked.

"Yes," he said.

"Are more coming?"

"I don't know," he said after a few seconds.

She didn't reply to this.

Norman wanted to ask her questions, but before doing so he decided to shift himself around so that he could see her and she him. It took several minutes, the squared wooden edges difficult to work around as pieces dug into his back and arms, but eventually he succeeded in the endeavor and found himself facing into the barn rather than a wall.

Abigail was against an old wooden livestock stall about ten feet to his left, her wrists now threaded through one of the rails behind her head rather than being locked behind her back, the tape that had been around her mouth earlier now dangling around her throat, the new position having allowed her to work at it with her fingers until her lips were free.

They stared at each other for several seconds, an odd awkwardness present.

"Were you in the van?" Norman asked.

"Yeah."

"What happened?"

She shifted herself a bit, a wince escaping. "I have no idea. One moment I was in this wooden box that he had put me in, the next I was bouncing all over the place thinking I was going to die." A weak laugh escaped. "I thought the girl was helping me when she finally opened the box, but I guess not because she simply dragged me all the way over here into the barn."

Norman considered this, trying to figure out what to ask, but then she asked her own question.

"Where are we?"

"Smallwood," he said.

"What state?" she asked.

"Illinois."

"Jesus."

"Where did you think we were?"

"I had no idea. He grabbed me while I was walking home from school in Casewell, North Carolina."

"When was that?"

"Shit, I don't know. What day is it?"

"Thursday."

"Tuesday then." She shook her head. "He snatched me right off the road and put me into the box, and then we drove for hours and hours until he finally got to wherever it was he was taking me, his home, I guess, and then he pulled me out of the box." She wet her lips. "I thought he was going to rape me or something right there, but instead he dragged me into this house, into a cellar, and chained me to a wall and left me there."

Norman waited.

"I think it was my Apple Watch that freaked him out."

"Apple Watch?" Norman asked.

"It's like an I-phone, just it's a watch. I had one in my backpack since I'm not allowed to wear it during class."

"Why did it cause him to freak out?" Norman asked.

"I guess he thought the police could track it or something." She shrugged. "Who knows, maybe they can. All I know is he came down with it to where I was chained and started demanding to know if it was making a map on Facebook. He kept saying 'like those penis outlines students do' and shaking me to answer, and then eventually he unlocked me from the wall, dragged me back into the van, and put me back into the box."

"Penis outlines?"

Another shrug. "People do things like that with activity trackers. You just turn it on and start walking and it will map out your route, so if you want to make a design you simply walk a route that will create it."

"And your watch could do that?" Norman asked.

"Probably. I never used it like that, but I'm sure it could."

"And would it map out a route from North Carolina to here?" Norman asked.

"I doubt it."

"But he seemed to think it was possible."

"I guess."

"And it has some sort of GPS or tracking in it?"

"Yeah, just like a phone."

Norman considered this and then asked, "Any idea where the house was, the one with the cellar you were chained in?"

"No."

"How long do you think you were in the box this second time?"

She thought about this and said, "I really don't know. Not as long as the first time. And we only stopped once, I'm thinking for gas."

Norman nodded and then regretted it, the movement causing blood to run down the back of his throat, choking him, which in turn caused pain to flare up within his broken nose.

She decided to bury her daddy, which was what she had been planning to do when the policeman had shown up, the old shovel she had found in the barn having worked well as a weapon when he had gone inside and spotted the schoolgirl on the ground. The only problem, she didn't know where Daddy would want to be. If at home, she would have put him next to her mother, who had been buried beneath the second peach tree not far from the old well, her sweetness seemingly having an influence upon the peaches that grew from that tree because they always tasted far better than the ones from the others. But now that wasn't possible, her excitement over the Apple Watch having made it so she could not bury him near her mother, or anyone else he knew, the spot she eventually picked, wherever it ended up being, one that would produce nothing but loneliness from here on out.

Tears appeared once again, and this time she didn't fight them and simply let them flow, dropping to her knees in the field, sobs echoing.

Several minutes passed, her shadow growing as the sun slowly but surely made its way toward the horizon.

She needed to start digging, for once it grew dark she didn't want to be outside, not in this field away from home, uncertain of what might be lurking.

But first she needed to find a spot for him, one that would be pleasant and help with the loneliness of being way out here.

An idea arrived.

Maybe she could make it so he wasn't lonely.

Maybe she could bury him with the schoolgirl he had brought home.

Would that make him happy?

At home, he had always been excited once he had a new schoolgirl to play with, and in the videos he always seemed to be enjoying himself, so maybe if he couldn't be by her mother, being by one of his girls would be the next best thing.

She looked around the field while considering this, her eyes trying to see something that he would like to be buried near, but nothing jumped out at her. It was just a field, and not a fun one with trees and streams. Instead, it had weeds.

One spot is as good as the next.

Or was it?

She had no idea, but given that the sun was continuing to fall, she decided to start digging, her goal being to have him within the hole and sealed away before the sun disappeared.

Such was easier said than done.

Digging was harder than she expected it would be.

She needed Bitsy.

They always made a good team when digging the holes for the schoolgirls that Daddy was finished with, Bitsy doing the digging while Misty stood over her in her prison mistress outfit, a whip in hand, cracking it against Bitsy's back whenever she slowed, threats of a punishment echoing.

But Bitsy was gone, and without her they couldn't play the digging game. It needed two people.

Did she really go for help?

The memory of being shaken by her was stronger now than it had been earlier and didn't seem like something her mind had fabricated. But if she had gone to get help, why wasn't she back yet? Had something happened? Had someone found her and decided to take her home to their daughter? Would someone do such a thing knowing she already belonged to someone else?

Would Bitsy tell them about her?

Or was she so upset about the other night that she decided to stay with the new family?

Regret appeared.

Bitsy had only been doing what Misty had asked, which was what she was supposed to do. Such was her purpose in life, and she had simply been fulfilling it.

All because of the videos.

Was that why Daddy had never wanted her to watch them? Had he known she would grow curious about what she saw and eventually want to try it? Had he known that Bitsy would act like a boy with her and help her experience what she saw? Was that why he had wanted to get rid of her last year, statements on how Misty was too old to have toys like Bitsy being made?

His stance had softened with her tears.

It always did.

She sighed, focus shifting to the hole she had dug.

It wasn't deep enough.

Wouldn't be for hours, at the rate she was going, but with the sun nearly set and the darkness settling in, she couldn't keep going.

The hole could wait a day.

Daddy wouldn't mind.

In fact, it would probably be better because once morning came and she had more time, she could explore a bit more and maybe find a spot that was better. Plus, Bitsy might be back by then and they could make a game out of it. She had her prison mistress outfit and her whip. Both were in her bag along with all the other things she had packed after Daddy told her they had to leave. And she had Daddy's bags, and though she wasn't sure what exactly he had packed, she had a feeling there would be lots of fun things in there that she and Bitsy could play with.

Or would he rather she buried all his things with him?

Indecision gripped her.

Many of the items were things he used with the school-girls he brought home, so putting them in the ground along-side him might be the proper thing to do.

She would have to think on this.

Did he bring the black toy?

The question brought about memories that she didn't need to dwell upon at the moment, so she pushed them away. One thing she did know: if he had brought the black toy, she wasn't going to bury it with him. No, no, no. She was going to keep that one as a gift to herself. And maybe the pink toy.

Actually, there was no "maybe" about it.

She was keeping both.

Her daddy wouldn't mind.

Both items made her happy, and while he probably would have been upset if he knew what she was doing with them while he was at school or away on his hunts, now it would be different. He was gone and she was in charge. She wouldn't have wished it to be this way, but it was so. If she wanted to play with the black and pink toys, she could. If she wanted to play with the policeman in the barn, she could. If she wanted Bitsy to act like a boy again, she could.

Thinking about Bitsy and what they had done the other night forced her to a sudden stop as the memories brought about a sensation that made walking impossible, her hand quickly pressing itself into the fold between her legs to stifle the warm tingle that began to build, a soft moan escaping her lips.

Once it faded she was able to continue her journey back toward the house and barn, her elongated shadow reaching them first now that the sun was nearly at the horizon, and then continuing beyond as she came upon it, eventually stretching all the way toward the overturned van.

Would it attract more police officers?

With the sun setting she didn't think anyone would be able to see it from the road the way the first police officer had, but come morning, once the sun was back in the sky, light shining down upon the world, it would be visible again.

And what about the police officer's car?

That would be visible as well and would attract even more attention than the van.

She needed to move it.

But how?

For several months now she had been begging her daddy to teach her how to drive, but he had always been reluctant, making statements about how she didn't need to learn because he would always take her wherever it was she wanted to go. Plus, he didn't really want her leaving the house on her own, not when her existence might bring about questions that were best left unasked.

But now he wasn't there and she would need to know how to drive, first so she could move the police car, and then, once she had the van unflipped, so she could do things like go shopping for food.

Would she be able to unflip the van?

Doing so by herself wouldn't be possible, but maybe with the help of the police officer?

Would he help her?

What if he simply tried to get away once she unlocked him from the post?

Getting him with the shovel had worked because he wasn't expecting it, but now he would be more cautious of her and wouldn't turn his back on her. And once he was unlocked from the post, she doubted she would be able to control him given how big he was. Just dragging him from the floor of the barn to the post had been difficult.

His gun.

She could threaten to shoot him if he tried to get away.

But what if he still tried to get away and she missed him?

He would bring more police officers here, and they would lock her up and throw away the key.

But they'll do that anyway if you don't hide the police car.

The thoughts overwhelmed her, panic setting in.

She didn't know what to do.

She wasn't ready for this.

She needed someone to help her.

She needed—

Stop!

The voice was like her daddy's, though she knew it wasn't really his.

Couldn't be.

Or could it?

No.

Once someone was dead they couldn't talk with the living. He had explained this to her when she told him that Mommy still talked to her.

But maybe he was wrong?

Could he be wrong?

Maybe his mommy didn't talk to him after she had died, but her mommy did.

"Daddy?" she asked, voice sounding funny to her given that no one was around.

Nothing.

"Please, I don't know what to do."

Nothing.

"I'm scared."

Nothing.

He wasn't there.

Nor was Mommy.

She was alone.

With this thought, she headed back toward the barn.

FIVE

"How's she doing?" Gary asked while pouring coffee into Katie's mug.

"Hard to say," Katie said, reaching for a spoon. "She's really guarded. I've never seen anything like it."

Gary considered that for a moment and then took a sip of his coffee.

Katie mirrored him, the brew foul upon her tongue.

"We need a Keurig," Gary said.

"Oh no," Katie said. "I don't care how sludged up one of these pots becomes, coffee out of a plastic disc is a monstrosity that should carry a mandatory prison sentence."

"Spoken like a true rookie who is trying to impress."

"Watch it," Katie said. "I've patrolled streets and neighborhoods that would make most CPD officers piss themselves."

"I don't doubt that."

She was also the only one on this particular force who had taken a bullet, but that wasn't something she was going to bring up, especially since everyone already knew about it, the mayor having mentioned it during her homecoming all those years ago.

"So," Gary continued, "Any hits on the name or the picture?"

"No, nothing," Katie said, suppressing her frustration.

"And she won't tell you what happened."

"No, though that may start to change. I get the sense that we've connected a bit. Not much and not to the point where she'll feel comfortable talking, but a foundation has been set."

"Well, might want to kick things up a notch. I just spoke with Lieutenant Bell, and she has already notified the county about the girl and they're going to send someone out."

"What? Why?"

"Bell feels the county will be more qualified to handle her and that the van she escaped from was likely outside of our jurisdiction given that you were already on the edge of it when the two storm chasers found you." He held up a hand to stop her protest. "I think it's BS too, and that she's over-thinking, but she is the boss right now, and speaking on just a departmental handling capability, the county does actually have people for this kind of thing, whereas we don't."

"So what if they have a department for it? She has started to grow comfortable with me, and that is something you don't just toss away and start over on."

"I agree, and maybe the specialist will too."

Katie gave him a look. "Or they'll believe that their training makes it so they are the only ones who can possibly deal with a girl in this situation." She set her mug down hard, the coffee sloshing with the impact. "Any idea when they'll get here?"

"No, and given all the destruction, it may not be until tomorrow." He grinned. "Sometimes being this far north isn't such a bad thing."

"True," Katie said. Smallwood officers often grumbled about the distance because of how long it took them to transport someone to the county lockup. They were so far from it that the jail in the next county to their north was actually closer to them than the one within their own county. Same with the courthouse.

"Anyway, Bell agrees that you have built a bit of a bond with the girl, and thus she is leaving you in charge of her until the county gets here."

"Well, that's something at least," Katie said and then, knowing that Gary had likely suggested this to Bell, "Thanks."

"No problem." He took a large swig from his mug, grimaced, and then topped it off. "I swear, first thing tomorrow, I'm going to start a donation bucket for that Keurig."

Katie smiled.

"And the bigger one's donation, the better their patrol routes will be."

"And if one doesn't donate at all?"

"Permanent high school liaison duty."

"Shit, let me go get my wallet."

Gary grinned and left the break room, turning right in the hallway to head toward the dispatch desk where he was fielding all the patrols and directing the emergency responders. Most would think it an odd, almost demeaning position for someone with so much time on the force, but it was the position he desired after all these years, and one that required a person to be quick thinking and able to respond without hesitation. It also allowed him to be the so-called "man behind the curtain" when it came to authority within the department. No one would ever say it directly, but Gary was pretty much the ranking official when it came to the law enforcement in Smallwood.

Leaving the police station was easier than Bitsy thought it would be, her body simply following the red Exit signs through the hallways until she came upon a large heavy-looking door that was unlocked. Beyond it a square parking lot waited, one that she initially thought was walled in, but then, after crossing through it, she realized the large brick walls were simply other buildings that backed up alongside the rear parking area, alley-like driveways providing an entrance and exit for the vehicles pulling in and out.

The rumble of the generator faded as she walked along one of those alleyway-like driveways, quickly emerging onto a deserted street that had two-story brick buildings on either side and slanted parking spots for cars. No meters were present, which surprised her. Most of the TV shows and movies she watched with Misty always had parking meters in downtown areas like this, ones that often would result in tickets for the main characters and confrontations between them and the local police.

But not here.

Why?

No answer appeared.

Later, once she found Misty—if she found her—she would ask about this. Until then, it would simply be tucked away within her mind, stored with all the other little things that had made an impression during her years with Misty.

Which way?

Once again, no answer appeared.

She had no idea where Misty was, though from what she had overheard in the police station, she had been picked up on the southern outskirts of the town. All she had to do was figure out what that meant and then head in that direction.

But what if she couldn't find them?

What then?

She couldn't picture herself with anyone but Misty, and from what Misty had told her, the chances of anyone else ever wanting her were slim to none. People wanted new toys, not used ones that misbehaved and were no fun to play with.

Those toys ended up in trash heaps and landfills, or worse, with kids like Sid.

Did Misty still want her?

After the other night, Misty had barely spoken to her, and had it not been for them having to pack up and leave, she probably would still be in her box, left to wait and wonder when Misty would want to play with her again, fear that she would soon get a new toy to replace her dominating her thoughts.

What if she already has a new one?

What if she and the Daddy-man woke up, got the van back on its wheels, and drove away to their new home?

What then?

Katie?

Even though the young lady was a police officer, Bitsy liked her, an odd warmth present when she was with her. Plus, she hadn't treated her like a simple toy and had let her have a warm-water shower and as much pizza as she wanted. And soda. Misty let her have pizza and soda too, but not as much as she wanted, statements on how fat toys were no fun to play with always being made. Katie hadn't seemed to care about that. But she also no longer played with toys. Bitsy had asked her about this while Katie had been sitting at her desk, before Katie had suggested she go lie down on the sofa and try to get some rest.

"Never?" Bitsy had persisted.

"Well, when I was younger I had some dolls, but my brother ripped off their heads and then set them on fire," Katie had said, a laugh echoing.

A Sid!

"Does he still do that?" Bitsy asked.

"I don't know," she said. "Maybe I should bring one home and find out."

Horrified, Bitsy realized that she needed to get back to Misty because even if someone seemed nice like Katie, they might have a Sid-like brother that they couldn't protect her from. Misty didn't have any brothers. It was just her, and while she could sometimes be cruel, she would never pull off Bitsy's head and set her on fire. That was just—Bitsy couldn't think of anything to adequately label how horrible something like that was.

Would Katie really allow that to happen?

Or had she simply been joking?

As nice as she seemed, Bitsy knew she didn't want to risk finding out.

Couldn't risk it.

She had to find Misty.

But which way?

She decided to go left because to the right the street looked like it ended quickly and simply disappeared into the darkness. Plus, in the TV shows and movies she had watched, towns like this oftentimes had maps that people could look at, so once she found the main area of town she might find a large map to look at, one that would give her a better idea of where she needed to go.

A gust of wind hit while she made this decision, one that chilled her to the core, her arms quickly hugging herself as she journeyed down the cold sidewalk, bare feet somehow finding every little protrusion, the sharp edges trying to halt her progress as she went across the pockmarked surface.

"Bitsy?" Katie called into the bathroom, the couch where the girl had been resting empty when she returned from the break room, the blanket folded, pillow on top. "You in here?"

No answer.

She stepped inside and did a quick check.

No Bitsy.

Next she opened the men's bathroom and called into it.

Once again, no answer.

Shit!

She headed back to the sofa and looked around, eyes assessing which direction she could have gone.

Exit.

Oh no, no, no!

She hurried down the hallways to the rear entrance, one that required a key card when coming in, but not going out.

Cold air slammed into her as she opened the heavy door to peer out, a quick scan of the parking area revealing that Bitsy was nowhere to be seen.

Would she really wander away?

Or is she simply exploring the police station?

Though she desperately wanted it to be the latter, Katie was certain it was the former. Bitsy had left, her captivity-conditioned mind producing a desire to get back to her captors. Back to Misty.

And it's my fault.

While she had been getting coffee and venting to Gary about how she had made headway with the girl, Bitsy had wandered away. The irony of it would have been amusing if it had happened to someone else and didn't involve a child who had obviously been abused.

How could she be so careless?

How could—

A patrol vehicle pulled into the parking area.

Katie waited for the occupant to get out.

It was Dean, a five-year veteran of the force.

"Thanks," he said, assuming she was holding the door for him.

"No problem," she replied. "Hey, you didn't happen to see a young girl wandering around out there on Main?"

"No. Someone lose a kid?"

"Something like that," she said and pushed past him to go check the streets herself.

"Good luck," Dean said as the door shut behind her.

Knowing it was probably pointless and that Bitsy was gone, Katie hurried through the parking lot and down the alleyway to Main Street, ponytail whipping back and forth as she quickly scanned the deserted street.

No Bitsy.

Next she hurried around the corner on the right and checked McDowell.

Once again, no Bitsy.

From there she rounded herself around until she was near the main entrance of the police station.

Still no Bitsy.

The girl was gone.

And she was taking Katie's career with her.

Not her fault.

Still, she couldn't help but feel a bit peeved at the girl.

How could she do this?

How could she throw away her freedom to try to go back to whoever it was that had been holding her captive?

Katie knew the questions were useless and that her focus needed to be on finding the girl, who couldn't have gone far, not while on foot and wearing clothing that would stand out, yet she couldn't help but let them bounce around within her mind as she headed to her desk to grab the keys to her patrol vehicle, hope that she would bump into Bitsy as the girl finished a simple exploration of the police station going unrealized.

As humiliating as it was, she had to go tell Gary.

He would alert everyone to be on the lookout for Bitsy.

That was the most important thing at the moment.

Finding Bitsy and making sure she was safe.

After that, Katie could then deal with trying to repair the damage this would do to her career—if possible.

Goodbye FBI…

Stop!

Focus!

Gary was on the radio when she entered the dispatch area.

She waited a second, his eyes looking at a map he had laid out that he was continuously marking to show what routes were clear and which ones weren't, the importance of having such up-to-date information before him unquestionable when trying to guide emergency responders to scenes.

A memory of Iraq appeared, their unit having come under attack as it provided security for a contracted waste-removal convoy that had been transporting piss and shit from a coalition base to a dump site outside of Baghdad.

The routes they had been provided for the convoy had been compromised and an alternative one dispatched to them over the radio, one that apparently hadn't been noted as being unusable due to an attack three days earlier, the road nothing but a giant crater from the VBED that had hit an Iraqi police patrol.

"You okay?" Gary asked.

"Yeah," Katie said, shaking the memory away.

"You saw the BOLO?"

"BOLO?" she asked.

"About the van and kidnapping suspect."

"No, I was looking for Bitsy and was going to have you put out a message to everyone."

"Wait, what?"

"She left. While we were in the break room."

"Shit."

"Yeah. Was the BOLO about her?"

"No, but it mentioned a van, a possible kidnapping victim named Abigail Abbott from North Carolina, and the name Misty, which is what caught my attention."

"When did that come in?"

"Just a few minutes ago, while we were in the break room."

"But nothing about Bitsy?"

"No. But still, what are the chances she is talking about a different van and a different Misty?"

"Is this Misty listed as a kidnap victim as well?"

"That's what's odd about it. The kidnap victim for North Carolina is specifically listed as a kidnap victim, one that went missing a couple days ago while walking home from school. But Misty is simply listed as a young lady the perp is traveling with." He clicked around with his mouse a bit and then shifted his screen. "See."

Katie leaned in. "Out of Champaign-Urbana?"

"Yeah, the suspect in the kidnapping works for the university."

"Jesus. How did they link him with a missing girl from North Carolina?"

"Doesn't say. Why don't you give the investigator a call?"

"Okay, yeah, I'll do that. Can you put out word on Bitsy?"

"Yep," he said, picking up the radio.

Katie dialed the number of the investigator while he did this, his call going out as a phone down in Springfield rang in her ear.

Bitsy didn't find a map in the center of town, which was a bit upsetting because she figured that if there had been one, she would have been able to locate the cemetery on it, which in turn would have shown her the direction she needed to start walking in. No map meant no direction, so she walked aimlessly for quite some time, sticking to the darkest areas she could find and ducking out of sight every time she saw a vehicle that wasn't the van, which eventually led her into a neighborhood that bordered the downtown part of Small-wood, her feet finding that the sidewalks in front of the homes were, for the most part, less painful than the ones that had been in front of the empty businesses. Why this was, she didn't know, the TV shows and movies that she and Misty often watched never addressing such topics.

And then something pierced her foot, the pain causing her to yelp, a chunk of something black and gritty coming up with her as she tried lifting her foot away from whatever it was that had stuck her, the weight as it dangled bringing about more pain.

It wouldn't let go.

Dropping down to a knee and then her butt, she studied the issue, discovering that she had stepped on a torn piece of shingle, the small roofing tack having embedded itself into her heel.

Relief arrived.

Had it been a nail or some rusty piece of twisted metal, her ability to walk once it was pulled free might have been compromised, but it was simply a roofing tack, which she was familiar with and could walk on if needed. Not that she wanted to, her fingers quickly pulling the tack free, a bubble of blood following, but she could, Misty having used such tacks when teaching her to walk like a girl. Four tacks for each heel, lightly taped in place so that the tips were just pressed against her flesh, her feet forced to walk on her toes as if in heels so that the points didn't push through into her skin. Misty had done this for several weeks, until walking as if she were wearing heels became something Bitsy did without thinking. The training had been pure agony and led to many tears, but in the end it had been worth it, the heels she eventually stepped into feeling like an extension of her body. She could walk, run, skip, and jump in them without a problem. Misty...not so much. But then she hadn't been trained with roofing tacks.

She stood and took a test step.

As expected, the weight coming down hurt, but it was nothing like having four roofing tacks in there, or the candle flames while strung up. It was also a good reminder for her to watch her step and be a bit more careful. This time it had just been a roofing tack, but next time it could be something that sheared the flesh from her leg or twisted her ankle until it snapped. If that happened, she would never make it back to Misty.

"Sparky, no!" a voice shouted.

Bitsy twisted, eyes going wide as a dog charged toward her, a scream leaving her lips as she tried backing away and tripped over her own feet, the dog's paws quickly upon her chest, nose in her face. And then it started licking her.

"Sparky!" a young man said, yanking the dog off her. Then, "I'm so sorry about that. Are you okay?"

"I-I-I-" Bitsy said, unable to continue, hands checking her face for bite marks, but only finding goo where its tongue had struck. It was gross.

"I'm so, *so* sorry," he repeated. "Sparky gets excited when he meets new people."

Bitsy rubbed at the goo with her sleeve and then looked up at the young man, who held out his free hand.

She took it.

He helped her back up to her feet.

"If you give him a scratch behind his ears, he'll be cool and your best friend for life."

Bitsy hesitated. She had never touched a dog before but knew that they sometimes liked to chew on things. Would it want to chew on her? Would it try to make her squeak?

"It's okay if you don't want to," he said.

"It won't bite me?" Bitsy asked.

"Oh no, he's completely harmless. Just gets too excited. Right, Sparky?"

Sparky seemed to grow excited at hearing his own name.

Bitsy decided to give it a try and slowly reached out her hand to touch the dog behind his ears.

He swung his nose toward her hand, startling her.

"No, no, it's okay," the young man said.

Bitsy took a deep breath and tried again, this time managing to touch Sparky behind the ears and scratch at his fur.

Sparky smiled at her and started wagging his tail.

"She likes it," Bitsy said, her own smile appearing.

"He," the young man said.

"He?" Bitsy asked.

"Sparky's a boy."

"Oh." She continued to scratch at the fur. "Sorry."

"And my name's Andrew," the young man said. He held out a hand.

"I'm Bitsy," Bitsy said, carefully taking the hand.

Andrew smiled. "Sparky was excited at the door. I thought he needed to use the bathroom, but I guess he just wanted to say hi."

Bitsy didn't reply to that.

"Are you sure you're okay?" Andrew asked.

"Yes," Bitsy said.

"You have a bandage."

"Oh." She touched her head. "I bumped it in the storm."

He eyed her.

"But it's okay now."

"That's good. Do you live around here?"

"Oh, um...no." She looked down. "Our house is gone."

"I'm sorry," Andrew said. "Were you heading to the school?"

"The school?" she asked.

"Yeah, that's where everyone goes if they lost their house."

"Really?"

"Yeah."

"Why?"

"They have beds set up and people that help you find a place to stay."

"Wow. I didn't know that." Was that where the Daddy-man had been taking them? Were he and Misty there now? Hope started to build. "How do I get there?"

"It's actually not far from here. I can show you if you want."

"Yes," she said, nodding. "Please."

"Okay, yeah, let me just go get Sparky's leash."

Bitsy nodded again.

He smiled and started to turn, but then stopped and asked, "Did you lose your shoes?"

Bitsy looked down at her bare feet and for a moment was going to mention how she had outgrown her last pair of heels and didn't have any new ones yet, but then decided he might not understand and simply said, "Yeah."

"What size are you?" he asked.

"Um…" She shook her head.

He waved a hand. "Never mind. I have an extra pair for cutting the grass. They'll probably be too big, but better than being barefoot out here. Lots of shit from the storm, especially toward the school."

Bitsy nodded, though he didn't see, his body already heading back into the house, his hand on Sparky's collar, guiding the dog in with him.

She waited, uneasy about simply standing alone on the sidewalk.

A few seconds later, that unease faded as he returned, the end of a leash in one hand, a pair of old shoes in another. "Here you go. See if those will work."

They weren't heels, but she figured that since she was already in pants it would be okay. And if it wasn't, well, Misty would punish her, but that would be okay too because at least they would be together again.

That was all that mattered right now.

"They good?" Andrew asked once she had them on her feet.

"Yes, thank you," Bitsy said.

"Excellent, let's go." He gave Sparky's leash a bit of a tug. "Come on, boy."

Bitsy watched as Sparky started to walk, thoughts on how Misty gave similar tugs on her leash when they went on walks through the field behind the house entering her mind. She hoped such moments would happen again.

SIX

"You okay?" Abigail asked, having heard a grunt in the darkness of the barn.

"Yeah," Norman said, a heavy, wet-sounding breath echoing.

Coughing followed.

Abigail winced, the sound of his hacking something up turning her empty stomach.

"What were you doing?" she asked once he was finished.

"Trying to get—"

He started hacking again.

Abigail tried to block out the sound but failed.

"Sorry," he muttered.

"It's okay," she replied.

As disgusting as the sounds were, she knew he couldn't help them, not with his nose having been crushed. And honestly, she was no picnic herself, the smell of her urine-soaked panties and skirt filling the air every time she shifted herself.

Can he smell it?

He couldn't breathe through his nose, that much she

knew, but what about his sense of smell? Had that been compromised as well?

Ask him.

Do I smell like piss?

As crazy as it sounded given their situation, she couldn't bring herself to voice this, not with the embarrassment it would bring.

He took a deep breath, one that was louder than his typical mouth ones, and then, her eyes just barely able to see him given the darkness, folded himself over once again, his head leaning in while his back arched against the post, almost as if he was thrusting his chest toward his face.

Why?

Brain damage?

When not hacking up bloody clumps of mucus from his busted nose, he seemed pretty lucid and aware, so if asked she would say he was okay, but then one never knew what was going on when it came to head injuries. Every minute that passed could be a minute when his brain continued swelling against the skull, his mental capacity growing worse and worse, uncontrollable spasms occurring as signals within the gray matter got triggered and crossed.

Is that what this is?

A spasm as his brain malfunctions?

The sound of his straining ended with a curse and then more hacking.

She cleared her throat.

"Are you sure you're okay?" she asked.

"Yeah."

And if he'd said no?

Then what?

No answer appeared.

She wouldn't be able to help.

And screaming for the Misty girl wouldn't do anything.

"Oh, he's hurt. I better call the police."

Yeah, right.

She would probably pull up a chair and watch as he succumbed to his injury, an odd satisfaction and maybe even sexual release arriving.

Or would she?

Was she like the man?

On the surface the answer seemed to be yes, but maybe it wasn't really that simple. Maybe she was a prisoner just like them, but one that had been conditioned to the point of being able to roam free.

Abigail had heard about such things happening.

After years of being a captive, subject to sexual abuse and torture…

She shivered.

Norman started straining again, and like the other times, eventually gave up with a curse.

Thankfully, he didn't start hacking this time, just took several deep breaths through his mouth.

"What are you trying to do?" she asked, a clink of chain as she tried to adjust her own wrists into a more comfortable position reaching her ears. It didn't work.

"Trying to open my pocket," he said.

"Why?"

"I have a key."

"Seriously?" she asked, the word *key* bringing a sudden spark of hope into her mind.

"Yeah." Mouth breath. "And if I can get it out, I can get free."

"You're sure?"

"Yeah."

"But?" she asked, sensing the word within his voice.

"I can't reach it." He sighed, defeat present.

"Keep trying," she said.

"I will, I just…I can't stay bent over like that for long with my nose."

"Better that pain than whatever is going to happen later."

"I know."

"And your body will get more and more limber each time you try." She didn't know if this was really the case, but suggesting it couldn't hurt.

He took a deep breath and tried again.

And again.

And again.

Each time ended in failure, one that was either punctuated with a "fuck!" or the sounds of his hacking. Sometimes both.

It was disgusting and frustrating, yet she didn't want to lose the hope, not when the key was their only chance, her lips constantly voicing statements of encouragement.

And then an idea arrived.

"What about your feet?" she asked.

"My feet?"

"Yeah, could you bend your leg inward and open the pocket with your toes?" She moved her own foot while asking this, the darkness making the demonstration pointless.

Rather than answer, he simply tried, the sounds of his movements reaching her ears.

She shifted herself while he did this, the smell of piss appearing once again. Her armpits were bad too, and given the way her wrists were lifted up behind her head, her face was unable to get away from the sweaty pit fabric. It was nauseating.

But at least she wasn't in that box.

That had been unbearable.

Hour after hour, unable to move, body and backpack wedged in, ankles and mouth taped shut, cuffs so tight that her fingers were numb, each bounce of the van jolting through her, mind wanting them to arrive at wherever it was they were going just so she could be released from the tiny compartment, yet at the same time fearing that moment because she knew worse horrors would likely follow.

And then finally being released, her body screaming as he unfolded it and forced her to start moving, legs unable to support her weight, fingers feeling as if they were on fire once the handcuffs were removed and the blood started working its way back into them.

He had tossed her backpack onto a kitchen floor once they were inside and then dragged her down some wooden steps into a cold cellar, one that had a girl in it already, body hanging from her wrists, toes unable to reach the floor, eyes watching them from a face that seemed squished between her arms.

"Misty!" the man had shouted, Abigail wincing as the voice bombarded her eardrums.

Misty had come down several seconds later, Abigail trying to see her but unable to shift herself in the right direction as the man held her in place.

"Sorry, sorry, sorry," Misty said. "I was punishing her."

"Well, continue it somewhere else," he said.

With that, Misty had taken the girl down and helped her up the stairs.

Abigail had thought she would replace the girl, fear at what the pain would be like as she dangled there dominating her mind, but the man had chained her to the wall instead. Her hands were still over her head, but not to the point where all her body weight was supported by them, the position allowing for her butt to rest on the cold concrete floor.

He had then gotten her some water.

The first few sips were great, the moisture barely reaching her throat as the parched flesh within her mouth soaked it all up, but then it turned bad as he forced her to down several glasses, her stomach feeling as if it would purge it back up.

"Please," she begged, another glass held before her. "No more."

"It's either this or I put a funnel in your mouth and piss down your throat," he said.

She drank the water.

And then he left her alone, her eyes watching as his body disappeared around the corner and went up the stairs, wood groaning with the weight followed by a heavy door being secured into its frame, her mind left to wonder what was going to follow.

"I need to get my shoes off," Norman muttered.

His voice brought her back. "Can you slip them off?"

"I'm trying, but they're too tight."

"Can you undo the laces with your—" *Teeth* was going to be her suggestion, but then the door to the barn opened, startling her into silence.

It was dark.

Really dark!

Darker than outside, which was also really dark.

No windows.

Misty hadn't realized this earlier while in the barn, her focus always being on the two captives and finding things she needed to use like the shovel. But now, looking back, she should have noted this would be a problem given how dim the barn had been during the daylight hours. Light had managed to get in, but not much, and it had been more of an overall glow from the sunlight hitting the outside rather than a source itself.

She needed a flashlight or a lantern.

Something so she could see.

But she didn't have anything and had no idea where something like it would be.

Unless…

Did Daddy bring his hunting bag?

She had been so focused on getting her own bags together that she hadn't paid much attention to what he had brought, but she was fairly certain he would have taken that particular bag knowing he would need to hunt again once they were in the new house. Inside it was a police outfit that he sometimes wore to trick the schoolgirls into thinking they were needed to answer questions about a crime they may have been involved in, their looks matching a description from a witness. With that police outfit was a belt with a flashlight, one that she could—

Wait.

"Hey!" she called into the dark barn. "Mr. Policeman."

Nothing.

"Hey!"

Nothing.

"Mr. Policeman," she persisted. "I have a question."

"What?" a muffled, odd-sounding voice asked.

His nose?

I must have really hurt him bad.

"Where's your flashlight?" she asked.

One hadn't been on his belt when she took that, though he'd had other items of interest on there, all of them making the belt really heavy. She had also gotten his wallet, which had been in his back pocket.

He said something she couldn't understand.

"What?" she asked.

"He said it's in his car," the schoolgirl snapped.

The car.

It was still on the road.

She didn't want to walk all that way, but knew she needed some sort of light. She also still needed to move the car so that it didn't act like a beacon to other police officers. Only she didn't know how to drive.

Did the girl?

Could she risk taking her out of the barn and bringing her to the car?

She had the police officer's gun, and if she put Bitsy's

collar and leash on the girl, she could control her with that hand while holding the gun with the other.

Bitsy's collar and leash.

Thinking about them brought back the questions on where Bitsy was and whether she was okay.

Was she scared?

Especially now that it was dark out?

Misty wanted to find her but didn't know how. She wanted to bring her inside the barn where it was safe and cuddle up with her. She wanted to apologize for the way she had reacted the other night.

No, not in the barn.

Not in front of those two.

Going inside the house would be better.

That way they could maybe find a bed and lie down in it together.

Bitsy liked it when they did that. Misty was sure of this because whenever they were in bed together Bitsy would put her arms around her and curl up with her face on her chest and fall asleep with a smile. Plus, whenever she didn't allow Bitsy to sleep with her and put her in the toy box for the night, she would find dry tear crusts on her cheeks. She never heard her though, Bitsy always making sure to keep her sobs quiet so that she would not disturb Misty. It was nice and something that Daddy's schoolgirl toys wouldn't do. Whenever he tried to sleep with them, they would not only keep him awake, but her as well, and probably Bitsy, Daddy eventually having to put them back in the cellar.

"Hey," Misty called. "Schoolgirl?"

"My name's Abigail," the schoolgirl said from the darkness.

"Abigail," Misty said, testing the name. It was the first time she had heard the name of one of the schoolgirls, and while she knew they all had names, it somehow felt odd to now have a name implanted in her mind while thinking about her. "That's a nice name."

Abigail didn't reply.

"Do you know how to drive?" Misty asked.

Nothing.

"Abigail!" she snapped. "Do you know how to drive?"

"Yeah," Abigail snapped back. "I know how to drive."

Misty considered this and then without really thinking said, "Okay, I'll be right back."

"Ooh, I can't wait," Abigail said, voice carrying a nasty edge to it.

The statement stung, but then Misty realized the schoolgirl was probably irritable after everything that had happened since leaving the house. Probably hungry and thirsty too. Once she was back with the collar and leash, she would need to feed her, or at least give her some water.

But first, she would need some light so she could see what she was doing.

And to get light she needed to go to the van, and if Daddy's flashlight wasn't in there, she would need to go to the police car.

Back and forth, back and forth.

All because she hadn't planned well for the darkness.

Daddy would have planned better.

But then he was more experienced with things like this.

She wasn't.

For her, just leaving the house was a rare treat, one that brought with it anxiety because she never knew what to expect. Even with Daddy coaching her beforehand. And this was much different than simply getting to go to a restaurant or the grocery store or the bookstore or the mall. This had been a move. They were searching for a new home. And now since Daddy was dead she was in charge. Nothing he had ever done had prepared her for such a thing. She wasn't ready.

Ready or not…

She liked those words better when she was playing hide and seek with Bitsy.

Will Abigail help me find her?

Once they were in the car and she had the leash and gun, Misty could have her drive her around the area, looking for Bitsy rather than simply driving the car up and behind the barn, or off into a field somewhere.

Had Daddy been alive that was what they probably would have done—would have *been doing*.

They would have driven around looking for her.

Was it too late?

Would they be able to find her in the darkness?

Maybe it would be better to wait until morning.

Being in charge was hard.

She had too many decisions to make.

Go get the light.

And the collar and leash.

And the police uniform outfit.

She knew it fit since she had worn it several times while he was at school, Daddy being a short man who she had quickly matched in height during the last year and a half.

Did she need it?

Would wearing it help make others think she was a police officer if anyone else came to the farm to see if they needed help, or would they know she wasn't and simply laugh at her?

"I think she'll be gone for a bit," Abigail said once Misty had left the barn, mind shaking away the questions she now carried on why the girl wanted to know if she could drive. "How're the laces coming?"

"I can't reach them," Norman said, exhaustion present.

Jesus.

If their positions were reversed, she would have been able to get her shoes off without a problem, but with him, his middle-aged joints seemed to be saying *fuck you*.

"And you're sure you can't slip them off?" she asked.

"I'm trying," he said, the sounds of his heels kicking at the knotted laces appearing.

She waited, shifting several times, the position growing more and more unbearable with each passing second until she finally couldn't take it and stood up, the wooden stall rail vibrating a bit with her movement while her back and legs popped.

A spinning sensation hit, forcing her to lean against the stall rail.

"What're you doing?"

"Standing," she gasped, eyes closed against the turbulence, even though it was internal.

"You okay?"

She took several deep breaths and then said, "Yeah, fine."

"You sure?"

Another deep breath.

If I said no, what would you be able to do?

She opened her eyes, the darkness of the barn replacing the darkness of her lids.

Behind her she heard him working at the laces again.

Hands on the rail, she worked her fingers a bit, the cuffs not as tight this time around as they had been during her initial journey in the box, yet still causing circulation issues given that she was forced to rest her weight against the metal links while sitting.

Could I saw through the board with the chain links? she asked herself, hands slowly working the tiny chain back and forth for a moment against the edge to see what would happen, and then going a bit faster, the metal links digging into her flesh with each pull.

"Is it true that you can snap open handcuffs with a sudden

pull in opposite directions?" she asked, hands fisted in anticipation of giving it a try.

"I've heard of it but never seen it happen and"—deep mouth breath—"wouldn't recommend trying. You'll just end up tearing *into your flesh*." A horrible gasp for air punctuated this.

"You're probably right," Abigail said but then tried anyway, her hands coming together for a moment into a prayer-like clasp before bouncing out in opposite directions.

It didn't work.

Teeth clamped, she tried again, her thinking being she needed to make sure each wrist pulled against the part of the link that swung open and closed.

Once again, it didn't work, and this time a bit of a cry slipped out from her lips.

"Told you," Norman said.

Abigail ignored that and braced herself for a third attempt, her hands making fists once again in anticipation of the sudden pull and pain.

Focus.

Deep breath.

PULL!

It was the most painful attempt yet, and one that caused the link around her right wrist to tighten rather than open when she banged it against the edge of the wooden rail beneath the one she was threaded through, the sound of the ratchet clicking tighter echoing through the barn as she screamed.

"Did it open?" Norman asked, obviously misinterpreting the ratchet sound.

"No!" Abigail cried and then cussed several times. The link was too tight now. Far tighter than it had been while she was in the trunk.

She could actually feel the blood slamming up against the sudden closure within her hand, like cars on an interstate coming up on a blocked lane. It was horrible. And painful. Too painful.

"Easy," Norman urged. He likely didn't know what had happened, just that something had.

If "easy" meant body-slamming the rail, she complied with his suggestion, her body hitting it hard enough for the hinges to squeal.

"Abby, what are—"

She slammed herself against it again, her mind picturing the wood cracking and then snapping, all while it simply wobbled a bit in its supports, her body doing little to compromise its structural integrity.

"Stop!" Norman urged. "You're going to hurt yourself."

She knew he was right but couldn't give in, not when it meant admitting defeat.

"Once I get my shoe off—"

"But you can't!" she snapped. "The key is in your pocket, but it might as well be on the other side of the barn for all the good it's doing us!"

"Yeah, but hurting yourself won't"—mouth breath—"do any good either." Another mouth breath. "Those stalls were designed for"—mouth breath—"keeping animals inside."

Abigail knew he was right.

"It will be okay."

"Will it?" she asked, teeth clenching once the words were spoken.

"Yes," he insisted. "I'll either get the keys or someone will find us." Mouth breath. "She can't keep us here forever."

"What if she decides to kill us?" Abigail asked.

"I don't think she will," Norman said.

"Bullshit!"

"Honestly."

"Why not?"

"I don't know. I think she's a victim like us, but just

doesn't realize it yet." He choked a bit, but this time it didn't sound like anything came up.

Abigail squeezed her right hand into a fist to fight the numbness, a horrible chill already spreading through the fingers. It was worse than when she had been in the box.

Would the girl loosen the handcuff when she came back?

Would she care?

"Got it," Norman said.

"The key?" she asked.

"The laces."

Abigail sighed.

"Hang in there."

She didn't reply to that, her only thought being the pain in her wrists and the numbness in her fingers as she opened and closed her fist, her body eventually sliding back down into a sitting position, her weight adding to the discomfort of the cuffs as her wrists were forced to offer some support.

The walk back to the van was uneventful and much easier than Misty's previous journeys given that she wasn't carrying or dragging anything or anyone. The only downside was the darkness, which slowed her, the inability to accurately see what it was she was stepping upon in the old field inducing quite a bit of hesitation with her steps. An odd fear of snakes was also present. They liked fields. She knew this because she had come across many in the fields behind the house, some of them being rattlers.

"Don't mess with them," Daddy had warned when she told him about them. "If you get bit, you know I can't take you to a doctor."

Misty knew that and assured him that he didn't need to worry. She wouldn't get close to them, her fear of the slithering beasts and their potential for harm if they bit her making it so she would always keep her distance. Bitsy too.

The trouble was, what if they didn't see one while playing their games? What if they rounded a tree trunk or jumped down from a rock and landed upon one? Would Daddy really deny them medical treatment? With Bitsy, the answer was yes, but with her, she didn't know. He had said he couldn't because it would raise too many questions about who she was, but at the same time she doubted he would be able to sit around and watch the poison kill her.

Doesn't matter.

Daddy was dead and would never have to face such a decision.

Even so, the question lingered.

As did questions about her future.

Where would she go?

The police car wouldn't be able to get her far, even if she was in a police uniform, not when it would call attention to itself once the town realized it was missing, and she didn't think she would be able to get the van back on its wheels.

But maybe she could find a different car.

One that she could have the schoolgirl drive until they found a new house, one up north like Daddy had wanted, in the woods near a lake. Such a place had always been his dream. A dream that she was interested in experiencing. A dream that could still be a reality.

She thought about his body.

Maybe her inability to dig a hole for him had been for the best.

Being entombed by a lake in the woods would make him happy, and once there, she would be able to visit with him rather than simply picturing the area of dirt that she had left him in down here. And he would have the schoolgirl with him, her body buried alongside his once she had finished being a driver for her and Bitsy.

Bitsy.

Sadness threatened to return but then was quickly stifled

as she did her best to push the thoughts of Bitsy away and focus her attention upon the van, which was looming before her, its dark shape sticking out against the nighttime darkness.

Was it still visible from the road?

If so, then staying at the farm for the night might not be the best option.

It's the only option.

No…

If she wanted, she could have the schoolgirl drive her around until they found a new car and then take that northward.

Or maybe it would be better to have the policeman drive her—that way the schoolgirl could keep Daddy company in the trunk. Given his age, the policeman probably would be a better driver, and he might know the way up north better than the schoolgirl would.

But could she really control him?

If she had Bitsy with her, then yes. Working together, the two could keep him secure. Without her though…

Think about it later.

Right now she needed the bag with the flashlight so that she could move around the barn without too much trouble, and she needed the collar and leash so that she could have the schoolgirl drive the police car.

Or…

She looked out toward where the road was, thoughts on trying to drive the car herself once again entering into her mind.

Could she do it?

She had the keys with her.

And it didn't really look all that difficult, her eyes having studied what Daddy did several times on those occasions when he had allowed her to accompany him on errands and for special dinners, her hope always being that when he finally did start teaching her that he would be impressed by how much she already knew.

Hesitation gripped her.

Get Daddy's bag.

And change into the uniform

Once she did that, she could make a decision on how she was going to handle the police car.

"It's not going to work," Norman said.

"It has to!" Abigail snapped, his statement and the pain in her right hand threatening to push her over the edge.

"It won't. I can't bend it that far."

"Then try something else!"

"Like what?"

"I don't know, just stand up and start hopping up and down until the keys bounce out."

"The pocket's buttoned shut."

"Then try with your mouth again, or your toes. Fucking do something!"

He didn't reply.

She stood up again, her wrists unable to take the weight that sitting down produced.

A grunt appeared.

And then several mouth breaths.

He was trying with his teeth again.

She shook her head.

After all the work to get his shoe off, they were back at the mouth attempts.

Such a waste.

But really, now that she thought about it, the chances of him getting the pocket open with his mouth were better. Trying to bend a leg toward one's body without being able to grab it and pull was pointless if one wasn't already flexible enough to touch it to his face, which he obviously wasn't.

Why she hadn't considered this before while encouraging him to get his shoe off, she didn't know, but now she chided herself for the lapse in judgment.

"Are you able to swing it?" she asked, left hand exploring the cuff link around her right wrist.

"What do you mean?" he asked, an exhausting ring present within his voice.

"Can you sort of like buck your chest upward to swing the pocket toward your mouth and catch it?"

"I'll try."

The sound that followed was bizarre.

Pathetic too.

Had she not been in so much pain, she would have felt sorry for him, but her mind couldn't go that route, not when he was her only chance at freedom.

Several more odd sounds followed, her mind picturing the noises as being pre-thrust motivation sounds. Sort of like karate shouts as one swung his fists and feet.

And then there was a muffled shout that could only be one of triumph.

"You get it?" she asked.

Nothing but a muffled sound followed, which was good because it meant his mouth was likely full of cloth.

And then he let out a gasp and took several breaths.

"What happened?" she asked.

"I had…it," he said.

"But?"

"Couldn't breathe."

"But you still got it," she said. "That's encouraging."

"Yeah."

He took another breath.

She wanted to tell him to keep trying, but knew he would even without her saying it.

The odd thrusting grunt echoed, followed by a curse.

"What happened?" she asked.

"Something stuck me," he said. "This post is full of splinters."

"Same with this rail," she said. "How old do you think this barn is?"

"Not sure."

With that, he made another attempt, the muffled sounds as he caught the cloth in his mouth once again appearing.

And then what?

Did he try to undo the button with his tongue and teeth, or simply pull until the button came free?

Or maybe grind his teeth behind the button trying to sever the thread?

Whichever it was, he was right in the middle of it, and this time it didn't seem like he was going to stop until it was free or he choked to death, the sound of him taking deep breaths while the button was likely between his teeth appearing.

She continued exploring her cuffs while he did this, her fingers desperately trying to figure out a way to loosen the grip of the right link.

"Got it!"

She spun toward him, cuff links digging into her flesh with the movement, momentarily afraid to ask what he meant, but then finding her voice.

The door to the barn opened, Misty stepping inside, the beam of a flashlight scanning back and forth until it found Abigail, the light blinding her.

Misty then shifted it toward Norman.

"What are you doing?" Misty asked, flashlight beam back on the schoolgirl Abigail, who was standing up rather than sitting, her face looking guilty. Pain was present as well.

"My cuffs are too tight," Abigail said. "Can you please loosen them?"

Misty eyed her.

"Please. I bumped one of them and it tightened and it's cutting off the blood flow. Please! I can't feel my fingers."

Something wasn't right.

Misty could sense it.

She swung the light back onto the police officer, who shifted his eyes away from the beam.

From what she could see, he was still secure, as was the girl, light reflecting off both their cuffs, yet something was up. She couldn't put her finger on what it was but knew it to be so.

His shoe!

Had it come off earlier when she had been dragging him toward the post?

Was that what was wrong?

No.

It was something else.

But what?

No answer arrived.

"Please," Abigail said again. "My cuffs."

Misty turned back to her, light bathing the girl.

"You were trying to get free," she said.

"No," Abigail said.

"Yes." *But only managed to make things worse.*

"Please!"

Misty sighed and stepped toward the girl, left hand holding the collar and leash. "You're coming with me for a bit."

"Why?"

"I need you to move his car."

Abigail looked toward the policeman and then back. Pain was still present upon her face, yet it had changed. Misty couldn't make out what exactly the change was, but for some reason it chilled her.

She turned to the policeman, light upon him.

His eyes squinted against it but did not look away.

His nose looked terrible, mucus having crusted upon his upper lip and parts of his chin. It was also on his shirt, almost as if it had been oozing.

Or had he hacked it out, but not gotten it clear of his own body?

Misty grimaced at the thought but didn't let it dominate her focus as she shifted the light, eyes looking for any signs of what it was that had taken place while she was away.

Nothing jumped out at her.

She looked at the shoe.

It was from his right foot.

"What happened?" Misty asked.

"I kicked it off," Norman said.

"Why?"

He made a shrug-like motion. "Had an itch."

Misty considered this and then stepped around behind him to check his wrists.

The handcuffs looked secure.

She knelt down and tested them.

Secure.

She stood and turned back to Abigail.

Hope.

That's what it was.

She had hope.

But why?

Was it simply because she knew her cuffs were going to be opened in a moment and the pain she was in would fade?

No.

It was something else.

But what?

She studied both of them again, but nothing more was revealed.

It has to do with the policeman.

What would Daddy do?

Several scenes from various videos he had made played

out across her mind, but none of them offered up any realistic ideas.

She turned back toward Abigail.

"You better not have been lying about being able to drive," she said.

"Why would I lie?" Abigail asked, almost as if she was insulted by the suggestion.

Misty didn't reply to that and simply stepped forward to put the collar around Abigail's throat, the flashlight tucked up under her arm while she did this, thoughts on Bitsy and how much she missed her trying to work their way into her focus.

"Jesus," Abigail whined once it was in place, throat making a swallowing noise. "It's too tight."

Misty gave the leash a tug to silence her complaints, one that would have sealed Bitsy's lips until she was told she could speak again. This was not the case with Abigail, who let out a choking noise and then called her a bitch.

"You want me to be a bitch?" Misty said, getting close. "Because I can be a bitch."

With that, she reached out her free hand and closed her fingers across the cuffed wrist, squeezing it until she heard a ratchet click.

Abigail let out a scream while bucking against her, fruitlessly trying to loosen the link.

Misty stepped back and watched her struggle.

After a few seconds, she gave the leash a gentle tug. "Schoolgirl, look at me."

Abigail didn't look at her, eyes and fingers focused on the wrist and cuff link, tears present.

"Schoolgirl," Misty said again, giving the leash a second, firmer tug.

Abigail looked at her, tears now running down her cheeks. "Please, take it off!"

"Do you promise to behave?"

"Yes."

"Say it."

"I promise."

"You promise what?"

"To behave."

Misty nodded and then stepped forward to release the cuff link.

Abigail cried out as the blood raced back into her fingers, body dropping down to her knees.

Misty let her stay like that for a moment, one hand on the leash, the other returning the key to her pocket and grabbing the flashlight from beneath her arm.

She looked at the policeman.

Nothing had changed.

She turned back to the schoolgirl. "Put the handcuff back on."

Abigail complied, fingers carefully clicking the link closed, the sound of three ratchet clicks echoing.

"Let me see."

Abigail stood up and stepped forward, wrists out in front of her.

It was tight but could be tighter without causing harm, her fingers giving it another click.

Abigail winced.

"Knock it off," Misty said and gave the leash a yank. "Let's go. The sooner we move the police car, the sooner you can be back, and this time you'll have some food and water."

Abigail did not protest.

The two left the barn.

SEVEN

"He thinks he's a girl," Andrew said with a chuckle as they waited for Sparky to finish with the fire hydrant.

"What do you mean?" Bitsy asked, a bit confused.

"He won't lift his leg. Always squats. Has ever since he was a puppy."

"Oh," Bitsy said.

"In the world of dogs, it's odd, kind of like if I started using the women's bathroom or you the men's room."

Bitsy nodded.

Nothing else about the leg lifting was said as the two waited for Sparky to finish up with the fire hydrant.

Andrew fidgeted with the leash.

It was cloth rather than leather.

Same with the collar Sparky wore.

She liked hers better.

A gust of wind arrived, her sweatshirt providing very little protection against it.

Andrew, noticing this, shrugged off his jacket and handed it to her.

"No, it's okay," Bitsy said, waving a hand.

"No, no, I have on two shirts and a sweatshirt. I'll be fine."

She smiled and put the jacket on.

It was warm, like a cocoon.

"Just don't let me forget about it once we find your family," he said. "My dad will kill me if I lose it."

Her eyes went wide.

"Not literally," he added, seeing her look.

Bitsy didn't reply, questions on his daddy and whether he was like the Daddy-man entering her mind but going unasked.

Sparky finished and they started walking again, the shoes he had let her wear, while way too big, proving to be a good idea given all the debris they started to come across.

"Oh my God, look at that!" Andrew said, voice nearly a shout.

Startled, Bitsy followed his finger but couldn't tell what he was pointing at. "What is it?" she asked.

"There's a freaking toilet in the yard over there."

She saw it.

"Can you believe it?"

"It's crazy," Bitsy said, unsure how to answer his question.

"Yeah," he said.

They continued onward.

"There it is," he said a few minutes later.

This time Bitsy didn't need him to indicate what it was he was referring to and simply said, "It's big."

"I guess." Then, a few seconds later, "Where do you go to school?"

"Nowhere. I stay at home."

"Oh, home school?"

Bitsy thought about the school games that she and Misty played, she being the student, Misty the teacher, paddle always within reach if she couldn't read the sentences correctly, and nodded. "Yep."

"That's cool."

Again, Bitsy wasn't sure how to respond to that.

Up ahead a police car rounded a corner and started down the street toward them.

Fear tickled her bowels.

It drove past without stopping.

Bitsy let out a silent sigh.

Andrew himself didn't seem fazed.

They kept walking.

"So, what was the tornado like?" Andrew asked.

Does he know about the van?

Should I tell him?

No!

"I'm sorry," he said. "Probably too soon."

"It's okay."

"I'll tell you, I was scared shitless."

"Me too."

"I've seen movies and some of those storm-chasing shows, but this wasn't anything like that. It was intense."

Bitsy nodded, watching him as he spoke.

"And I'm guessing it was way worse for you."

Bitsy continued to nod.

"But at least you're okay."

"Yes."

"And pretty soon you'll be back with your family."

"Yes." *I hope so.*

Would they really be inside?

If so, why wouldn't Katie have simply taken her here?

She had overheard Katie and others talking about wanting to find Misty and the Daddy-man, yet at no point had they said anything about going to the school. It seemed weird. But then maybe they didn't realize the house was gone. She had only mentioned the van.

"I think we'll probably need the main entrance, which is over there," Andrew said as they neared the end of the sidewalk, a street between them and where it began again on the school side.

She followed his finger, which pointed to an area between a large field and the school building.

A parking lot was there as well, tucked up behind the entrance area.

Beyond that were more fields.

The rumble of a large vehicle echoed.

Bitsy turned and saw a yellow school bus approaching along the road, one that eventually turned into the school entrance area.

"I bet those are people they've picked up from the storm areas," Andrew said.

The school bus pulled up outside of the entrance they themselves would be using.

People began to get out.

"Wow, hard to believe so many people lost houses," he said.

"Yeah," Bitsy said, trying to see if Misty and the Daddy-man were among them.

"And these are in addition to all the people that are already inside."

She didn't see them, but maybe they had arrived earlier.

What would they say when she appeared?

What would others say?

Would everyone around them wonder about her and Misty?

Misty always explained that people would not understand them and would ask too many questions if they all went out together. Would that be the case here? Would they ask questions?

"He's probably just tied up with helping people," Gloria said, her eyes scanning the people as they entered the school. Some had items in their hands, things they had grabbed from their wrecked homes; others had nothing. One kid had a gerbil in a yellow plastic cage.

"He would still answer his phone or at least send me a text," Lindsey said. "I haven't heard anything since just after the storm."

Even Judy had been left in the dark, the woman having texted Lindsey several times asking if she had heard from him. At first Lindsey had planned to ignore the texts, but then, fearing Judy might think something had happened to her and decide to head to the house to try to act like a parent, had texted her back.

"Well, I'm sure he's fine," Gloria said. And then, as if spotting something that would win her a prize, loudly proclaimed, "There she is!"

Lindsey followed her pointing finger, as did a few other curious people.

Sure enough, Liz and her family had just entered the school and were moving toward the processing table that had been set up, one that had originally been so close to the doors themselves that people had started to stack up outside, in the cold, until an officer had finally suggested they pull the table farther back into the hallway so that people could at least get out of the elements while awaiting their instructions.

"Is that Gizmo?" Gloria asked, spotting an orange cat in Liz's arms.

Lindsey focused on Liz and the orange object she held, and shook her head. "I think that's a stuffed animal."

"A stuffed animal?" Gloria said.

"Looks like Tigger."

"Oh, Jesus Christ." Gloria sighed. "I thought she burned that thing."

"She said she did, but…" Lindsey shrugged.

Tigger was a stuffed animal that had been won at a carnival by Alex, aka He Who Can't Be Named. The two had been a thing from seventh grade through the homecoming dance last fall. The perfect couple. And then he fucked the Macy girl. Literally fucked her since she was now expecting a child that would be born sometime in May. It was a huge scandal, one that Gloria and Lindsey had minor parts in. Gloria enjoyed her time in the spotlight and often could be relied upon for the latest updates in the Smallwood High School saga. Lindsey, however, just told people to fuck off when they tried to get information.

Will the tornado tragedy finally usurp the pregnancy scandal?

Fingers crossed.

Gloria bounced up and down as Liz and her family were processed, her excitement odd and feeling a bit misplaced given that all these families were here because they no longer had homes they could go to. Making it even more awkward, she and Gloria hadn't lost their homes, and while most of these families wouldn't know that, Lindsey did, which only fueled her shame.

And then Liz and her family were approaching, Gloria waving to her and calling her name.

Liz's eyes went wide as she saw them but then changed, an indescribable look spreading across her face. And then she walked by them without a word.

"Liz?" Gloria said.

Liz continued walking toward the gymnasium while her mother turned to see who had called her daughter's name, as did her little brother Danny. Her father for some reason had stayed behind at the table talking with someone.

"Hi, Mrs. Haldeman," Lindsey said. "I'm sorry about your house."

"Thank you," Mrs. Haldeman said. She shifted her gaze toward her daughter, who had stopped by the doorway, arms crossed, Tigger trapped against her chest. "Liz, honey, you okay?"

"I'm fine," Liz called.

"Your friends are here."

"Where? I don't see any friends." With that, she turned and headed into the gymnasium.

Gloria looked at Lindsey and then back at the doorway Liz had disappeared through.

"She's pretty distraught," Mrs. Haldeman said.

"She can't find her stupid cat," Danny said.

"Daniel!" Mrs. Haldeman snapped.

"What? It's true!"

Mrs. Haldeman shook her head and then shifted her gaze as Mr. Haldeman approached. "Everything okay?" he asked.

Mrs. Haldeman nodded and then turned back to Gloria and Lindsey. "I'll talk to her. Maybe come on by in a little while. I know she could use the company."

"We will," Lindsey said.

Gloria, however, simply crossed her arms and then, once the Haldeman family was beyond earshot, said, "What's up her ass?"

"She just lost her house, and then we promised we would come help her find Gizmo but never showed up."

"How's that our fault? We kept getting turned around from debris."

"Yeah, well, she probably isn't thinking clearly right now."

"I'll say." She turned toward the exit. "Come on, let's go."

"What? No. Let's go talk to her."

"Did you hear what she said? We're no longer friends. She made that very clear." She started walking toward the exit.

"Gloria!" Lindsey hissed.

Her friend did not stop.

"Gloria!" she snapped, heads turning.

"What?"

"Don't be a tard. Let's go." She nodded toward the gymnasium.

Gloria stayed right where she was, arms crossed.

Lindsey shook her head and said, "Fine." With that, she

headed toward the gymnasium, the sound of families getting settled echoing within.

Once through the doorway, it took a while for her to find Liz and her family. They had four cots all the way in the far end by the doors that led to the locker rooms. Everyone but Liz was getting the sheets and pillows ready. Liz simply sat on her cot, holding Tigger in her lap, staring at the folded-up bleachers.

Lindsey walked over, eyes going from Liz to the other families whose homes had been destroyed, recognition hitting several times as she saw fellow students with their parents getting cots ready. All seemed to have the same stunned expression, one that had elements of horror and thankfulness mixed together. Many were crying.

Guilt that she still had a house, one that she would be returning to later that evening, began to appear but then was knocked away when she realized it was foolish to feel guilty for something like that. After all, she couldn't control the weather.

"Lindsey?" a voice called, halting her as she approached Liz. "Over here," it added when she failed to pinpoint who had spoken her name.

Oscar!

No, not Oscar.

It was his older brother, the two sharing an uncanny resemblance despite being several years apart.

"Gordy," she said, looking around.

"He's not here," Gordy said.

Lindsey didn't know how to reply to that.

"I was kind of hoping maybe he was with you, but…" He didn't finish.

"I'm sorry," she said, unsure what else to say.

An awkward silence settled between them, one that was bombarded on all sides by the sounds of the gymnasium.

And then Lindsey spotted Gloria looking around.

"If you hear from him…" Gordy started, but once again did not finish.

"I will," Lindsey said and then watched as Gordy headed back to the cot area his family had staked out. They did not have a cot waiting for Oscar. Seeing this was like a kick to the stomach. She wasn't sure why, but it nearly toppled her.

They know he's dead.

"Hey," Gloria said as she neared.

"Hey," Lindsey replied.

"Sorry."

Lindsey nodded and then nudged her shoulder toward where Liz's family was. "Be cool."

"I will."

Lindsey nodded again and then turned, leading the way over to Liz.

"Ramsey," Tess said. "Look!"

Ramsey was about to win an Angry Birds level that he had been struggling with all evening, a win that was riding on his launching of a final egg that he knew was positioned perfectly to take out the last pig outpost.

"Look!" Tess said again, nudging him.

Goddammit! he silently snapped, but then saw that the egg still hit the tower as planned.

Relief spun through his system.

"What?" he asked.

"And now they're gone."

"Who's gone?"

"You don't care."

"Who's gone?"

Tess hesitated for effect and then said, "The girl that we picked up after the storm and brought to the police station."

"What?"

"She was walking around with a young man."

Ramsey struggled to understand the significance of this. "So what?"

"Why would the police let her wander around in here?"

"I don't know," Ramsey said. "Are you sure it was her?"

"Of course I am."

Ramsey knew she probably was, her mind noting and storing things that would barely leave an impression on others like himself. He also knew she was correct. Given the marks that had been on the girl, and the obvious mistreatment she had suffered at the hands of some unknown person, bringing her to the school and letting her go off on her own didn't make any sense—unless they had established that the marks were from a game like she said

"Maybe the police are here with her but let her wander in with the young man as cover," Ramsey said. He didn't really believe this, but knew he had to say something that would appease her concern.

"Why?"

"Because they think the person that abused her is here, and they want her to point them out."

"And without them knowing the police are here looking for them," Tess said with a nod.

"Exactly." He clicked the Continue button on his phone screen and watched as the next level opened.

"Do you think it worked?" Tess asked.

"I don't know."

"Hmm."

A rickety yet daunting tower with pig lookouts appeared on screen, one that he could tell was going to be a pain in the ass to take down due to a rocky outcrop that stood in the middle of the screen and offered a support base for the center of the structure and a shield for the rear part.

"Maybe we should—"

"Not get involved," Ramsey said, cutting her off.

"But—"

"No, Tess, it's a police situation, one that they're handling."

"But maybe we should just make sure."

"No. We could screw it up for them."

"How?"

"By interfering."

"But we would just be making sure she really is with the police still."

"That is not our responsibility."

"But what if she escaped?"

"Escaped?"

"From the police."

"Why would she do that?"

"Stockholm syndrome."

"Stockholm syndrome?"

"Yes, it's a condition that develops when a captive begins to bond with their captor."

"I know what Stockholm syndrome is."

"You didn't seem so sure."

"I wasn't asking—never mind. You think that girl has Stockholm syndrome, and what, fled the safety of the police to head back to whoever it was that had kidnapped her?"

"Remember what the police said? That she had said there were others, but then wouldn't talk about them. And they think she wanted us to help the others, rather than just her."

Ramsey thought back and nodded. "Yeah, sort of."

"Well, maybe it wasn't that she wanted the police to help someone escape, but to help someone that was hurt, and once she realized that they weren't going to do that, she left."

"But what about the marks on her wrists? Someone obviously had her tied up."

"I know, but if she is suffering from Stockholm syndrome and her captors were hurt, she might feel the need to try and help them rather than escape from them."

"Okay, maybe," Ramsey said with a nod.

"Come on," Tess said, standing. "Let's go make sure everything is on the up and up."

Ramsey sighed and stood up.

Getting involved with the mystery girl and whatever situation she was a part of was the last thing he wanted to do, but if meeting up with her in the hallways of the school would appease Tess and get her to leave him alone, then he was game. Plus, he needed to move around. Sitting on the cot wasn't all that comfortable, especially since he had no back support. Sleeping on it would be fine, but being hunched over while staring at his phone just wasn't ideal.

A pop echoed from his joints as he took the first steps.

Tess gave him a look.

"What?" he asked.

"I heard that."

"Don't start."

"Mom's right. You sit around too much. You need to start walking like we do."

He gave a simple nod and then let Tess lead the way, her steps becoming slow as they neared the doors that would lead them out into the main hallway.

"Sorry," Andrew said. "I thought for sure they'd be here."

Bitsy didn't reply, a sense of hopelessness once again creeping in. She was never going to find Misty.

"Do you want a soda or anything? They have machines around the corner."

Bitsy nodded but did not get up from the cushioned seat she was on.

"What kind?" he asked. "They have Coke, root beer, Mountain Dew, Sprite."

"Coke," Bitsy said, voice hinting at her exhaustion.

"You know, they may still be on the way. You could check in and get a cot, and then when they get here they'll join you." He waited for a response, but when none arrived, he added, "Might be the best option at this point."

Bitsy looked up at him and smiled.

"Let me go get that soda."

"Thanks."

He nodded and started away from the bench, eventually disappearing around a corner where some kids were playing a game of tag. It was three boys and a girl, all of whom seemed to be enjoying themselves, the girl being the tagger, the boys running from her.

She thought about Misty and wondered what type of games they would have played if she had been here. Would the Daddy-man have let them play, or would he have made them stay on the cots in the gym area? And what about the game of tag? If the Daddy-man let them go off and play, would the kids let them join in their game?

"I got you!" the girl shouted.

"No!" one of the boys replied.

"Yes!"

"No."

"She got you."

"No she didn't!"

Bitsy hadn't been able to see if the girl had really tagged the boy, the action having moved beyond her line of view, but given how adamant the girl was, and the fact that one of the other boys agreed, she had a feeling a tag had occurred.

Someone approached.

Bitsy shifted her gaze from the kids on her right to the sound on her left, eyes blinking in recognition as a young woman neared. *Is that…?*

"It is you!" the girl said.

The girl from the red car!

And the boy.

He was behind the girl.

"We picked you up after the storm," the girl added. "My name's Tess, remember?"

"Yes," Bitsy said. "I remember."

"And this is my brother Ramsey," Tess said.

"Hi," Ramsey said.

Bitsy nodded a greeting.

"What are you doing here?" Tess asked.

"Trying to find my family, but they're not here," Bitsy said.

"Oh, did the police bring you here?" Tess asked.

"Andrew did," Bitsy said.

"Andrew? Who's that?"

"He's getting me a soda. He has a dog named Sparky. We had to leave him outside."

Tess looked at Ramsey, who shrugged.

"What happened with the police?" Tess asked.

"They couldn't help me," Bitsy said, concern starting to build. At first she had been thinking maybe these two could help her find her way back to where they had picked her up, but now she was starting to think they would probably just bring her back to the police. To Katie. And this time Katie probably wouldn't be so nice.

At that moment, Andrew returned, a can of Coke in each hand.

Bitsy took the one he offered and quickly opened it so she could take a sip.

"Are you Andrew?" Tess asked.

"Yes," Andrew said, opening his own Coke. "Bitsy, is this your—"

"No," Bitsy said, anticipating his question. "They tried to help me earlier."

"Oh?"

"We brought her to the police station after the storm," Tess said.

"The police?" Andrew asked, looking down at Bitsy.

"They couldn't help me," Bitsy said. She took another sip of the Coke.

This is going to get bad, she told herself. *They are going to call Katie.*

As if on cue, a police officer appeared in the hallway up ahead. It wasn't Katie, and at the moment he didn't seem interested in Bitsy, his focus being on the young lady that was sitting behind the check-in table, but once he noticed her sitting on the bench at the end of the hallway, he would probably call Katie.

Laugher echoed.

Tess turned toward it, likely spotting the police officer.

Bitsy stood up, said a quick thank-you to Andrew that left him with a puzzled look, and started walking away, feet taking her down the hallway that the kids were playing in, their game of tag having resumed with one of the boys being the tagger.

"Hey," Tess called. "Wait!"

Bitsy ignored her and hurried around the corner, nearly crashing into a kid that came around from the other side.

"Bitsy!" another voice called, this one Andrew.

Bitsy ran.

She had no idea where she was going, but knew she had to put distance between her and those near the bench. And find a door. That was the most important thing. She needed a door that would lead outside and then needed to hurry away so that she could resume her search for the old graveyard she had wandered through. Once she found that, she would be able to find Misty.

If they are still by the van.

Pushing the fear away, she continued to run, rounding one corner after another, always expecting to see a set of doors to the outside, but only discovering more hallways. It was like a maze, one designed to keep kids within so they couldn't sneak out while they were supposed to be in school.

"Bitsy!" a voice echoed.

It sounded like the girl.

Tess.

Bitsy didn't like her.

Or Ramsey.

They were the reason she was in this mess.

If they had just helped her like she had asked when first finding them, then none of this would have happened. It was their fault.

Up ahead, another corner loomed.

Please!

She rounded it.

A set of doorways was at the end.

Thank you! Thank you! Thank you!

She pushed through them and emerged onto a side of the school that was free of people, one that looked out at some sort of sport field. Beyond it were trees and what could have been houses.

Though somewhat fragile, a truce was eventually established while the three sat on Liz's cot, Lindsey explaining that they had actually tried to drive down to Liz's place to help her look for her cat, but every road they had turned on had been blocked with debris.

"Then how did the bus get through?" Liz had demanded during the initial peace talks, her stuffed animal squeezed within her crossed arms.

This led to a discussion on how crews were slowly but surely opening up the roads, and while Liz had stayed skeptical of the effort the two had made, she eventually cracked and decided that staying mad was pointless, a whispered offer of heading back to Lindsey's place so that they could indulge in some of the grass stash that Gloria had hidden in her locker helping to cement things.

"Seriously?" Lindsey asked as Gloria pulled a battered Teavana tea tin from the top shelf.

"What?" Gloria asked, fingers fishing out a baggie that was hidden beneath the loose tea leaves. "This works."

"Yeah, but last time it ruined it."

"Last time it was Earl Grey. This time it's…" Gloria's face went blank "Fuck, I don't even know. Something that my mom raves about but tastes like yesterday's glass clippings."

"Yesterday's grass clippings," Lindsey repeated. "I'm totally reassured."

"Hey, I don't see you producing anything from your locker."

"She has a point," Liz said.

"Okay, okay," Lindsey said, hands up in surrender.

Dope secured, they left the school, heading out through a side entrance near their locker area.

"Shit, another one," Gloria said as a bus turned into the school.

No one added anything, a somber silence settling in as the bus passed and they began heading toward Lindsey's house.

"By the way, you won't believe what is sitting in the middle of Lindsey's front yard," Gloria said a few minutes later.

"What is it?" Liz asked.

"Just wait. It's hilarious."

"It's not," Lindsey said.

"Oh it is, trust me."

Lindsey shook her head.

"What is it?" Liz asked again.

"You'll see."

Lindsey thought about spoiling the surprise, but then realized if it did get a chuckle from Liz, then it would be worth waiting. Anything that put a smile on their friend's face was welcome at this point.

Another few minutes passed, the three simply walking,

feet occasionally having to step around obstacles that were on the sidewalk. Some people had started the cleanup process of their yards, others hadn't, but now that it was dark, everyone seemed to have headed in for the night, candles and flashlights illuminating some windows, others looking dark and empty.

"You know, once we get some candles lit, we could pull out the Ouija board," Gloria said.

"No way in hell," Lindsey said.

"Come on, what else are we going to do once we're finished with"—she tapped the baggie in her pocket. "It's not like we have many options."

"I don't know, with the power out and so many people having died…" Lindsey shook her head.

"Lindsey's right," Liz said.

"Fine, forget I suggested it," Gloria said, voice a bit defensive.

No one replied to that, the three eventually rounding the corner that put them onto Lindsey's street.

"You know what sucks?" Liz said.

"What?"

"Of the three of us, my house was the only one that had a generator."

"Shit, you're right," Gloria said. "Didn't your dad get it last year, after that blizzard?"

"Yeah, well, two years ago. Remember. It was so fucking cold that we actually had to sit by the fireplace all day and all night until the power finally came back on. After that, he was like 'never again' and got the generator."

"Ever use it?"

"Nope. And that's the worst part of all—is that a fucking toilet?"

"Yeah!" Gloria said with a laugh.

"That's hilarious."

"I know, right."

"I'm taking a picture of it," Liz said.

"Why?" Lindsey asked.

"I don't know, but it's funny."

Lindsey rolled her eyes.

Gloria took some pictures too.

"Now we have to think of something to say about it so we can post it," Liz said.

"Yeah," Gloria agreed. "Oh! We should hang up a roll of toilet paper next to it."

"Come on," Lindsey said. "That's gross."

"Or a sign that says to bring your own."

"Ha!"

Lindsey shook her head and said, "Let's go inside."

"What if your dad walks in?" Liz asked.

Lindsey halted, thoughts on him and the fact that he hadn't contacted her at all since that afternoon and wouldn't answer his phone returning to the forefront of her mind.

"What?" Liz asked, sensing something.

"She's worried about her dad," Gloria said.

"Oh, what happened?"

"It's nothing," Lindsey said, having heard enough of the "he's probably just busy" statements for one night. No one seemed to agree with her that his lack of contact was something to be alarmed about, and she was tired of trying to convince everyone differently. "Let's go."

Bitsy heard a rustle in the brush beyond the chain link fence as she made her way alongside it, and then a menacing growl that chilled her to the core.

She paused to peer into the darkness.

The rustling stopped.

She took a deep breath and sighed, the run from the school and through the backyards having taken a toll. She was exhausted. But she couldn't stop. She needed to keep moving. First to return the jacket so that Andrew's daddy didn't kill him, and then . . .

She had no idea.

Misty and the Daddy-man could be anywhere.

It was hopeless.

No.

If she could find the cemetery, she could find them. And once she did that, all would be well.

Would it really?

She pushed the doubt from her mind and continued through the backyard, her goal being to reach the toilet Andrew had pointed out to her so that she could leave the jacket on it for him.

Will he see it?

It was on the way to his house, so she was sure he would. Hoped he would. If not . . .

No. No. No.

She could not focus on that, her own situation far too desperate.

She needed to get to the toilet and then find the cemetery before Misty and the Daddy-man left.

The clock was ticking.

One more yard.

She started through it, a burst of laugher forcing her to take cover.

Confused, she looked around, but didn't see anyone.

More laugher.

And then voices.

It was all coming from within the house.

Moving carefully, she crept up alongside it and started walking toward the front, her mind fairly certain that this was the house with the toilet in the yard.

The sounds of a vehicle halted her, body taking cover in the bushes.

More laughter and voices.

She waited.

The vehicle drew nearer.

It was moving slowly.

And then it passed by.

It was not a police car.

Relief arrived.

She took a deep breath.

"Hey!" a voice cried.

Bitsy twisted to the right, the voice having come from the house next door.

A young man had stepped out onto the front porch, his body angled in a way that it could look at her between the houses. "What are you doing?" he demanded.

Without a word, Bitsy turned and ran.

"Hey! Stop!"

"You hear that?" Liz asked, fingers passing the half-finished joint to Lindsey.

"Someone's shouting." Gloria said, blinking.

Lindsey took a hit and passed it back to Liz, who then handed it to Gloria, who took her own hit.

"I thought I heard a scream," Liz said.

"I didn't."

"There it was again!"

They all went quiet for a moment, eyes turned toward the open porch door, which Lindsey hoped would help in eliminating the odor from the joint, an incense stick and scented candle also working toward that end.

Barking erupted, followed by another shout from someone and then a high-pitched scream.

"Shit, that's Cujo," Lindsey said, standing, knee knocking the coffee table, nearly toppling the incense stick from its slot.

"Jesus!"

Another scream.

"He's got someone!" Liz cried.

"Come on!" Lindsey urged and headed toward the door.

"Whoa," Gloria said, still on the couch. "What? Hey."

Lindsey stumbled out onto the back porch, her foot catching the lip of the sliding door, and then turned to the right toward Cujo's backyard.

The screams had stopped.

And the barking had been replaced by a low, menacing growl as Cujo paced back and forth, body nothing but a shadow beyond the fence.

Two figures were struggling.

"Hey—" Lindsey started, wishing she had grabbed a flashlight.

"They're fighting," Liz said.

"I got'em," a voice said.

"Dennis!" Lindsey snapped. "What're you doing?"

"Call the police," Dennis said.

"Dennis, it's just a kid," Lindsey said.

"What the fuck is going on!" a new voice demanded, flashlight illuminating them.

Lindsey shielded her eyes.

"Knock it off or I'll sick the dog on you."

"Fuck you!" Lindsey shouted. "You release that mutt and I'll blow his fucking head off."

The flashlight went away.

"Dennis, let her go," Lindsey said.

Dennis sighed and complied.

"Come on, it's okay," Lindsey said, holding out her hand.

The girl simply stared at it.

"She was casing your place—"

"Dennis, for the love of God, shut the fuck up," Lindsey said. "No one is casing or looting anything." She turned back to the girl. "Come on, let's get you cleaned up."

Liz put a hand on the girl's shoulder and said, "It's okay, we're here to help."

The girl looked between them, nodded, and took Lindsey's hand.

The three started back.

Dennis stayed where he was.

Gloria was waiting for them in the doorway on the back porch.

"Whoa, who's this?" she asked.

"Um…" Lindsey looked down at the girl.

"Bitsy," the girl said, voice soft. "My name is Bitsy."

EIGHT

"The basement was a dungeon," Tina Powell said. "And we're not talking a fun *Fifty Shades of Grey* one. More like *Silence of the Lambs.*"

"Jesus," Katie said, unsure what else to say. Given her position as a simple patrol officer with a department that didn't even have an investigative unit, she was stepping outside of her role big time and feared what might result if the detective on the other end realized this.

"And with the North Carolina connection, this thing is blowing up fast."

"Sounds like it," Katie said. She could hear voices in the background. Lots of them. For all she knew, the scene contained more personnel than the entire police population of Smallwood. "FBI there yet?"

"Yeah, they have two agents here. As does the state and county and college."

"College?"

"The man that owned this house was a professor at the university."

"Oh God!"

"Tell me about it. I have a daughter that will be going to

college in two years. Now I'm going to be wondering about every professor that could cross her path, as well as all the other potential threats one would expect at a university." Tina let out a laugh. "Anyway, you said you think you found the van?"

"Um, maybe." She eased the phone from her ear a bit, her hand having had it pressed tightly against it for some reason, which was now starting to hurt. "Honestly, we're not sure what we have. As you may have heard, our area was hit by several tornadoes. Afterward, a girl was found wandering about in a daze by two storm chasers. She had suffered a minor head injury and had evidence of her wrists having been restrained. She wasn't very forthcoming with information and wouldn't let us look at her body beyond her head, but I was able to learn that she had been in a van that was flipped by the storm and crawled out. She also said that one of the occupants of the van was a young woman named Misty." She hesitated a moment. "That's what caught our attention. It's an unusual name. And then the mention of a van in connection with her really brought it home."

"Does the girl you found match the picture of the kidnap victim?"

"No," Katie said. "And given her determination to get back to this Misty and the van, it seems like she must have been a captive much longer than"—she glanced at the alert —"Abigail Abbott."

"Was she dressed in a school uniform?"

"Um, no, a dress."

Tina Powell considered this and then asked, "Do you have any evidence whatsoever that Abigail Abbott may be there in...where did you say you were?"

"Smallwood."

"Which is where exactly?"

"You know Bloomington?" Katie asked.

"Sure."

"Okay, we're north of that by about half an hour, just west of 39."

"What's that, like two, two and a half hours from here?"

"Sounds about right."

"And when would you say the van was likely flipped?"

"Around three."

"Okay, and the fire looks to have started around noonish, so the timing fits."

"Fire?" Katie asked.

"They tried to burn the house down, but it didn't quite work out the way they planned. Don't ask me for details since it's way beyond my understanding at the moment, but something about there not being enough oxygen within the room it was started in, so it eventually burned itself out rather than spreading throughout the house. A mailman called it in around two o'clock. Could smell it from the front door."

"And how do you know Abigail Abbott was there?"

"Her backpack was sitting on a kitchen table, along with her wallet, driver's permit, student ID, and all her notebooks and schoolbooks."

"Wow."

"If the fire hadn't died out and if all of that had burned, it would have probably taken weeks to realize there was a connection between the two. Shit, it might have taken that long just to realize this professor was bad news."

A beep in her ear told her she had a message.

It was from Gary.

About Bitsy?

"Any idea why they tried to burn the house down and flee?" she asked while standing up and heading toward the dispatch area.

"That's still the big question. Something obviously spooked him, but what it was exactly we have no idea. The kidnap itself was clean. No witnesses. The girl simply never came home from school. And doing a check on this guy brings up nothing. Not even a simple parking ticket. As far as everyone knew, he was an upstanding citizen that loved academia and was living his dream—the one about being a tenured professor, not the raping, torture, and slaughter of innocent teenage girls."

"So you're certain this isn't a one-time thing?"

"Oh no, no, no. Whatever it was that caused them to flee meant they were in quite a hurry and left tons of stuff behind. We're talking pictures, torture items, clothes, and all the stuff one would expect to find within a house of a successful literature professor. He thought the fire would take care of it, but whatever intelligence he had, it wasn't enough for him to realize he should have opened some windows in the room where the fire was started. Good for us, bad for him."

"I'm guessing the pictures are not your typical family photos?" Katie said, entering the dispatch area.

Gary looked up.

Katie pointed at the phone and mouthed the words *Detective Powell*.

He nodded and started writing on a piece of paper.

"No," Tina said. "They're teenagers, all dressed in school uniforms. Chained up, in cages, hanging from ropes, stretched out on a rack, spread eagle on a bed—if you can imagine it, he probably took a picture of it. Several show girls in the process of being violated. Both with sex toys, random objects, and the man himself. He liked taking shots of his penis pressed up against their faces and down their throats, their mouths held open by a painful-looking gag device." She paused. "I've only seen what was scattered about in his bedroom, likely because he wanted them to burn and simply dumped them out onto the mattress, one box after another. We're not touching them, so those that are covered or turned over haven't been examined yet."

"Sounds awful."

"Awful doesn't even begin to describe it."

"Can you tell me about this Misty? Who do you think she is?"

"Ah yes, that's where things really take a turn for the bizarre."

Gary handed her the note. It said: *Bitsy was just seen at the high school.*

Katie pulled up alongside the main entrance of the high school just as a bus was leaving, a group of disheveled residents making their way through the doors to the check-in table. Seeing this, Katie was reminded of the fact that the town had been devastated, the twisters having left a good chunk of its residents homeless. Others had been killed. It was the worst disaster to ever befall Smallwood, yet for her it was nothing more than a backdrop. Bitsy was her focus. She needed to find her and get her back, not just to save her potential career, but because of what Detective Powell had described was found down in Champaign-Urbana.

Are the two really connected?

They have to be.

Two things were certain about the serial killer that had fled Champaign-Urbana. First, he had an old VW Van. Second, he had a daughter named Misty, yet no wife or a record of ever having been married. A daughter who apparently lived among the captives that her father brought home and held in the cellar dungeon. Where she had originally come from was unknown, but given what was found in her bedroom, it was clear that she not only knew about the captives, but that she would occasionally torment them herself.

"Alongside the professor?" Katie had asked, horrified.

"It's hard to say," Tina had replied. "Obviously someone was behind the camera taking the pictures of her with the captives, often while she was wearing what I can only describe as a kinky female prison camp warden outfit—one that looks really bizarre given that she probably is only thirteen or fourteen in the photos—but if it was the man, he didn't seem to be taking part in the activities the way he did in his own pictures, which he always took himself, not with a partner. And in one you can see some of the picture-taker in a mirror on the side of the wall. It isn't enough to make out an identity, but one thing is clear. Whoever is taking the picture is wearing a pink dress."

"That could be Bitsy," Katie suggested.

"Who knows? We're still going through everything. Misty's pictures were kept in pink photo albums that were in a box under her bed. Normally it would have been locked, but someone obviously opened it and grabbed stuff. These albums were likely the rejects while she looked for others that might be more significant. I also suspect she had a digital camera, one that could be hooked up to the photo printer we found in the professor's home office. Both took their cameras, but not the printer. Our tech guys are going to go through it to see if they can find anything."

"Can you do me a favor?" Katie asked, eyes on the note that Gary had written, one that was urging her to get to the school. "I'm going to send you a photo of Bitsy that I took earlier. If you can, try to see if it matches any of the photos left behind. That way we can nail things down and say for sure that the family fled this way and got themselves stuck here in Smallwood."

"Okay, yeah, send that over."

"Will do."

"Great."

A few moments later, the photo she had taken while in the interview room was texted over. Whether this was standard procedure for situations like this, Katie didn't know, but it seemed the quickest way to get things over to the detective.

Now, while walking into the school, her phone buzzed with a text.

It was from the detective and simply read: *It's them.*

Katie stared at the message, a question of "now what?" echoing.

The phone buzzed again.

Katie thumbed open the new text. It was a picture of Bitsy. She was standing next to a newly planted tree, wearing a dress that was similar in style to the one that she had been in earlier that day, one that was currently folded up in a box as evidence.

Buzz.

This one was a selfie of Bitsy alongside another young woman. Both were smiling.

Misty? she wondered.

Buzz.

This one read: *The girl next to her is Misty.*

Several more texts followed, all pictures. They were simple shots of Misty modeling outfits for the camera, photos that would have looked like those of any teenager who was excited about her new outfit—if the outfit hadn't looked like something one would see at a fetish event.

Another buzz echoed, only this time it was the first ring of a call rather than a text.

She answered.

"Sorry to photo bomb you like that, but I figured you should see what it is we are dealing with here since you've found yourself on the front line," Tina said.

"No worries, this is good stuff and will be very useful," Katie said. Up ahead she could see a fellow officer named Owen standing with three young adults, two of whom were the storm chasers from earlier, the other a young man she did not recognize. "Up until now, we didn't know who Misty was or what she looked like, so this will really help." She hesitated and then asked, "Are you going to come up here?"

"Eventually. Your department is going to get swamped with investigators from several agencies, though that will take at least a day, especially with the storms having wreaked havoc upon much of the state. So for now you are going to be on your own in locking this thing down."

Owen saw her and waved her over.

Katie held up a finger and was about to let Tina know that she had to run, when Tina said something else.

"I also hope you realize something. Those outfits that Misty is wearing in the pictures, they aren't things that a teenager her age can simply walk into a store and buy—even if we had stores that sold such things around here."

"Ah, good point," Katie said. "How would she secure clothing like that?"

"My guess, her father bought it for her, which really adds a dimension to this that I don't want to think about. It also means that if you do find her, be careful. She may be just a teen, one that has likely suffered in ways we can't even begin to imagine, especially if she was originally born from a captive, but she is also an accomplice in everything that was taking place here, and will need to be treated as such to ensure your own safety when apprehending her. Simply put, don't look at her as a victim that needs rescuing, because she likely isn't going to be viewing you as a rescuer freeing her from captivity. Instead, you're a threat, one that she will likely try to defend herself against."

Katie thought about Bitsy and how they had miscalculated her view toward them to the point of her walking out of the station when their backs were turned. She wasn't going to be making any more mistakes like that. "Don't worry, once we find her, we won't let our guard down."

"Okay," Tina said. "Good. I have to run. Impromptu meeting. But I will keep you posted on what we learn down here."

"Same here."

The call ended.

. . .

"There we go," Lindsey said. "Good as new."

Bitsy looked down at her leg, the sting from the disinfectant fading now that the gauze was in place.

"Do you want me to change the one on your head while we're in here?" Lindsey asked.

Bitsy looked up at her, the flickering light from the candle reflecting itself in the mirror, which bathed the girl in brightness. "Do you think it needs to be changed?" she asked.

"It couldn't hurt."

"Okay."

"We can clean off your face too. Seems you got splattered with mud."

"While being tackled by that boy," Bitsy confirmed.

"Dennis," Lindsey said.

"Is he your boyfriend?"

"What? Ugh. No way!"

Bitsy was quiet for a moment and then said, "That dog wanted to eat me."

"Cujo wants to eat everyone."

"Cujo! Does he have rabies?"

"What?"

"Cujo had rabies."

"Well, no, he's not the actual Cujo. That's just what we call him because he's mean."

"Did he used to be nice?"

"I don't know. Maybe when he was little before he lived there. Everyone in that house is mean."

"Cujo was nice in the beginning, but got sick because he chased the rabbit into the hole."

"Is that what happened?"

"Yeah, it's sad. He was a good dog, but then became a bad dog because of the rabies. Did you see it?"

"Not really. Just bits of it on TV from time to time."

"I watched it with Misty. It was on Amazon. We ordered a pizza and breadsticks with garlic dipping sauce."

"Ah, fun. Do you and Misty like scary movies?" Lindsey asked, finger gently rubbing at the edge of the tape on her forehead so she could snag a corner and peel away the muddy bandage.

"Yes, especially while the Daddy-man is gone."

"The Daddy-man?"

Bitsy winced as the tape was peeled away.

"Sorry," Lindsey said.

"It's okay."

Lindsey leaned in close to look at her forehead.

Bitsy studied her while she did this, eyes going from her face down to her body and then back up to her face. She was very pretty, though her eyes looked funny.

"This isn't as bad as I thought it would be," Lindsey said.

"The nice man that covered it said it looked worse than it really was. He said heads bleed like crazy, which is scary, but that it wasn't anything to worry about."

"I bet you weren't scared though."

"I was." She looked down while saying this.

"Well, that's okay," Lindsey said, handing over a wet washcloth. "I was scared too when the storm hit."

Bitsy smiled and twisted toward the mirror.

Lindsey watched from over her shoulder.

"What's wrong with your eyes?" Bitsy asked, holding the washcloth.

"My eyes?"

"Yeah, they look funny."

"Oh, it's nothing. Don't worry about it."

In the other room, one of the girls laughed.

The other cussed.

Something crashed.

"I'll be right back," Lindsey said.

Bitsy nodded while rubbing at a spot of mud on her cheek.

It came away easily.

Some of the others were a bit more stubborn, but even so, she managed to scrub them free.

Following that, she put the washcloth into the sink and then turned on the faucet to wash the muddy residue from her fingers, carefully rolling up her sleeves so that they didn't get any mud on them from her fingers and wouldn't get wet once they were under the water.

"Those two," Lindsey said, coming back into the room. "They rolled another blunt and pulled out the Ouija board."

Bitsy spun toward her, water splashing.

"Ouija boards are dangerous!" So dangerous that the Daddy-man once spanked Misty right in front of her for ordering one from Amazon with the gift cards. She had said she wanted to try and talk to her mommy with it, but he burned it before they could even open it.

"Oh don't worry, they're not going to do anything with it," Lindsey said.

Bitsy sighed, but then wondered if using one might be helpful. Would the spirits on the other side help her find her way back to Misty and the van?

"Christ, what happened to your wrists?" Lindsey asked.

"What?" Bitsy looked down at them. "Oh, that was from a game that me and Misty played."

Lindsey gently took her right wrist and examined it. "What's it from?"

"Rope."

"Rope? What in the world were you two playing?"

"Misty wanted to try being a schoolgirl again and had me be the daddy and act like a boy, but then afterward Misty got upset with me and tied me up to hang from the ceiling in the dungeon."

"Dungeon?"

"Yeah. The Daddy-man built it in the cellar."

"And Misty hung you up in there from your wrists?"

Bitsy nodded.

"For how long?"

"I'm not sure. I think maybe a day. I passed out for a while."

"Jesus."

Bitsy pulled her hand back and pushed the sleeve down. "It's okay. We play games like that a lot."

"Why?"

"Misty likes them."

"And you?"

"What?"

"Do you like them?"

Bitsy thought about this for a moment and said, "I liked being able to act like a boy the other night." She had liked that a lot. "And I think Misty liked me acting like a boy. She made lots of happy noises."

But then why did she get mad later?

Bitsy was still confused by this.

"And your dad is okay with these games?"

"I don't have a daddy," Bitsy said.

"But…who is the Daddy-man?"

"That's Misty's daddy."

"I thought Misty was your sister?"

"No."

"Cousin?"

"No."

"Mother?"

"What? That's silly."

"Okay, maybe you should explain it to me. Who are you exactly?"

"I'm Bitsy Cole."

"Yes, I know, but how are you related to Misty and the… um…Daddy-man?"

"What do you mean?"

"You live with her, right? You said they are your family,

but if he's not your daddy, and Misty is not your sister, cousin, or mother, how are you all related?"

"He gave me to her after her mommy died."

"What?"

"To keep her company so she wouldn't be sad."

"He gave you to her?"

"Yeah."

Lindsey didn't say anything for several seconds.

Bitsy wondered if maybe she had said too much about her home life. Misty always said they were supposed to keep things secret, but that was before she got lost.

"What's Misty's last name?"

Bitsy shook her head. "I don't know."

"And it's not the same as your last name?"

"No."

"You said your name is Bitsy Cole."

"Yes."

"Is Bitsy your real name?"

"Oh, well no, it's Elizabeth. Elizabeth Cole. But Misty calls me Bitsy."

"Like the American Girl doll?" a voice asked from the hall.

"What?" Lindsey asked.

Liz, the girl that had given her the stuffed tiger earlier, stepped into the bathroom. "Elizabeth Cole, aka Bitsy Cole. It's the name of an American Girl doll." She turned to Bitsy. "You're named after a doll?"

"I am a doll."

"She said she lost her home and couldn't find her family, so I figured maybe they were here at the school," Andrew said.

"And then what, you two recognized her and came to find out what was going on?" Katie asked Tess and Ramsey.

"Tess did," Ramsey said.

"I thought it was odd that she was here without any police," Tess added.

"And I just thought she was lost," Andrew said. "I didn't know she had escaped. Jesus, I didn't mean to..."

"Aid and abet?" Tess asked.

"Yeah!"

"It's okay," Katie said, his fear obvious. "She didn't really escape since she wasn't in custody. We were just trying to figure out who she was, given her confusion."

"And you just let her wander away?" Tess asked.

"Pretty much," Katie said, holding back a glare. "And it was my fault. I thought she was sleeping and went to get a cup of coffee. After that, she was gone." She turned back to Andrew. "Did she tell you anything else about herself, or give any indication of where she was heading?"

"Not really," he said with a shrug. "She was just looking for her family."

"And then ran away when you two approached?"

"Yep," Ramsey said.

"After she saw the police officer," Tess added.

Katie nodded.

Officer Owen Collins, who worked part time for the department, had been at the school helping keep things organized and had had no idea about Bitsy until Tess told him that she had been brought to the police station earlier and might have been a victim of kidnapping. A bit skeptical, Owen had radioed in to find out if there was any truth to what Tess had to say, which was when Gary informed him that yes, they were looking for a young girl named Bitsy that had wandered away from the station. Unfortunately, by then there was no sign of her outside of the school.

Buzz.

She ignored the phone for the moment and turned to the storm chasers. "I know earlier you told me that you couldn't say exactly where it was that you picked her up, but do you think we could try to pinpoint it? I have a map and can show you exactly where I was flaring things. Maybe we can backtrack from there."

"We could try," Ramsey said. "But I doubt it will be much more than a general 'this area' description. We went back and forth quite a bit trying to find a road that wasn't blocked."

"At this point, anything you can add will be helpful." She turned for a moment and called to Owen.

"Yeah?" he asked, returning to where they were talking.

"Can you find us a map of the town and surrounding area?"

"Sure."

Her phone buzzed again, and this time she pulled it out to see what Detective Powell had sent.

It was another picture.

Of Bitsy.

What?

No.

"Jesus Christ!"

"Lindsey!" Liz snapped, voice seemingly trying to be a whisper but failing. "She thinks she's a fucking doll."

"Liz is right," Gloria said. "This is fucked up. We need to call the police."

"But she's terrified of the police," Lindsey said.

"Yeah, because she's been brainwashed into believing she's a doll."

"What if it's not that simple?" Lindsey asked.

"Of course it's not that simple. This is some seriously fucked-up shit. She thinks she's a doll."

"Which is why we need to really think about this and figure out what exactly is going on," Lindsey said.

"No. We need to call the police so that *they* can figure out what is going on."

"Lindsey, you of all people should know this. Your dad is a police officer, for Christ's sake."

"Yeah, and did you see the sweatshirt she was wearing?" Lindsey asked.

"Yeah," Gloria said.

Liz nodded.

"I'm sure you've noticed that I have one just like it," Lindsey said.

"So, what about it?" Gloria asked.

"Think for a moment. They don't sell those to the public. There are no Smallwood Police Department sweatshirt sales. The reason I have one is because my dad gave it to me."

"So?"

"Do I have to spell it out for you?"

"Isn't that what you're doing now?"

"Her dad, or whoever this Daddy-man is, could be a police officer."

Liz and Gloria didn't reply to that, understanding appearing on their faces.

"Well, shit," Gloria eventually said, and then laughed.

"And you two are high as fuck."

"We kind of are," Liz said.

"What do we do?" Gloria asked.

"I don't know," Lindsey said.

She wished her dad were there. Or at least answering his phone. He would know what to do. He always did.

In the bathroom, they heard the toilet flush.

"Guess she's one of those dolls that pisses," Gloria said, another laugh escaping.

Lindsey and Liz simply stared at her.

"Sorry."

"We need to think of something," Liz said.

"What about this Misty she keeps talking about?" Gloria asked.

"What about her?" Lindsey asked.

"Maybe we can find a picture of her in the yearbook and then at least have a last name. That way we can see if her dad is a police officer."

"Shit, that's not a bad idea."

The door to the bathroom opened.

A moment later, Bitsy joined them in the family room.

No one said anything for several seconds, the awkwardness heavy.

Bitsy looked at each of them, almost as if she were studying them.

She then turned and looked at a picture on the wall, one that featured Lindsey with her parents back before her mother had died.

"So, Bitsy," Lindsey said. "How old is Misty?"

"Um...I don't know." She frowned. "Sorry."

"That's okay. Look at me for a moment. Do we seem similar? Height, weight, age, hair?"

"Your boobs are bigger."

Gloria let out a snort.

"They are nice," Liz said, her own laugh appearing. "Been meaning to mention that."

"Shut up," Lindsey said, voice trying to stay serious.

"I wish I had boobs," Bitsy added.

"When you get older you will," Liz said.

"I don't think so. Misty says I wasn't made with them, but one day I might be able to get some put in."

Lindsey looked around, waiting to see if there would be any more comments about boobs, and when there wasn't, asked, "Does Misty have a driver's license yet?"

Bitsy shook her head. "No, but she's been asking the Daddy-man to teach her to drive. She says she's old enough. He keeps promising that they will go out one of these days."

"Okay, that's good. That means she is probably our age and we can help you find her."

"Really?" Bitsy asked, excitement appearing.

"Maybe. Come on, we need to show you something." Lindsey motioned for Bitsy to head down the hallway toward her bedroom.

Liz and Gloria followed.

"Wow, is this your room?" Bitsy asked, eyes wide, head swiveling around to look at everything once they entered.

"Yep."

"Look at all the books!"

"You like to read," Lindsey asked.

"Yes. Misty taught me. Sometimes she lets me have a book and a light while I'm in my box for the night."

"In your box?" Liz asked and then looked at Gloria and Lindsey.

"The toy box. It's where she keeps me when she isn't playing with me," Bitsy said, voice almost dismissive as she looked at the books. "You have Harry Potter!"

"I do," Lindsey said. "Have you read them?"

"I'm on the fourth one now," Bitsy said. "Misty says her mommy used to read them to her when she was little."

"Speaking of Misty," Lindsey said, joining Bitsy at the shelf. "I want you to take a look at a yearbook and see if you can spot her, okay."

"A yearbook?"

"Yeah, it has pictures in it."

"And Misty will be in it?"

"Probably."

"Okay."

Lindsey looked at the lower shelves, which were for taller books, light from the candle she held illuminating everything, but didn't see it. She thought for a second, unsure of where she would have put it, the last time she'd looked at it being right after they were handed out at the end of her sophomore year, her eyes on the lookout for pictures of herself in the various activities she had taken part in throughout the year.

"Huh," she said and turned toward the closet, wondering if it was on the shelf in there.

"Can't find it?" Liz asked.

"Not sure. I thought it was down there, but maybe"—she opened her closet—"I put it up here."

Nope.

Books were present on the shelf, along with sketch pads and various magazines, but no yearbooks.

"Huh," she said again.

"Not there?"

"No." *Where would I have put it?*

"You sure it's not on the shelf?" Gloria asked, stepping up to the shelf herself and kneeling down to look, head tilted sideways. She used the flashlight app on her phone to look at the covers.

"Pretty sure," Lindsey said and did a scan of her room.

"Misty hides things under her bed," Bitsy said. "Maybe you put it under there."

"Not sure why I would, but…" She got down on her knees and lifted the bed skirt.

Bitsy joined her.

"I don't think it's under here," Lindsey said, hand stretching to push a box out of the way. Nothing but a year's worth of dust was behind the box.

"Misty always keeps her photo books under the bed."

"How come?"

"So the Daddy-man won't look at them."

"Does he not like her having pictures?"

"Sometimes." She pointed. "Maybe in the box?"

"Let's see." Lindsey stretched her arm once again, this time grabbing the top of the box and pulling it toward them.

It wasn't in the box.

Instead, items from her mother's battle with cancer were, items that caught her off guard because she had forgotten that she had put all this stuff in a box and tucked it under the bed.

"Is this your mommy?" Bitsy asked, lifting up a picture.

"Yeah," Lindsey said. The picture was of just the two of them at a breast cancer walk. Another version of the picture was downstairs on the wall, that one having been taken by a friend so that her father could be in it as well.

The pink scarf that her mother had worn during the walk was in the box, as were several pins and ribbons.

"Just like Misty."

"What?" Lindsey asked, blinking away emotion. Several years had passed, yet somehow it all came flooding back.

"She keeps pictures of her mommy under her bed."

"How come?" She rubbed at her eyes, clearing away the moisture that had welled.

"Her daddy doesn't like her to have them." She frowned. "Does your daddy not want you to have these?"

"No, it's not that." She didn't know how to explain why she had tucked these away. It felt like a protective measure, one that would keep everything safe. "Let's put this stuff back." She started to fold the flaps back up on the box, but then stopped when Bitsy reached down and grabbed a pamphlet from the box. "Whoa, hey!"

"This is where they are!" Bitsy said, excitement present.

"What?" Lindsey asked. The pamphlet was from the funeral.

"Misty and the Daddy-man!"

"They're at a cemetery?" Gloria asked, leaning in over their shoulders.

"They are near it," Bitsy said. "I walked through it after the storm."

"You live near the cemetery?"

Bitsy looked confused.

"Your house," Lindsey added. "It's by the cemetery?"

"Oh no, our house is gone."

"Well, yes, I know, but it was near the cemetery?"

"No, that's where our van is. We were looking for a new house. But our van got flipped over into a field."

"Your van?" Lindsey said, a sudden memory of her father mentioning a van arriving. One that had been flipped over. Could it be the same?

Bitsy nodded. "Can you take me to it?"

Lindsey didn't reply to that.

"Please!"

"What kind of van?" Lindsey asked.

"What do you mean?" Bitsy asked.

"Was it an old Volkswagen van?"

"I don't know what that is."

"Okay, um…hang on a second." She pulled out her phone, thumbed in her password, and clicked the Internet icon. It took a second, the phone having to use data rather than the home wireless, but eventually it connected.

She typed *VW van* and then hit the Image selection once the search results appeared.

"Does it look like any of these?" she asked.

Bitsy took the phone and looked at the pictures, while the three crowded around her.

"Can you make it bigger?" she asked and then felt Lindsey's boob press into her arm as she leaned in to look at the screen.

She started acting like a boy.

"Which one?" Lindsey asked, boob still pressed into her arm.

No! No! No!

The pressure did not fade.

"Bitsy? Which one—"

"This one," Bitsy said quickly, pointing to the green one.

"Just touch it," Gloria said and reached over to show her, knuckles hitting the phone as Bitsy lifted it toward her.

It slipped from her fingers and landed between her legs.

"Oops," Gloria said, reaching for it.

Bitsy reached as well, trying to block Gloria's hand, the thin fabric of the sweatpants doing little to mask her lack of control.

It was no use.

Gloria's hand rubbed against it as she secured the phone.

Bitsy froze.

Gloria sprang up from the bed, face showing surprise.

"I'm sorry," Bitsy said, crossing her legs.

"What?" Lindsey asked.

Gloria didn't say anything.

"What?" Lindsey repeated.

"She's a...she's a boy!"

"Huh?" Lindsey said, looking from Gloria to Bitsy.

Bitsy shook her head, lips trying but failing to apologize.

"She has a dick!" Gloria shouted.

"Fuck me!" Liz said, stepping forward and peering at Bitsy's lap.

Lindsey looked down.

Bitsy could see her eyes go wide.

Crossing her legs hadn't helped, not with the sweatpants and lack of underpants.

And then, as if she didn't believe her own eyes, Lindsey reached down and took hold of her, and then let go and pulled away.

"Jesus fucking Christ!"

"See," Gloria snapped.

Bitsy felt the tears flowing, all while her body tried to fold upon itself to mask her boy part. "I'm sorry," she sobbed. "I didn't mean to act like a boy." The other night she had, because Misty had wanted her to, but not just now. This time, it had simply happened. "Don't tell Misty."

Down below, her boy part continued to display itself.

Go away! she silently screamed at it.

It didn't.

In fact, the more she wanted it to, the more it seemed to stay put.

Just like the time with the matches and the firecracker.

"*I will blow it off,*" Misty had threatened, half the fire-cracker sticking out of her pee hole, "*if you don't learn to control it.*"

"*No! No! Please!*" Bitsy had screamed, the pain from the firecracker that had been stuck inside nothing compared to the fear of seeing Misty holding a lit match.

"*Make it go down!*"

"*I'm trying!*"

"*Try harder!*" She brought the match close.

Bitsy shrieked, hands fighting at the ropes that held her to the tree.

Misty put the match out against Bitsy's groin before it burned her fingers, the relief of the flames' disappearance masking the initial sting of the burn.

But then she lit another one.

"Bitsy," a voice said, a hand landing on her shoulder, one that made her flinch.

She blinked.

"Are you okay?" Lindsey asked.

She blinked again and then rubbed at the tears with her right hand while her left continued pressing down on her boy part. "I'm sorry," she said. "I didn't mean to."

"Honey," Lindsey said, sitting down and putting an arm around her. "You don't have to apologize."

Bitsy tried to pull away, the press of Lindsey's body making it impossible for her to stop acting like a boy.

"And we're also sorry for freaking out," Lindsey said. "Right?"

Liz and Gloria didn't reply.

"Right?" Lindsey repeated.

"Yeah," Gloria said.

"Sorry," Liz said.

Bitsy looked at them and tried to smile, but failed.

"Why does Misty make you dress like a girl?" Gloria asked.

"I am a girl."

"But you're—"

"Gloria," Lindsey said, cutting her off.

Gloria didn't continue.

"I wasn't supposed to have a boy part," Bitsy said. "It was a mistake."

No one replied to that.

"But Misty says that one day when I get my boobs they can fix it."

"Do you want it to be fixed?" Lindsey asked.

"I want Misty to be happy."

"But what about you?"

"What do you mean?" She rubbed her eyes again.

"It should be up to you to decide what you want to do with your body."

"But I'm Misty's," she said.

Again, no one replied to that.

Misty was right. They don't understand.

"Are you still going to take me to her?" Bitsy asked.

"Oh…um…yeah," Lindsey said.

"Lindsey," Gloria hissed.

Lindsey waved her away. "You said the van looked like one of these?" She picked up the phone and thumbed the password back in to bring up the picture.

"Yeah, only the windows in back have boards over them. And curtains to hide the boards."

"Lindsey, we need to talk right now," Gloria said.

"Fine," Lindsey said. "I'll be right back."

Bitsy nodded.

The three left the room.

Bitsy waited, unsure what to do, fear that they were lying and wouldn't really help her find Misty starting to appear.

"Bitsy's a boy!" Katie said.

"What?" Gary asked. "Are you sure?"

"Yeah. Powell found pictures of her at the house they tried to burn down. In most, her genitals are covered, but in one of them…" She didn't even want to voice a description of what had been displayed, but then forced herself to share it.

"Jesus!"

"Tell me about it. We need to find her before she gets back to Misty and her father. And we need to find them because it seems likely they have this Abigail Abbott with them."

"I'm going to brief the lieutenant on all this right now."

"Okay." She saw Owen returning with a map. "I'm going to try and pinpoint the area where they might be. Let me know if anything comes up."

"Will do."

Katie ended the call and returned to the storm chasers, who were now looking at the map that Owen had spread out.

NINE

Misty was worried.

Walking toward the police cruiser was uneventful, the schoolgirl obediently complying with her instructions to stay in front of her and not tug at the collar. She also wouldn't slow to the point where they became parallel with each other, Misty having given her a solid snap on the back with the leash as they set off to show her what would happen if she did.

It wasn't right.

The schoolgirl should have tried something. A fake fall before an attack, or a sudden yank to get the leash free from Misty's hand. Instead, she had simply walked, feet somewhat cautious given the darkness, but not to the point where it felt like a stall tactic.

Why?

She was not subdued yet.

Two to three days wasn't enough for that.

Two to three months sometimes wasn't enough, Daddy eventually throwing up his hands and giving up on them.

Yet here she was, acting like a good little schoolgirl on a

leash, one that followed Misty's instructions to the letter during their fifteen-minute journey from the barn to the car.

The policeman was up to something.

What exactly, she didn't know, but her initial instinct coupled with this display of obedience solidified the fear.

They had to get back to the barn.

"Give me your wrists," Misty instructed once the schoolgirl was in the driver seat, her own body standing in the open doorway.

Once again, the girl complied.

Misty unlocked her left wrist and hooked the cuff to the steering wheel, and then hurried around to the passenger side.

"Well?" Misty said once she was inside.

"What?"

"Drive."

What if she doesn't know how?

What if it had all been a lie to simply get her away from the barn for a while?

The schoolgirl twisted the key, the engine coming to life.

Voices appeared.

Police radio!

Misty reached for the handset before the schoolgirl could even consider taking hold of it.

"I wasn't going to try for it," the schoolgirl said.

"Why not?" Misty asked.

The schoolgirl shrugged.

"Let's go," Misty said.

The schoolgirl nodded and then started looking around.

"What's wrong?"

"It's a bit different than my parents' car," the schoolgirl said.

"You said you know how to drive."

"I do, but every car is different." She bent her head a bit.

"Ah, there we go." She took hold of a lever sticking out of the steering-wheel area, shifted it, and then turned to look back.

"What're you doing?" Misty asked.

"We need to back up and turn around."

"Why?"

"Because I'm pretty sure the driveway is back that way." She pointed with her free hand.

"Oh."

The schoolgirl was right. Given the layout of the house and barn and the part of the driveway they had walked on to get to the front of the house, the entrance to the driveway was likely behind them somewhere.

"Ready?" the schoolgirl asked, voice a bit apprehensive for some reason.

Misty nodded.

The car lurched backward and then came to a jarring halt.

"Why'd you do that?" Misty demanded.

"Sorry, I'm still a bit new to this."

"You said you knew how to drive."

"I do, I do, but it's been like a week."

"Since you drove?"

"Yeah, but I did well during that lesson."

"Lesson?"

"For my driving class."

"You're in a class?"

"Yeah, to get my license."

"You don't have one?"

"No, just a permit."

"What's that?"

"It's what they give you when learning to drive."

"But you have driven before, right?"

"Yeah."

"How many times?"

"Um…four times, no, five."

"Five?"

"Yeah, and last time they let me on a road rather than just a parking lot, though no stoplights yet."

Misty had no idea what that meant.

The schoolgirl took a deep breath and then turned backward once again.

The car started moving, this time without the sudden lurch.

"Shit!"

The car jolted to a halt.

"What?" Misty asked.

"It's hard to turn the wheel like this, especially while going backward."

"Why?"

"It's like crisscross."

Is she faking?

Is this all part of a ruse?

"Try again."

"I can't, not when cuffed like this."

"Try!"

The schoolgirl sighed and tried again, this time jolting them to a halt with the vehicle nearly sideways in the road.

"This is too hard," she said.

"We're halfway turned around," Misty replied.

"But I can't get it all the way around with my hand attached to the steering wheel, and if we back up any further, we might go off the road."

"Then pull forward a bit."

The schoolgirl considered this and peered forward, her eyes squinting to see through the darkness.

Misty squinted as well, but couldn't see much beyond the car. It was just too dark.

More voices echoed from the radio, something about the high school.

"Do you have the headlights on?" Misty asked.

"Shit! I forgot." She started looking around, hand touching things. "I think this one is it."

"You think?"

"I've never driven at night before." She twisted something.

Both jumped as the windshield wipers squealed against the dry windshield.

"Sorry!" the schoolgirl said and quickly shut off the wipers.

Another switch turned on the siren.

"You know what, just turn on the spotlight and use that," Misty said, pointing.

"Hang on, I think it's this one."

This time the headlights came on.

Misty sighed.

"You're right," the schoolgirl said, leaning forward once again. "I got plenty of room to pull forward."

They went backward, the car jolting once again as she slammed on the brake.

"Oops. Forgot to put it in drive."

Misty didn't reply.

The schoolgirl took a breath and then eased the car forward a bit while turning the wheel.

"Stop!" Misty cried as they neared the ditch in front of the car.

Another jolt.

The schoolgirl backed them up a bit, the car turning slightly.

No jolt followed, the girl easing the car to a halt.

And then they started going forward, speed increasing with each second that passed.

"Too fast," Misty said.

They halted with a screech of brakes, Misty hitting the dash.

"Sorry."

Misty stared at the girl for a moment, trying to figure out if she had done that on purpose, but then decided she most likely hadn't. She also decided to put on her seat belt.

They started forward again, initially at a crawl, but then speeding up.

"Slow down," Misty said.

The schoolgirl did.

And then a mailbox appeared.

It was on the opposite side of the road, but it marked where the driveway was.

The turn was too fast, gravel spraying everywhere as they left the pavement, the car skidding rather than jolting to a halt as the schoolgirl slammed on the brake.

Norman waited for several seconds after the two left the barn before he tried bouncing the keys out of his pocket, his teeth having managed to rip out the button moments before Misty had entered with the flashlight.

It took three buck-like thrusts before the keys cleared the fabric lip and landed in his lap.

Yes!

All he had to do was get the keys into his hand, find the handcuff one, and thread it into the keyhole.

Once he did that—

Outside he heard something. It sounded like a yelp, one that was close to the barn.

Nothing followed.

He waited.

Did Abigail try something?

Even though she knew I was close to getting the key?

Would she do that?

He wanted to say no, but after going through what she had gone through these last two days, he couldn't say for sure that she wouldn't make an attempt at freedom if one presented itself. He also couldn't blame her for trying. No. All he could do was focus on freeing himself. That way, if her attempt had failed, which, given the odd yelp, sounded likely, he could still salvage things with his own attempt and put this thing to an end.

Outside, the silence continued.

Were they heading toward his patrol vehicle?

If the yelp had been the result of Abigail trying to make a break for freedom, one that Misty had countered, it seemed unlikely that she would then willingly walk toward the patrol vehicle. Instead, she would likely continue to fight, the sounds of the struggle echoing.

But no sounds of a struggle echoed.

There were no sounds at all.

Had the yelp really been an escape attempt?

Or had one of them simply stumbled in the dark.

Just get the keys!

Shifting himself around the post once again, the edge digging into his back, he eventually managed to get himself into a position where his hands could grab at the keys, his fingers finding them quickly, the handcuff one easy to single out.

He then tried to find the keyhole.

Fuck!

Misty had locked the cuffs so that the keyholes were facing away from his fingers.

Had the holes been on the same side, fitting the key into one would have been fairly simple; now it wasn't, his wrists having to twist around painfully so that he could get the key in one of the narrow openings and turn it, the angle such that he was forced to make blind stabs at where he hoped the hole would be.

The first dozen attempts failed, the key often falling from his fingers given how difficult it was to hold at such an angle, silent cusses echoing within his mind.

And then he did it, his mind not even processing that the key was in the slot, his fingers thinking they had lost it once again when the sensation of it between his fingers disappeared, a brief scramble in the dirt adding fear as he realized the key wasn't there, a brush with the keychain that was dangling from the handcuffs alerting him to his success.

One good twist and he would be free.

It was not as easy as it seemed.

His fingers could barely get hold of the key, and whenever they did, twisting it was almost impossible.

Seconds turned to minutes, his panic growing.

He was so close, yet it could all come crashing down.

If Misty stepped inside…

They'd be fucked.

Plain and simple.

It was one thing to have the keys in his pocket, or even on the ground beneath his body, but dangling from the keyhole of the handcuffs themselves…there was no hiding that.

Come on!

He got his fingers across the key chain and started working his way back up to the handcuff key, wrists screaming as they were forced to bend at odd angles, his fingers using the key ring as a sort of anchor to bring the fingers, wrists, and handcuff key all together.

The cuff popped open.

One moment it was secure, the next his hand hit the ground, the other swinging around under the force of the crazy contortion attempt.

Disbelief overwhelmed him, his brain unable to process the reality of his freedom.

Get up!

He tried, his legs and back locking up on him while the room spun.

Several dry heaves hit, nothing but a tiny speck of bile appearing.

And then came the bloody mucus, the heaves having torn whatever healing had occurred within his nose.

Once finished, he carefully worked his way up to his feet, the pole acting as a brace, edges tearing at his finger flesh.

The keys were still dangling from the keyhole.

He waited several seconds for the world to still and then pulled the key free and used it to unlock the other wrist. After that, he pocketed the keys and cuffs and turned toward where he thought the door would be, the darkness so great he couldn't make out anything within the barn.

Deep breath.

And another.

Five total, the last one marking the start of a lap around the post, one hand on it for support just in case the world twisted again.

It didn't.

Another breath, and then he stepped away from the post, his bloody fingers leaving the jagged edges and shifting out to feel the area in front of him as he walked, his lap around the post having made him a bit uncertain on just which direction he was facing, though he felt chances were good he was heading toward the door.

Abigail had been hoping to get the police car stuck on the turn into the driveway, thereby making it a marker for other police officers should Norman fail in his endeavor to free himself while they were retrieving the car, but the skid into the field as they turned didn't lock them into the mud like she thought it would. Even worse, the farther up the driveway they went, the more unlikely it would become that someone would spot the police car, which meant she might have missed her only opportunity.

I should have just put it into the ditch alongside the road.

The trouble was, she had wanted the act of getting stuck

to look like an honest mistake. Had she simply put them in a ditch from the start, Misty might call into question whether it had truly been a mistake. By the time they made it to the driveway, there would be no doubt.

Only they hadn't gotten stuck.

Muddied up, yes, but stuck, no, though at first she had thought her plan successful given how much the tires spun before graining traction and jerking them forward onto the gravel.

Misty had too, her screams of frustration and belittlement of Abigail making that clear.

"You're lucky we got out of that," Misty said.

Nothing else was said.

Abigail considered speeding up again and then losing control, her frantic, inexperienced hands "accidentally" bringing the car to the left and back toward the road, but feared that she wouldn't be able to go far enough into the field to where it could be spotted from the road within the darkness. Once morning came, people would see it, but at that point, the van would be a marker, and though a disabled police car would probably bring about attention quicker, she felt that might be too late.

No.

She needed to do something that would bring the police there now, something that would act like a backup to Norman's attempt at freedom.

But what?

The radio?

It seemed like an option, though only if Misty let her guard down to the point where she could get control of the handset. Another was the phone that was sitting in a tiny slot between the cup holders, a phone that she was sure Misty hadn't noticed, because if she had, she would have likely grabbed it the way she had the radio handset.

Moving slowly, they crept along the driveway, Misty

seemingly relieved that Abigail wasn't pressing on the gas, her thinking likely being that she had made a big mistake in letting Abigail behind the wheel.

Then again, what choice did she have?

She obviously had never learned to drive, and since she wasn't about to let the police officer free, not when he was bigger and stronger and could easily overpower her even while cuffed, Abigail and her apparent lack of driving skill were the only real option.

Crash it?

Into the barn?

Not at a suicidal speed, but at one that would be enough to distract Misty to the point where she could grab the phone without her knowing, thumb 911 into the dial pad, and then drop it beneath the seat.

Once that was done, all they had to do was wait.

The police would track the call and respond, so even if Norman hadn't managed to free himself, they would still be rescued.

And once again, her apparent inexperience while behind the wheel could be blamed.

It was perfect.

The only downside was that Misty had put on a seat belt, so the chances of her being injured in the impact were slim. Still, even a slow-speed crash would be jarring enough to throw her off balance.

Up ahead, the house appeared in the headlights.

House or barn?

Barn.

That way she could act like she'd lost control while turning the car to face it, and then hit the gas a bit in her panic.

Are you really going to do this?

Yes.

No.

Indecision gripped her.

"It turns up there," Misty said, caution present.

"I see it."

"Maybe slow down a bit."

"We're good." She pressed on the gas.

"I think we should slow down."

"It's cool." More gas.

"*Please!* Slow down!" Misty cried, grabbing the armrest.

The car came upon the large turnabout area, Abigail twisting the wheel to point them toward the barn, tires skidding in the gravel.

"Abigail, please!"

She pointed the car toward the barn door, foot still on the gas.

Too fast! her own mind warned.

Releasing the gas, she moved her foot toward the brake.

"Stop!"

She tapped the brake a bit, hoping to slow the car as they sped toward the barn, her own panic beginning to set in.

The barn door opened.

Norman's eyes went wide as the car came toward him, headlights trapping him like a deer.

"Shit!" Abigail cried, twisting the wheel while hitting the brake.

The car wobbled and fishtailed, Abigail trying to steer the car away from the doorway without effect.

Misty screamed.

The front driver side of the car slammed into the barn, the impact throwing Abigail toward the steering wheel, the airbag catching her. It wasn't soft. More like a firm pillow that would not yield.

Norman felt cold and knew something horrible had happened as he opened the door to the barn, one that had taken him far too long to find after having walked straight into one of the livestock pens that Abigail had been hand-cuffed to earlier.

Abigail.

What happened?

He tried to get up but couldn't, the movement causing a tug within his belly that was impossible to ignore. It didn't hurt, not yet, but was far from pleasant, almost as if...

Oh God!

His hands found his stomach and whatever it was that had skewered him, the object protruding about five inches from the left of his belly button.

A cramp hit.

With it came the pain.

It was the worst thing he had ever experienced, the intensity of it blocking out everything else.

And then it faded.

Shit.

He could smell it.

At first he thought it had oozed out of his butt during the spasm, and while that may have happened, he realized it was his opened bowels that he could smell. And feel. A loop of them had come up with the object as it punched through him.

Another spasm hit.

Fluid bubbled up, his hand trying to hold it in but failing.

A hissing sound followed.

At first, he didn't know what it was or what it meant, but then it dawned on him. He had just passed gas through his opened abdomen.

Light appeared.

He shifted his face away from it, a sudden memory of the headlights coming at him as he opened the door filling his mind, a cry of *no* echoing.

Legs.

He could see them behind the light.

They approached.

A gasp reached his ears, and then a gagging noise.

An odd apology left his lips, one that was likely too soft for her to hear. Then, "Help me."

No reply.

"Help me!" he said again, this time mustering up all the sound he could manage.

Blood punctuated the request.

Lots of it.

Another spasm hit, this one knocking all sense from him.

"I'm sorry," a voice said.

Lindsey?

No.

An explosion deafened him.

He blinked.

Gunshot?

His ear felt like it was on fire.

Another gunshot, this one hitting his shoulder.

If there was pain, it was masked by the agony from his bowels, which were continuing to ooze.

And then something seared the side of his head.

He tried turning away but couldn't, an image of her pressing the gun barrel to his temple appearing just as she pulled the trigger.

Misty took three steps and then vomited, the smell of cordite mixed with that of the policeman's bowels, blood, and brain tissue too much for her. She had seen death before. Had even caused it once by mistake. And as horrible as that was, this was worse.

Voices.

They echoed behind her.

She turned and looked at the car.

• • •

"...*Volkswagen van...kidnapping suspects...Abigail Abbott...*"

Abigail heard but didn't process the statements being made on the radio, the only thing that fully registered being the use of her name.

Kidnapping?

The box!

She was in the box, body folded, unable to breathe.

She needed to get out.

She needed—

The radio!

Call for help!

It all started to come back to her, her hands fighting against the fabric of the airbag in an attempt to reach the handset that was dangling somewhere, her fingers just needing to snag the cord, which was clearly visible.

She got it!

The door opened.

"What were they saying?" a voice demanded.

Abigail didn't reply, her only focus being on getting the handset to her lips so she could call for help, the cord seemingly going on forever and ever.

"I heard them say my name!" the voice continued. "And Daddy's and Bitsy's."

The handset appeared.

"Did they say where she was?"

Abigail lifted the handset to her lips, finger pressing on one of the buttons. "Help!" she cried, the sound of her own shriek startling.

"No! No! No!" the voice said.

"Help me! I'm Abigail Abbott. Misty has me and Norman —" An image of his body smashing against the hood and then being thrown somewhere unseen flashed before her eyes.

Was he okay?

No.

"Norman's hurt! Please help—"

The handset was ripped from her fingers, the cord eventually torn free from the radio itself.

And then Misty was trying to pull her from the car, screams of "you stupid bitch" and "I'm going to kill you" raining down upon her, all while the handcuff that was still looped through the steering wheel kept her body from being pulled free, the metal digging into her wrist.

Voices erupted on the radio, her name being spoken by several different people.

Did they know where she was?

Could they tell that by a radio call?

Did the car have a GPS or some other sort of tracking device?

The phone!

Misty continued to pull, Abigail's body feeling like it was going to be ripped in half, the flesh on her wrist breaking against the cuff.

"*Handcuffs!*" Abigail screamed.

Misty didn't seem to understand and kept pulling.

The radio voices continued.

"*Handcuffs!*"

She screamed the word over and over again, until finally Misty released her grip on Abigail's arm, her body falling to the dirt next to the driver-side door, handcuffed wrist stretched all the way up to the wheel, the sight of it hidden by the airbag.

The phone.

I need the phone.

The radio call might not be traceable, but the phone call would.

Misty pulled a key from her pocket and tried to get into the driver side of the car to find the keyhole.

Abigail stood up and shoved Misty as hard as she could, a

gasp exploding from the girl's lips as she crashed backward to the ground, flashlight bouncing across the gravel.

"You stupid shit!" Misty cried. "I lost the key!"

Ignoring her, Abigail climbed back into the car, body fighting the airbag, which had now deflated, so that she could pull the door shut and lock it. She then reached across and tried to reach the other door, but couldn't get it.

Just get the phone.

She reached for where it had been, but the slot was now empty, the impact having likely bounced it free.

But where?

She peered over the edge of the passenger seat, hoping to see a reflected gleam from the screen.

Nothing.

She then scrunched herself down and patted the floor by her feet, but found nothing but carpet.

The same was true of the area beneath the seat, though she couldn't reach the full length.

How the phone would have even gotten all the way under there was beyond her, but it didn't seem to be anywhere else, so…

Misty appeared on the right side of the car.

Without really thinking about it, Abigail shifted the car into reverse and pressed her foot on the gas.

The grinding squeal from the engine was unlike anything she had ever heard before, and given the agony it was generating, she knew she wouldn't get very far, but that was fine. All she wanted to do was move the vehicle enough for the passenger-side door to shut when she hit the brake so that she could lock it and find the phone.

Misty would get in, of this she had no doubt, but the delay would be costly for her if Abigail could get to the phone. In fact, it might just put an end to this entire thing.

Or she will kill you in a rage.

It was a risk she was willing to take.

The car died.

She had gone maybe ten feet, the momentum not enough to even move the passenger door, let alone slam it shut.

And then smoke appeared, along with the smell of something burning.

Oh shit!

She pulled at the handcuff link, fist squeezed, flesh continuing to tear, all to no avail.

The burning smell got worse.

Abigail continued to fight the handcuff link, blood now dripping.

She then attacked the steering wheel itself, hoping to rip it free.

Could she even do such a thing?

The answer was no.

She pulled and pulled, but it would not come off. Next she tried twisting it until it snapped, but that was useless as well, her knuckles white with the effort yet achieving nothing.

Light appeared.

The car was on fire.

And then Misty was in the passenger doorway, screaming at her that the car was on fire.

No shit!

"The police officer has a key!" Abigail shouted.

"What?" Misty asked.

"That's how he got free. They were in his chest pocket."

Misty turned and ran toward the barn.

A buzzing noise echoed.

It was near her feet.

The phone!

She peered down, but once again could not see it.

And then the buzzing stopped.

But it was there, somewhere, and if she got it she could pocket it before Misty came back with the key.

She reached down and started patting the ground again, but like before, she could not find it.

It didn't make any sense.

She knew it was there.

The buzzing sound left no doubt.

Frustrated, she sat back up and checked the hood of the car.

The flames were growing.

And Misty was nowhere to be seen.

The keys in the ignition!

Would they have a cuff key?

The stench of the policeman's body had gotten worse during the short period of time that Misty had been dealing with the stupid schoolgirl, and instantly produced a sensation in the back of her throat that would lead to another bout of vomiting. Or at least dry heaving since there was nothing left in her body. She didn't want this, yet at the same time she didn't want the schoolgirl to burn to death in the car, even though the bitch deserved it after what she had just done.

No.

She needed the girl.

Not just for her driving abilities, as lacking as they were, but also for her company and companionship.

Going off alone just wasn't something she wanted to do—couldn't do—especially if she failed to find Bitsy. The loneliness would be too much, as would the sheer volume of everything around her. Total information overload, her experience with the world beyond that of her father's house too limited for her to make it to a new home and get it up and running. Not that she wouldn't try if forced to, but having someone like Abigail with her would make things easier—even with the moments of disobedience.

I can curb that.

But only if I get her out of the car.

Taking a deep breath, she headed into the cloud of fecal stench and began searching the stiffening body of the policeman, eyes watering as the smell seeped in through her nose, her attempts at not breathing in the stench becoming more and more difficult.

The heat from the flames was starting to bake the inside of the car when Abigail slipped from the driver seat into the gravel, her left hand holding her right wrist where the handcuff link had encircled it, the fingers flexing and unflexing as she contemplated her next move.

Misty was still in the barn.

Go!

A buzz echoed.

The phone.

Just go.

Hesitation hit.

She peered back into the vehicle, her eyes now level with the brake and gas pedals.

The phone was sitting between them, screen side down, the dark case making it almost invisible.

She grabbed it.

Lindsey Call.

Abigail hit the End button and then hit the main button to bring up the password screen. Near the bottom was the word *Emergency*. She hit it and then darted away from the burning car toward the side of the barn, eyes on the lookout for anything she could use to hit Misty with when she emerged from the doorway.

Misty found the keys in the front right pants pocket, which had been caked with bloody fecal crud that had oozed from the chunk of skewered bowel. It was one of the most disgusting moments of her life, the sludge sticking to her fingers as she slipped them into the pocket.

Keys retrieved, she wiped her hands on the upper part of the policeman's shirt, near an area of the shoulder that still seemed clean, and then headed toward the door, startled by how big the flames had become.

The gas tank!

What if it explodes?

She had to act fast, her feet starting toward the car just as something came toward her face, her head twisting away while her arms went up, the object impacting her left forearm with a heavy ping-like *thunk* sound.

Pain flared, the entire arm going useless.

Another swing.

Misty dodged this one and watched as the shovel slammed into the side of the barn, Abigail wielding it with a fury that was eerily visible within the light from the flames.

"No, no!" Misty shouted, backing up several steps, one hand held out in a "stop" gesture while her other hand reached for the gun that was tucked into her waistband.

Abigail swung again.

Misty pulled her hand back but wasn't quick enough, the shovel clipping her knuckles.

And then she tripped, falling backward just as she pulled the gun free, butt hitting the wet ground, the impact painless.

Abigail came forward, shovel raised.

"Drop it!" a voice commanded, a beam of light spearing her.

Abigail froze.

Misty peered around, toward the light, eyes just barely able to make out a figure standing near the edge of the barn. She had a gun in hand, one that was aimed at Abigail's back.

"I said drop it!"

"My name is Abigail—"

"Drop it!"

Abigail took a breath and lowered the shovel. "My name is Abigail Abbott—"

"On the ground, facedown."

"You don't understand!" Abigail shouted.

"I'm not going to tell you again. On the ground now!"

Abigail glared down at Misty, the firelight still illuminating her face, and then eased herself down onto her knees.

"Facedown."

Abigail let out a sigh and leaned herself forward onto the ground.

"Hands out to your sides."

"You're making a big—"

"Hands out!"

Abigail put her hands out.

The woman stepped forward, flashlight beam staying on Abigail during the approach. She looked like a police officer, though her uniform was a different color than the man's had been. She also had on a hat.

The light shifted toward Misty. "Are you okay?" the woman asked, offering a hand.

Misty nodded and lifted her free hand for the woman to grab, the firm grip helping her to her feet while the officer's other hand held a gun on Abigail. She then released Misty's hand to take hold of her radio.

Misty lifted the gun and shot her in the face before she could make the call.

Abigail screamed as the gunshot echoed, her initial thought being that the police officer, or whoever it was that was behind her, had decided to shoot her in the back, her body actually bracing itself for the impact that never came.

No other shots followed, an odd calmness arriving.

A moan reached her ears.

It sounded like it came from behind her.

The officer!

She wasn't dead.

She could still—

Steps crunched by her head and then moved toward where the officer was, the sound of something being lifted from Abigail's side followed by a garbled plea and then a heavy *thunk* echoing.

Abigail shifted so she could see, her movements slow so as not to be noticed, and watched in horror as Misty brought the shovel down onto the police officer's face over and over again, and then, when that didn't seem to be enough, shifted it in her hands so that she could stab the pointed part into the officer's neck.

Blood spurted.

Abigail gasped.

Misty turned, the firelight reflecting in her eyes as she glared down at Abigail. And then she knelt down and grabbed something.

The gun.

And then a pair of handcuffs, which she tossed onto the ground next to Abigail.

"Put them on."

Abigail hesitated.

Misty aimed the gun at her face.

Abigail cuffed her wrists, the familiar sensation of metal against flesh returning.

TEN

"Lindsey, no!" Gloria said. "You need to let the police handle this."

"But they're not handling it!" Lindsey snapped. "I called them four times to find out why my dad wasn't answering his phone, and they kept telling me he was busy. And now—" She simply pointed toward the police scanner.

"You don't know if it was your—"

"How many other Normans do you know around here?" Lindsey demanded.

Gloria didn't reply to that.

"And the last thing I heard from him was that he was going to go check a van that had been flipped over. An old Volkswagen van that looked like it had been driven right out of the sixties. Those were his exact words. How many of those have you seen around here?"

Again, Gloria didn't reply.

"Lindsey?" Liz asked, coming down the hallway from her bedroom.

"Yeah?" Lindsey asked.

"Bitsy wants to know if she...he—" Liz shook her head. "Can Bitsy borrow one of your dresses?"

"One of my dresses?"

"She's worried that if she goes back the way she is that Misty will be mad that she is acting like a boy." Liz shrugged.

"Oh, okay, sure, whatever." She gave a dismissive wave, but then said, "Wait! Not the blue one."

Liz nodded.

"How about not any of them?" Gloria said. "How about we simply call the police?"

Liz looked from Gloria to Lindsey.

"The only reason you didn't want to call them before was because you were worried her dad might be one, but it seems pretty safe to say that he isn't. At least not one from here."

"I'm not going to sit around waiting for an inept police department to get their shit together and try to help him," Lindsey snapped.

"What happened?" Liz asked.

Gloria told her about the cry for help they had heard on the police scanner.

"Fuck. Do you think he's okay?" Liz asked.

"I don't know, but I'm not going to wait to find out." Lindsey turned and started toward her father's bedroom.

Gloria and Liz followed.

Lindsey went right to the closet and started reaching around on the top shelf, hands eventually finding the box she was looking for and bringing it down.

"Oh, no, no, no!" Gloria said.

"That's a fucking gun," Liz added.

"Lindsey, think about what you're doing!" Gloria urged.

"I am thinking about it," Lindsey said, opening the revolver so that she could load the cylinder, memories of her father always telling her to leave one chamber empty as a safety precaution echoing since there was no safety on this piece.

"I'm sorry," Gloria said, putting her hands up. "I'm not going to be a part of this."

"Fine." Lindsey turned to Liz. "Let's help her get a dress."

"Lindsey, I'm not really cool with this either."

Lindsey stared at them both while tucking the gun into her coat pocket, and then, without a word, pushed by them and headed into the hallway toward her room.

Bitsy was sitting on her bed, waiting.

She stood, hands folded.

"Liz said you wanted a dress so that Misty doesn't get mad?" Lindsey said.

"Yes," Bitsy said. "If it's okay with you."

"Go ahead," Lindsey said, motioning toward the closet. "Pick out whatever you want. Just not the blue one."

"Thanks," Bitsy said, quickly moving toward the closet.

"Lindsey," a voice said from the doorway. It was Liz.

"Yeah?" Lindsey asked.

"You're really going to go do this?"

"I am."

Liz nodded. "Okay, then I'll go with."

"And Gloria?" Lindsey asked.

Liz shook her head. "She left."

"Are you a schoolgirl?" Bitsy asked.

"What?"

"You have a schoolgirl skirt."

"I do?"

Bitsy pulled it out to show her, the tartan pattern barely visible in the flickering candlelight.

"Oh that," Lindsey said. It had been part of last year's Halloween costume. "You can wear it if you want."

"No, no, the Daddy-man doesn't like it if I wear stuff like this. But if you did, he would like it. All the girls that come home with him wear them. And Misty has one that she got online, but it is a surprise. She wore it the other night when she wanted me to act like a boy so she could see if she really likes being a schoolgirl."

"I think I'll stick to wearing this," Lindsey said.

"Okay, but the Daddy-man won't like it."

"That's fine with me," Lindsey said. She touched the butt of the gun within her coat pocket, a thought on how the Daddy-man wasn't going to like her no matter what she wore arriving.

"Maybe you should wear it," Liz said.

"Why?"

"Because if he likes stuff like that, it might catch him off guard, which could be to your benefit."

Lindsey considered that and said, "Shit, you're right." She turned to Bitsy. "Okay, I changed my mind. If you think the Daddy-man will like it, I'll wear it."

"He will," Bitsy said, face brightening. "And maybe you can then come live with us once we find our new home. You, me, and Misty can play games and have parties. Do you like *Mario Kart*?"

"Um, yeah, I do," Lindsey said.

"Me too. It's my favorite." Bitsy handed her the skirt. "Hopefully the Daddy-man will let you play with us."

"Do you have a second one?" Liz asked, motioning to the skirt.

"I don't."

"The Daddy-man has some," Bitsy said. "Leftover ones from the other schoolgirls. I'm sure you can wear those if you want to stay with us too." She pulled out a frilly dress that one of Lindsey's aunts had given her for Christmas two years earlier. "Can I wear this one?"

"Sure," Lindsey said.

Bitsy smiled and then said, "You need a shirt too."

"Ah, yes."

Bitsy reached back into the closet and pulled out a white long-sleeved blouse.

"Wow, going all out," Liz said.

"You suggested it," Lindsey said.

Liz shrugged.

It really was a good idea. Anything that could cause a moment of hesitation with this Daddy-man would be an advantage for her.

She looked at the schoolgirl outfit and then over at Bitsy, who was holding the dress up to herself.

Are you really going to do this?

Maybe Gloria is right.

She then heard the scream from the scanner replaying itself in her memory, the statement about Norman being hurt echoing over and over again.

The girl had gotten on a first-name basis with her father, which didn't seem good, and he was hurt, which was even worse.

Topping it all off, someone had ended her most recent call several rings before it normally would go to voicemail.

She couldn't sit around waiting for the police, not with this department.

No.

And if what Bitsy said was true and the van was in the cemetery that her mother was buried in, then she likely knew more than the police did.

"Okay, let's get changed and then head out," Lindsey said. "Don't want to risk missing them."

Bitsy nodded and then said, "I might need help with the back."

"I'll help you," Liz said.

"Thanks."

Katie stared at her radio for nearly two minutes following Abigail Abbott's sudden cry for help, waiting—hoping—for more.

Nothing followed.

"Was that the girl?" Owen asked. "The kidnapped one?"

"Yeah," Katie said, still shocked. "I think so."

"Norman's hurt!"

Their Norman?

Did he come upon the scene only to be attacked while trying to help the girl?

As crazy as it sounded, that had to be the case, for how else would Abigail have gotten hold of a Smallwood Police Department radio?

Shit.

"Now what?" Owen asked.

Katie looked at him and then at the two storm chasers who had been looking at the map with them, Tess trying to be helpful in determining the area that Bitsy had been found in, Ramsey looking bored and as if this was all a big inconvenience to him.

"I have no idea," she said.

Owen didn't reply to that.

Katie pulled out her phone and called Gary.

"Yeah, I heard it," he said before she could say anything. "We all did."

"Did Norman say anything about where he was?" she asked. "It sounds like he must have stumbled upon them and tried to help."

"We're trying to establish that," Gary said.

"What do you mean?"

"Turns out Norman never checked in during the six o'clock. And no one has heard from him since right after the storm."

"What? How is that even possible?"

The same way it's possible for convoys to make wrong turns and for soldiers and contractors to get into firefights with each other because no one thought to mention they would both be hitting the same area, her mind said. *People!*

"I don't know," Gary said. "We got overwhelmed."

Katie shook her head, but then realized she wasn't one to

talk, not after Bitsy had simply walked out while under her watch. "So, what's Bell doing?"

"She's on the phone with the county right now trying to get manpower out here to help with what she feels will likely be a hostage situation, though that is proving difficult given that the entire county was devastated by the storms. Same is true with the state. Most of those boys are trying to clean up a hog truck that was flipped and is blocking most of 39."

"Jesus."

"Yeah. It's a mess."

Katie couldn't even begin to imagine.

"Bell has also talked with Powell."

"Oh jeez. Am I going to get it for playing detective?"

"I wouldn't worry about that."

Something in his voice told her she should do just the opposite, especially if Bell was worried about her own failures and tried to deflect attention away from them.

Not now!

Focus.

"What are we doing about Norman?" she asked. In her mind she pictured dozens of officers converging on an area, a determination to rescue a fallen comrade guiding them. Unfortunately, they didn't even have a dozen officers, nor did they know what location it was that they needed to head toward.

"We're trying to figure that out right now. He isn't answering his phone, but it is on, so we're going to try and pinpoint its location, though that could take some time. And of course, everyone is going to be on the lookout for his cruiser."

In other words, they had no idea where he was and didn't know where to start looking.

"I think he is somewhere south of town, likely around the same area where Bitsy was picked up," Katie said. "We should have everyone converge on that area and start sweeping."

"That's my—" A conversation developed away from the phone, Gary's voice recognizable, but not what was being said.

Katie waited.

And waited.

And waited.

"A call just came in from the county," Gary said, the return of his voice startling her. "They say one of their deputies reported seeing what appeared to be a fire in a field off of Route 7 and was going to check it out. Now they can't reach her."

"Seriously?"

"Yeah."

"Did they say the address?"

"No. She wasn't sure. Most of the road signs down there are gone. She also didn't know if it was something that needed fire and rescue or was just a fire that a homeowner had going for debris. That's why she decided on checking it out before calling in anything. Didn't want to divert anyone away from something serious by mistake."

"And now no one can reach her," Katie noted. "It has to be connected."

"Hard to say," Gary said.

"Come on, you and I both know it is. She probably approached the area without realizing she was walking right into the middle of situation involving a serial killer, one who had already gotten a jump on Norman as he approached earlier to offer help."

Gary didn't reply.

"I'm going to head down that way and see what that fire is all about."

"I'll get some backup for you as well. Let me know what road the fire is on once you locate it."

"I will."

"Also, be careful on Route 7. Most of the stop signs from the cross streets are gone. We've already had two accidents from people pulling out onto 7 without stopping."

"Jesus."

"Yeah, between that and the electrocutions from people trying to take selfies next to downed power lines, the post-storm stupidity is on its way to being more deadly than the tornado itself."

Katie didn't even know what to say to that.

Gary went quiet as well.

And then a thought arrived, one that chilled her to the core.

"Oh shit," she said.

"What?" Gary asked.

"They might have access to patrol vehicles."

"Christ, you're right."

"I better get down there," Katie said, turning to head toward the doors.

"Yeah, you do that. I'm going to put out word about the cruisers." He sighed. "This is fucking crazy."

Katie agreed.

"I feel ridiculous wearing this," Lindsey whispered after closing the door to the back seat of her car. Bitsy was inside, wearing the red and white frilly dress that Lindsey had only ever tried on, comments about looking like a candy striper echoing from her lips while her father tried not to laugh.

"Are we really doing this?" Liz asked, ignoring Lindsey's wardrobe statement.

"I am," Lindsey said. "If you don't want to…"

Liz stood by the passenger door, contemplating.

"It's now or never," Lindsey added.

Liz answered by getting into the car.

Lindsey followed, the stupid schoolgirl skirt riding up to the point where the back of her legs got a shock from the cool leather of her seat, the moment bringing back memories of wearing it to the Halloween party last year, the outfit one that she had to sneak by her father because of the garters that showed, garters that had kept coming unhooked throughout the night until she had finally given up on reconnecting them and simply let them dangle, her thinking being that a zombie schoolgirl would do the same.

And then she had been tagged on Facebook, her father seeing everything anyway.

She shook her head.

This time around she didn't have a garter problem.

Instead, she had a "gun keeps digging into my side" one.

Call the police.

No.

She looked in the rearview mirror, her eyes finding Bitsy, who was looking out the window, seat belt buckled across her body, hands folded in her lap.

Kind of looks like a doll, she noted to herself, the frilly dress one that she would have seen on Liz's dolls when they were over there. Then, *This is fucked up.*

"You okay?" Liz asked.

"Yeah."

"He's going to be okay," Liz added.

Lindsey nodded, though deep down inside she wondered. On the day her mother had died she had somehow known her mother was gone before her father had come out to tell her. It had just clicked. Would the same happen here?

"Officer Adams?" Tess called.

Katie turned, right hand slipping her phone back into her jacket. "Yeah?" she asked, hearing her own impatience.

"Is there anything we can do to help?"

"No. Not at the moment. Just stay here. If we need anything, Owen will come get you." She glanced at Owen, who nodded. She then turned to continue toward the doors.

A girl came barging through them, looking winded, almost as if she had been running.

"You need to help me!" she cried.

"What is it?"

"She has a gun!"

"Who?" Katie asked, hand going to her own sidearm.

"My friend. Lindsey." She took a breath, a hand pressed into her side. "We heard on the scanner that her dad was hurt, and now she is going to go and try to help him."

Scanner?

Lindsey?

Fuck!

Katie had met the girl a few times during holiday events and on the shooting range, Norman often bringing her there and boasting about how she was a better shot than he was. It was true too. Lindsey was a better shot than most of the Smallwood officers. She could probably give all the county deputies and state troopers a run for their money as well.

"I called nine-one-one, but they're all fucked up," the girl continued.

"What do you mean?"

"They kept asking if I was in Smith's Grove. Said they couldn't find the address I was talking about. So I said fuck it and ran here."

"Okay," Katie said, noting that people were gathering. Owen and the two storm chasers had stepped closer as well. "Take a breath and tell me what happened. Where is she right now?"

"At her house. Right down the street." She motioned toward the doors. "But they won't be there for long. They're going to go find her father."

"They know where he is?"

"Yeah."

"How?"

"This girl, or boy…fuck, I don't know." She threw up her arms. "Says her family is by the cemetery."

"Bitsy?" Katie asked.

"What?"

"The girl, was her name Bitsy?"

"Yeah, how—"

Jesus! "You said the house is right down the street?"

"Like two blocks that way. It's the one with the toilet in the front yard."

"Show me," Katie said and then, while stepping toward the door, turned to Owen. "Radio this in."

Owen nodded.

"What's your name?" Katie asked once the two were outside.

"Gloria."

Katie nodded.

A few seconds later, they were getting into her patrol vehicle, Katie throwing on the switch for her emergency lights.

"Ramsey, the cemetery," Tess whispered.

"What about it?" Ramsey asked.

"We know where that is."

"So?"

"We should head down there."

"No way!"

"Why not?"

Ramsey simply stared at her, lips slightly opened.

"Why not?" Tess repeated.

"Because, you heard the radio. People are being hurt down there, maybe even killed."

This time it was Tess who simply stared.

"It's too dangerous," Ramsey added.

"You drove us into a fucking tornado."

"That was different."

"How?"

"We were trying to film it. To make money."

"And is tornado footage the only thing that the news stations will buy?"

Ramsey didn't reply, his mind suddenly focused on all the times he had seen amateur footage used in news broadcasts, the most memorable being the grainy shootout footage from the Boston bombers a few years back. Had the news stations paid money for that, or had they simply taken it from Twitter? If the former, how much would they be willing to pay, and if the latter, had it boosted the original poster's notoriety and social media reach?

And we have a professional camera.

"How do we get there?" he asked. "The car is wrecked."

"It's in bad shape, but not even close to being wrecked," Tess said.

"True."

"And if you get some good footage of a standoff, maybe even a shootout, and it's the only stuff available, and news stations pay for it, it might pay for the repairs."

He nodded.

No reporters were present in Smallwood yet, but once word spread that there was a hostage situation underway that involved a serial killer who had kidnapped a high school girl, all the reporters that had gone out to gather storm-damage shots would be diverted. This area was going to be crawling with news vans and camera crews, likely before the sun came up.

And most likely, none of them would arrive in time for the good stuff.

If any good stuff unfolded.

"So…" Tess pressed.

He hesitated, thoughts on their mother and how she

would kill him for bringing Tess into something like this working their way to the forefront of his mind.

"Ramsey?"

She's going to kill me anyway for what happened earlier with the storm.

"Let's do it," he said.

Tess clapped her hands.

Across the hall, Officer Owen Collins was talking on the radio, having moved as far as he could from all the curious onlookers that were filtering in, the distance doing little to keep his words and those that came from the radio itself private.

"We might not be the only ones that head to the cemetery," Ramsey noted, the soft words of *Old Grove Cemetery* leaving the lips of several people that had gathered.

"Most came in on the buses," Tess said.

"But not all."

Theirs had not been the only car in the parking lot when they had arrived at the school, and even those who didn't have vehicles in the lot would likely have phones in their pockets and could call others who did have vehicles. Word was going to spread. They would not be the only ones trying to get a piece of the action.

"Let's go."

The house was empty, though not dark, the flicker of candlelight easily visible through the windows.

"What's her car look like?" Katie asked.

"Um...blue, I guess. Four doors. It's a Hyundai."

"Plate number?"

Gloria shrugged.

"Anything else? Dents, ribbons, stickers?"

"Oh, she has a breast cancer ribbon thing and a pride

sticker. Someone tried tearing that off, so it's kind of messed up."

"Okay. Anything else?"

Gloria shook her head.

Katie took out her phone. "What's her number?"

"Um…" Gloria pulled out her own phone, thumbed it a bit, and then read off the digits.

Katie dialed while she did this and then hit Send.

The phone on the other end rang three times before being picked up.

"Hello?" a voice asked.

"Lindsey?" Katie asked.

"No, this is Liz. Lindsey's driving."

"Liz, this is Officer Katie Adams with the Smallwood Police Department. I want you and Lindsey to pull over right now, tell me where you are, and wait for me."

Liz conveyed the message and then came back on the phone. "Lindsey says no."

"Lindsey is committing a crime right now, and if you two don't pull over and stop this foolishness, you will both be charged."

"*Bullshit!*" a voice, likely Lindsey's, cried.

Katie shook her head. "Liz, do you have any idea what she is dragging you into?"

"Yes," Liz said, though there was hesitation in her voice.

"I don't think you do," Katie said. "The girl you heard on the radio is a kidnap victim, the most recent by a man who has been kidnapping, raping, and killing girls like you two for years. Do not—"

"*I called the station four times to let them know my dad was missing!*" a voice on the other end shouted. "*And they did nothing!*"

"Lindsey, I'm sorry. There is no excuse for what has happened, but that doesn't mean you should—"

"It's still Liz," Liz said, cutting her off.

"Okay, then tell her that she knows better than to do what she is doing. Tell her that we have officers heading down that way to the cemetery, and that this will all be over soon."

The phone disconnected.

Katie sighed with frustration.

"She's stubborn," Gloria said.

"Yeah," Katie agreed. "You live near here?"

"Just a few streets down."

"Okay, I want you to head home and stay inside."

"Maybe I should come with you, so I can point out their car when you come upon it."

Katie considered this and then nodded, her hand motioning for the girl to get into the passenger seat once again. "And you stay there unless I say otherwise, understand?"

Gloria nodded.

Lights still flashing, Katie shifted to drive and started toward Route 7, her hope being that Lindsey would have gone that way as well given that it was the most direct and quickest way to get to the area of the Old Grove Cemetery.

And if not?

Maybe they would get there first and be able to keep the situation from becoming even more fucked up.

"That was Katie?" Bitsy asked after the phone call was finished, her ears having listened while her eyes stayed focused on everything beyond the window.

"It was," Lindsey said.

"She's nice."

"You know her?"

"Yes," Bitsy said. "She's the one that gave me the sweat-shirt and pants. And some pizza and soda. But she wasn't really going to help me find Misty and the Daddy-man. She pretended she was, but I heard them talking about it when they thought I was sleeping."

Lindsey didn't say anything.

Bitsy shifted her gaze down to the dress she was wearing. She liked it but wondered if Misty would.

Was she still mad about the other night?

Had it all been an elaborate test?

One that she failed?

No.

Misty had enjoyed what they had done, her mind having been curious and wanting to try the activities for quite some time—ever since stumbling upon the old video of her mother and hearing what the Daddy-man said while holding her down and putting his boy part into her butt, her wrists bound behind her, fingers fisted, knuckles as white as her blouse.

"I'm going to raise her to be my very own schoolgirl slave," he had said while thrusting, Misty's mother squirming and screaming against the ring gag that held her mouth open. *"Her only purpose in life will be to bring me pleasure and to endure whatever torments I decide to inflict upon her."*

"Nooo!" echoed from the wide-open mouth, the gag unable to prevent the word or its meaning.

"Yes," the Daddy-man hissed and then pulled himself free from her butt and twisted her around so that her mouth was before him, ring holding it wide, his hips thrusting his boy part through the ring and into her mouth until he finished, several silly-sounding grunts echoing from his lips.

He then left her on the ground for several minutes, the camera only showing part of her body as it lay bound, mouth still held open, boy juice flowing out, breasts exposed from where her blouse had been opened, the noise of her breathing heavily through her sobs the only sounds.

And then…

"I'm going to teach her to like it," he said while sitting on the edge of the bed, his sticky boy part shrinking. *"She's going to*

crave it, her tiny lips begging for my cock, her pussy and ass trained to take it whenever I please, all because you're a lying sack of shit."

The gagged mouth tried to speak, the word inaudible.

"What?" he asked.

She repeated herself, the words slower.

"You didn't know?" he asked.

She nodded.

His fingers grabbed a chunk of her hair and lifted her by it, bringing her back to her knees, gag barely masking the scream from her throat. *"They had a special about your disappearance last night on* Dateline. *They said you and your boyfriend fought the night before I took you."* He punctuated the statement with a slap across her face. *"Because you wouldn't have an abortion."* Another slap. *"You knew it wasn't mine from the beginning!"* He threw her onto the bed, his boy part having firmed up again. *"You lied to me!"* He pressed himself against her butt, his firmness not yet to the point where it would go in. *"I thought she was mine."* Tears exploded, his eyes leaking as if a dam had been broken. *"All this time, I thought she was mine."* He crumpled until his back was against the bed, sobs echoing. Misty's mother joined him, body slowly working its way down until his head was able to rest upon her chest while her back was supported by the bed, a word that might have been "sorry" leaving her gagged lips.

Misty had watched it over and over again, Bitsy sitting on the ground beside her, unsure of what to say.

"I'm supposed to be his schoolgirl slave?" Misty finally asked.

"That's what it sounds like," Bitsy confirmed.

"But he hasn't taught me anything."

Bitsy didn't reply.

"Does he not like me?"

"He likes you. You're his—" She had been about to say "daughter" but then caught herself since that obviously wasn't the case, according to the video. Instead, she said, "Maybe he's worried you won't like it?"

"Bitsy?"

Bitsy blinked, her focus returning to the car.

Lindsey was turned around, looking at her, the car having stopped at some point.

"Yeah?" Bitsy asked.

"Do you recognize any of this?" Lindsey asked, hand motioning to the window next to her.

Bitsy looked toward the glass, eyes taking a moment to focus.

"Yes!" she said, seeing one of the brick columns of the gate she had passed after walking through the cemetery and finding the road, which she had crossed, her hopes being that the house beyond it in the field would have someone that could help Misty and the Daddy-man. It hadn't, her journey continuing across the field until she found another road, which was when she saw the red car making a turn and ran out to try to stop it. "This is it!"

"And Misty and the Daddy-man are in there somewhere?"

"No, behind it." Bitsy pointed. "There is a field that leads to a house, and the van is in front of the house."

"Wait, you crossed through a field first before coming to the cemetery?"

"Yes."

"Shit!" Lindsey snapped and hit the wheel.

"How long did it take you to cross?" Liz asked.

"I don't know. My head hurt and I was dizzy." Bitsy hadn't meant to upset Lindsey. "I'm sorry—"

"Did you cross any roads between the van and here?" Lindsey asked, cutting her off.

"Roads? No."

"So the barn that the van is at is on the opposite side of this field," Liz said. It had not been a question and had been directed at Lindsey rather than Bitsy, so Bitsy simply waited.

Lindsey considered this for a moment and then said, "There should be a road up here, right, one that will connect us?"

"I think so," Liz said. "The bus uses it to pick up George and Martin."

"Okay."

Bitsy sensed a newfound optimism within Lindsey, one that made her think that the girl was no longer mad at her, which was nice.

Would it be the same with Misty?

Or was that situation different?

Were her actions unforgivable?

If so, Bitsy would allow the necessary cuts to be made so that it would never happen again, though not without a sense of loss given how much she had enjoyed the sensations that her boy parts had experienced that night. She liked acting like the Daddy-man with Misty. So much so that she wanted to do it again.

And not just with her.

She wanted to do it with Lindsey.

And now that she realized that Lindsey was able to be a schoolgirl, her desire was even stronger.

Would she be able to act like the Daddy-man with Lindsey?

Would Misty allow it?

Would the Daddy-man?

Misty might, but the Daddy-man wouldn't, but that was okay, because he often was gone during the days, during which Misty and she would play with the schoolgirls.

But what if he finds out?

The Daddy-man didn't like her.

It made her sad.

And scared.

The only reason the Daddy-man put up with her was because Misty liked her, and if the other night had ruined that, then she might decide it was okay for the Daddy-man to get rid of her.

Would it be better to just stay with Lindsey?

Would she want to keep her?

No, she had to try with Misty.

After all these years, and all the fun they'd had, one night couldn't ruin it completely.

If it had, she wouldn't have wasted time punishing her. Instead, she would have just gotten rid of her.

The car began moving again.

They were heading to the road beyond the cemetery, the one that Liz said would take them to the road the farm was on, the one that the van had been driving down when the tornado caught them.

They were getting close.

So close that she started to examine her dress while seated, fingers making sure everything was done up correctly and that her boy parts were tucked away like they should be, Liz having given her a pair of Lindsey's panties to make sure everything was kept secure and wouldn't poke out the way it had while in the pants.

She was acting like a boy!

She felt it when reaching down to make sure those parts weren't going to be a problem.

It was the stupid thoughts on the night with Misty and acting like the Daddy-man.

She had liked putting her boy parts inside of Misty and now couldn't help but feel an excitement building even though she didn't want it to be there. And the panties weren't doing a good job keeping it hidden.

No! No! No!

Closing her eyes, she tried to think of things that would make it go away, things that Misty had done in response to moments like this.

The firecrackers came to mind, yet for some reason didn't work.

Nor did the memory of the cigarette tip.

Being kicked had always hurt too, but didn't make it disappear.

Or the rope tied around the dangling sacks and being lifted to the tips of her toes while her hands were tied behind her back, Misty threatening to lift her off the ground by them if she didn't shrink it back down.

It hadn't worked then, and the thought of it didn't work now.

Nothing ever did.

ELEVEN

Like the uniform, the police car that the policewoman had arrived in was different from the one that the policeman had been in, the colors and the words *County Sheriff* being the biggest differences on the outside, the computer the big one on the inside.

A picture of the schoolgirl appeared on the computer screen.

Misty nearly gasped at the sight.

Words were present as well, ones that she had to lean in to see.

They described the circumstances of Abigail Abbott's abduction, and then mentioned their home and that an attempt had been made to burn it down.

Attempt?

Misty leaned in closer to touch the mouse pad, finger carefully scrolling down so she could keep reading, her eyes quickly drawn to a picture of her daddy. It had been taken in front of the college where he worked, the sweater vest he wore one she had gotten him as a gift from Amazon. All the gifts she bought for him, and the things she bought for herself, came from Amazon, her daddy having been initially surprised and then angry when he found out she had used a Visa gift card that she had found in the purse belonging to one of the schoolgirls he had brought home.

After that, he had gotten her her own gift cards to use, the money he put on them a type of allowance for the chores she was assigned around the house while he was working, ones that she often had Bitsy do while wearing a frilly maid outfit. One that Misty had, naturally, gotten from Amazon.

Bitsy.

A picture of her and Misty was present beneath the one of her daddy, both of them smiling for the camera that Misty held.

How had they gotten it?

From the house?

The box beneath her bed?

She had frantically searched it in hopes of finding all the pictures of her mother, ones that she didn't want to leave behind to be consumed by the fire. But now it seemed that nothing had been consumed by the fire. Daddy had been wrong. Just like with the storm. He had said everything would be fine when she had been worried about how dark everything was getting. And he had made the mistake with the schoolgirl that had forced them to leave the house.

It was unthinkable.

Never before would she have thought he could make so many bad choices.

It was—

Smallwood!

The name was on the computer screen, written beneath the picture of her and Bitsy.

It was also on the policeman's car.

They obviously were in or near Smallwood.

She had known this after seeing a sign while in the van, but now the police seemed to know.

How?

Had it been the cry for help that the schoolgirl had made?

If so, how had everything come together so quickly?

Misty didn't know much about the police—beyond what she saw on Netflix and Amazon and read in her books—but even so, she didn't think the one radio call would have been enough for them to figure all this out and send out bulletins like this full of pictures.

Bitsy?

Had she told them everything?

Is that where she had ended up?

With the police?

The thought twisted her insides, nearly forcing her to the ground beside the open car door where the schoolgirl sat.

Why would Bitsy do that?

Why would she talk to them?

After all the fun they'd had together, and all the things she had bought for them to play with?

Why would she betray her?

It didn't make any sense.

Unless—

She thought about all the times they had pretended that Bitsy was a prisoner being tortured for information. Though Bitsy was tough and could endure quite a bit, there were certain things that would always get her to talk, things that would probably make anyone with boy parts talk.

Had the police done that to her?

Had they burned her?

Had they threatened her with clippers?

No.

Even if the police here in Smallwood had resorted to such measures, they would have had to have a reason to do so, and coming across a frightened girl that was weary from the storm wouldn't have been one.

Bitsy had talked.

She had betrayed them.

Betrayed her.

It was the only logical explanation.

Movement!

On the ground, just beyond where her feet were while leaning in the car.

Misty tugged on the leash, a muffled yelp pleasing her ears.

"I told you to stay still."

The girl didn't reply.

Couldn't reply.

Misty had seen to that with an item she had grabbed from her daddy's bag, one that had been retrieved from the van. It was an item she had worn herself many times while Daddy was working, her mouth trying to get a feel for it to see if she would truly enjoy taking on the schoolgirl slave roll he had envisioned for her all those years ago. It was a future she had not known she was originally destined for, one that she only learned about when trying to find videos of her mother because she had grown curious to hear her voice again, her hope being that Daddy had taken some video of her reading Misty bedtimes stories when she was little, her tiny head resting on her mother's thigh while her mother read from the book, her mother always trying to stay still so that the clank of chain didn't disrupt the tale. They were nice memories, ones that she wanted to relive with more than just the pictures she had. She wanted video. Only there was no video. At least none that she could find. Instead, she saw the scenes of her daddy and mommy together at night, scenes that sometimes made her sad because she didn't think her mommy liked what Daddy was doing to her. Other times they made her laugh, the noises her daddy made when he spurted his gooey spunk amusing.

He wanted to raise me to be one those schoolgirls, yet didn't.

And why did he continue to tell me I was his daughter if I really wasn't?

No answer would ever arrive.

She had spent too much time wondering about it and she had missed her opportunity for an answer.

All because of the schoolgirl and her stupid Apple Watch thing.

And the storm.

How could he make so many poor decisions?

It didn't make sense.

And now Bitsy had betrayed her.

Somehow that was the worst thing of all.

Her daddy dying was bad and something that would take quite a bit of time to recover from, but the reason for it was understandable. They had gotten caught in a storm. With Bitsy, she just didn't get it. How could she do this? And why?

She looked at the picture of the two of them together while thinking about this, a realization that she couldn't simply leave without knowing unfolding. She had to find Bitsy first. She had to know why. Bitsy owed her that much.

After that, if deemed appropriate, she would put an end to her.

With a knotted piece of rope.

Just like her daddy always did with the schoolgirls once he was finished with them.

But not Mommy.

Not after Misty had zapped her all those years ago, the tape she had put over her face to keep her from chewing off her other thumb to get out of the handcuffs once again having caused her to suffocate.

"Look out!" Liz shouted just as Lindsey saw the downed power line pole and hit the brakes.

They didn't see the wire.

It was dangling at headlight level, stretched across the road.

The car slammed into it just as the brakes engaged, the wire forced down beneath the car and lifting them up into the air for a moment before a loud crack echoed, the sound joining their screams, one end shooting toward the ditch on the left, an explosion of sparks shooting up into the air as it hit the standing water within, the other to the right where nothing happened, the car thumping back down onto the pavement.

No one spoke for several seconds, the light from the line that had sparked fading, the wire having danced right out of the water.

"Lindsey," Liz said, her voice nearly a whisper.

Nothing else followed.

Lindsey looked at her for several seconds and then through the windshield, the headlights illuminating the pole that lay across the road, its lines a tangled mess. Her eyes then shifted to the rearview mirror.

Bitsy was looking out the window, nearly touching it.

"Bitsy!" she snapped.

"What?" Bitsy asked, startled.

"Don't touch anything."

"Why?"

"We might be touching a power line."

"Won't the tires keep us safe?" Liz asked.

"I think that's just a myth."

"But they're rubber."

"Google it."

Liz did, Lindsey's phone still in her hand.

Several seconds passed.

"Shit, you're right," Liz said. "It says tires are too thin to offer protection." She scrolled down a bit. "Hey, does the car have a metal frame?"

"I don't know."

"It says that a metal frame inside the car will make it safer than one without."

"What? That doesn't make sense!"

"It says that it will conduct the electricity around the car and into the ground rather than through the car where we are."

"Does it say what we should do? How do we get out?"

"It says we should call nine-one-one and that we should only try to get out of the car as a last—"

Bitsy opened the back door, a door ajar beep echoing.

"Bitsy!" Lindsey snapped.

Nothing happened.

"They should be just across this field," Bitsy said, pointing.

"Bitsy!" Liz warned. "Don't step out."

"But we need to hurry!"

"If you touch the ground while a wire is touching the car, you could get electrocuted."

"Is a wire touching the car?"

"We don't know."

"Does it say how we get out if one is?" Lindsey asked.

"It says we need to jump," Liz said. "And that if we touch the car at any point while touching the ground we could get electrocuted."

"Jesus Christ."

"I think we should just call—"

"Are you coming?" Bitsy asked.

Lindsey and Liz turned.

Bitsy was standing outside of the car, looking in, her hands touching the doorframe as she peered down at them, a look of impatience on her face.

Lindsey shook her head, a statement of *wow* echoing within her mind, and opened her door, quickly looking at the ground to make sure there were no wires where she would be stepping, the light from within the car illuminating everything.

No wires.

She stepped out, eyes coming face-to-face with a wire that was stretched across the street, one that hovered several inches above the car, passing over the rear passenger side and going straight for the—

No!

"Liz!" she screamed while turning. "Don't step out—"

An explosion echoed, the air around them brightening for a moment.

Bitsy shouted.

Liz's body stayed standing for a second, a stunned expression present, and then collapsed.

Lindsey, ducking beneath the wire, hurried around the rear of the car, a horrific smell already hanging in the air.

Liz's body was smoking.

And then flames appeared.

Lindsey didn't know what to do.

She knew CPR. Had been trained at the police station during the yearly program. But this? Liz's body was on fire. *On fire!*

Call the police.

Where was the phone?

Liz had it.

It had been in her hand while in the car.

Now?

She didn't see it anywhere.

Had it actually been in her hand when she stepped out?

If so, it could have ended up anywhere once it fell.

And there was no telling where Liz's was.

Pocket?

Given the smoke and flames that were continuing to grow—

Do it.

Getting down on her hands and knees, Lindsey crawled to her friend, mind sensing the wire above, skin prickling and what was likely nothing more than an imagined charge in the air, and reached into her pockets.

Liz's phone was in the front one but was completely fried, and there was no sign of her own phone.

"Lindsey," Bitsy said.

Lindsey didn't reply, her body crawling back beneath the wire and away from Liz.

"She dead?" Bitsy asked.

Lindsey nodded.

"She was your friend?"

Lindsey nodded again, tears now present.

Bitsy didn't say anything else, simply turning and starting into the field.

Lindsey watched her for several seconds, and then followed.

No fire was visible as they approached Old Grove Street, which was disconcerting and caused Katie to bring the vehicle to a stop before turning.

"What is it?" Gloria asked, concern evident in her voice.

Katie didn't reply right away, her body shifting around to look northward, her mind thinking that the county deputy had likely been heading in that direction when she saw the flames.

Nothing.

Something wasn't right.

She opened her car door.

"What're you doing?"

"Just want to check—"

Burning rubber!

Tires!

The smell was hanging in the area.

A vehicle had burned.

She would never forget the smell, not after all the convoys that had been hit while on the roads in and around Baghdad.

But where was it?

"Officer?"

Katie ignored the girl and took a few steps toward the field alongside Route 7, trying to figure out if she could tell what direction the smell was coming from.

Nothing.

If it were daytime, she would have been able to see the smoke for miles, but at night, the darkness shielded it. And since she couldn't see the flames from where she stood, there didn't seem to be any way to tell—

A gust of wind arrived, and with it came a stronger smell and smoke particles from the vehicle that was burning.

And then she spotted it, the wind having billowed the flames a bit, the glow momentarily visible on the horizon before fading, a glow she would not have seen if she hadn't been looking to the south.

She hurried back to the car.

"Everything okay?" Gloria asked.

"They're south of here," Katie said, shifting the car back into drive.

"But the cemetery is that way."

"I don't think they're at the cemetery."

"Why not?"

Katie didn't reply right away, her focus solely on getting to the next road beyond Old Grove Street and taking a left, her hand grabbing the radio to call in a change of location on where the van likely was, but then hesitating, deciding to wait and make sure she was right.

Headlights!

Abigail saw them out to the west while leaning against the county sheriff car, her eyes blinking several times to make sure they were not a figment of her desperate imagination.

They weren't.

A vehicle was heading this way.

Would they see the fire?

It had died down quite a bit since the initial engulfment, but hadn't gone out, the glow from the flames still visible on the side of the old farmhouse.

If they didn't…

Abigail had already experienced two situations that should have ended her captivity, but each had failed. She wasn't going to let a third opportunity slip by. She needed to do something. She needed to get to the road and signal the occupants of the vehicle. She needed—

The headlights disappeared.

One moment they were on, the next they were gone, almost as if the driver had quickly shut them off.

So as not to be noticed while coming upon the farmhouse?

Hope appeared, her body shifting with anticipation, the movement causing another nasty yank on the leash.

This time Abigail didn't merely yelp, but took hold of the leash and yanked back, the sudden pull causing Misty to cry out as the looped end tugged at her wrist. It didn't do any damage, but it was enough for Misty to get twisted around a bit and then stumble while getting out of the vehicle, an angry shout leaving her lips, followed by a poorly placed kick toward Abigail's leg, one that Abigail caught with her cuffs, wrists quickly looping around and snagging the foot with the short bit of chain.

Misty screamed, pain clinging to the rage that left her lips.

Abigail twisted the foot.

Misty went down, hands fruitlessly scrambling to catch hold of the door to stop her fall, the pistol she had taken from the officer earlier slipping from her fingers and hitting the ground.

Abigail released her foot and tried to get the gun, but a yank on the leash from Misty pulled her throat to the left, her cuffed hands going up to try to stop the sudden assault.

And then Misty was reaching for the gun.

Abigail went for that hand, wrists using the chain to catch Misty's wrist and force it into the ground just as she got hold of the pistol.

The gun went off, Misty's finger having gotten around the trigger, the explosion less than a foot from Abigail's face, her ears feeling a horrific *ping!* and her face peppered with burning particles.

Don't let go!

She kept pressure on the wrist, her own flesh continuing to tear as the cuff edges dug in, her senses reeling from the gun blast, eyes burning and blinded from the tears that were trying to flush everything out.

And then a hand was in her hair, her scalp feeling as if it were being ripped free, a pathetic drool-filled scream leaving her lips.

She couldn't hold the wrist down any longer, cuffed hands releasing the pressure on it as her body went to the left, door catching her shoulder and digging in.

A crack raced through her head as something was smashed into her right ear, skull feeling as if it were splitting open, eyes still blinded, ears not working.

Her body hit the ground, back side down, mud seeming to take hold of her as Misty got on top of her, one arm pressing into her throat while the other held the gun muzzle to her face, the barrel opening searing the skin just beneath her nose, blistering her lip.

Fingers found flesh.

It was one of Misty's breasts.

She squeezed, skin opening beneath her muddy nails.

Misty screamed and pulled back, the pressure leaving her throat.

The weight left her body completely, fingers losing hold of the flesh she had held.

And then there was a tug at her throat.

Misty had backed up and was now pulling at the leash to bring her up.

The mud would not release her, the collar feeling as if it would tear through her neck, leaving her head rolling about.

A kick into her hip didn't help.

Nor did the shout for her to get up.

A second kick landed.

And then a third.

Abigail tried to tell Misty she was stuck but only managed to choke on her own drool.

Misty pulled on the leash some more and then, realizing that wasn't working, reached down and took hold of her blouse with both hands and pulled.

Fabric strained but held, her body popping free of the mud.

Misty released her, letting Abigail roll over.

The drool that was choking her ran out through the ring, as did several odd sounds as her throat tried to regain its composure.

A hand gripped her hair and pulled.

Abigail tried to spring up with the pull, hoping to knock Misty off-balance, but the girl seemed ready for such a thing and simply moved with it, the fist that was locked within her hair keeping her from falling back to the ground after she failed to connect with anything.

Where was the gun?

It obviously wasn't in her hand anymore, not with the chunk of blouse she had grabbed.

Was it in her waistband?

Or had she dropped it somewhere?

As if in answer, the gun was pressed into her back, Misty having had it within reach, it seemed.

"Misty?" a voice said, startling them both.

Katie heard the gunshot as she stepped from her patrol vehicle, her own gun coming free of its holster without her even thinking about pulling it, flames from the fire that she had barely been able to see while standing at the intersection of Route 7 and Old Grove Street now easily spotted up by the farmhouse.

The gunshot had been somewhere to the right of those flames.

Katie pulled her phone free and called Gary.

"We had the wrong area," she said. "They're south of the cemetery, at the old Sanders farm. Get everyone you can down here."

"Roger that," Gary said.

A second later she heard his voice echoing on the radio within the car.

Gloria looked at her, eyes wide.

Katie probably didn't need to say it, but she still instructed the girl to stay in the car.

Gloria nodded.

Katie started toward the farm, gun ready.

No other shots echoed, an eerie calmness settling in.

And then she saw the van.

It was on its side, just as she had pictured it would be, the description from Tina Powell spot-on.

This was it.

This was where it all started, and God willing, it was where it was going to end.

"Bitsy?" Misty said, surprise dominating her voice.

She stood about ten feet away, body just visible within the

darkness of the field, her clothes different, somehow more vibrant than they had been earlier.

"Yes," Bitsy said.

"Where have you—" She shook her head, the events too much for her to comprehend.

"I got lost," Bitsy said. "I tried to find help, but then couldn't find my way back."

Misty nodded and then said, "Get in the car. We need to get out of here."

A figure appeared next to Bitsy.

It was a girl, one who was out of breath.

For a moment, Misty thought it was her mother, the momentary resemblance causing her to do a double take, her eyes going wide, her voice failing as she tried to ask if was her.

"Misty," Bitsy said, voice cheery. "This is Lindsey. She's a schoolgirl I found for your daddy, one that helped me find you. She wants to come live with us."

Lindsey?

Not her mother, the resemblance quickly fading.

Something isn't right.

"Where is he?" Bitsy asked.

"Who?" Misty asked.

"Your daddy?"

"He's dead."

Bitsy's eyes went wide. "But—"

"Get in the car," Misty said, her hands still holding Abigail by the hair, gun pressed into her back.

Bitsy moved toward the car, the new schoolgirl following behind her and holding the back door for her while she got in and then closing it for her, an odd look of satisfaction on her face.

Why would she want to come with us?

None of the other schoolgirls ever did.

"Can you drive?" Misty asked, forcing the questions away.

The schoolgirl looked at her, almost as if she was trying to figure out if the words had been directed her way.

"Can you drive?" Misty repeated, voice more direct.

"Yes," the schoolgirl said with a nod.

"You have an actual driver's license?" Misty asked.

"Yes."

"For how long?"

"Almost a year."

"Good," Misty said and shot Abigail in the lower back.

Lindsey jumped, and then watched in horror as the girl that Misty had been holding by the hair crumpled to the ground, her mind not even registering the noise as a gunshot until she saw the gun in Misty's hand, one that Misty used to motion Lindsey toward the driver seat.

On the ground, the girl moved while letting out an odd sound, her cuffed wrists reaching for something.

Misty pointed the gun toward the fallen girl's head.

"Drop it!" Lindsey shouted, pulling her own gun from her pocket.

"Lindsey, no!" Bitsy cried from the back seat of the county cruiser. It was all she could do since Lindsey had trapped her within, the doors only able to open from the outside.

"Drop it," Lindsey repeated.

Misty stared at the gun, her own still pointed at the wounded girl's head.

"I'm not going to tell you again," Lindsey said, voice trying to mask the terror she felt.

Misty's eyes shifted from the gun up to Lindsey's eyes, nothing but pure hatred present within them.

She's not going to do it.

She's going to try and—

Misty swung the gun around toward Lindsey.

Lindsey pulled the trigger.

The hammer landed with a click.

Fuck!

Misty's gun fired.

Lindsey felt the bullet tear through her left arm, the sensation indescribable.

Another gunshot echoed, only this one was from neither of their guns, the bullet hitting the police car.

"Misty, drop the gun!" a voice cried.

Misty spun and fired toward the voice, and then dove toward the open driver-side door of the police car.

More shots echoed, all of them hitting the car.

"Misty!" Bitsy said from the back seat. "Are you okay?"

Misty didn't reply, her eyes frantically looking around at the various gears and levers within the car.

"Misty!" Bitsy asked again, ducking as another bullet hit the car.

Misty grabbed one of the levers and shifted it and then moved her body forward a bit, the sound of tires spinning on the gravel echoing.

They lurched forward, Bitsy's body slamming back into the seat and then into the door as Misty spun the wheel to turn the car.

"Misty!" Bitsy shouted. "You don't know how to drive!"

"Shut up!" Misty screamed.

Another bullet hit the car.

Misty spun the wheel again, this time throwing Bitsy's body into the center of the back seat, her fingers trying to find something to latch on to. Nothing but the mesh cage between the front and back was available. She threaded her fingers through the tiny squares and held on tight.

They hit a bump, car bouncing.

Bitsy screamed, the sound masking that of bones snapping within the fingers of her left hand.

Several more bumps followed, each one causing more and more pain as Bitsy tried to slip her broken fingers free from the mesh, one of them twisted so badly that it effectually trapped her hand within the squares.

Misty spun the wheel again and hit another bump, the angled finger becoming even more twisted.

"Stop!" Bitsy cried.

Misty ignored her, car finding three more bumps before it hit a wet patch of earth and came to a stop.

"Shots fired!" Katie shouted several times into her radio while running toward where the county patrol vehicle had been before it went tearing off into the field. "Suspects are fleeing northward in a county cruiser through the field toward the Old Grove Cemetery. EMS needed."

Gary acknowledged the request.

Katie came upon the scene.

Lindsey was sitting on the gravel, holding her arm, face white with shock.

The other girl, likely Abigail, was curled on the ground, face filled with pain, hands trying to undo the gag that held her mouth wide open.

"Lindsey," Katie said, flashlight beam searching for the gun the girl had. "It's Katie Adams."

Lindsey looked up at her, eyes blinking.

"Do you know where you are?" Katie asked. She spotted the gun. It was several feet from Lindsey, likely where she had dropped it after being shot.

"Liz's dead," Lindsey said.

Katie didn't know how to reply to that, the statement not what she had been expecting.

"My father?" Lindsey asked.

"I don't know," Katie said and knelt down next to Abigail, her fingers finding and releasing the buckle on the gag. "Paramedics are on the way," Katie said to her.

Abigail gave a nod.

Katie released her wrists from the cuffs.

"Am I going to die?" Abigail asked, a hand reaching for her back.

"Just stay still, okay," Katie said, flashlight pulled free so she could examine the wound, fingers moving the muddy blouse away from the flesh.

The bullet wound was not in a good spot, not if it had hit the liver, though from the look of the blood, that didn't seem to be the case. Unfortunately, that was not the only organ present on the lower right side of the body. She needed help, and fast.

Lindsey did too, though her wound was far from deadly at this point.

It could turn that way though.

"No! No! No!" Misty shouted, tires spinning uselessly as she pressed down upon the gas, car doing nothing but sinking farther and farther into the mud.

The radio came to life, a call for deputies in the northern part of the county to converge upon Smallwood, their help being needed in setting up roadblocks and securing an area to prevent their escape.

Hearing this, Misty tried pressing the gas again, lips urging the vehicle upward and onward through the field.

It didn't budge.

They weren't going anywhere.

Not in this vehicle.

They needed to run.

But where?

In the distance she could see the flashing lights of police

vehicles. They were still quite a ways away but closing in on the area fast. And with the county sending deputies, it wouldn't be long before they were trapped.

"Let's go," she said, opening her door, hand retrieving the pistol from where she had set it.

Bitsy didn't reply, her body hunched over in the back seat behind the wire mesh, one hand on her head while the other was held out before her, the fingers sticking out at odd angles.

Shit.

Bitsy was shutting down.

She did this from time to time when she became overwhelmed, either with pain or emotion, sometimes a combination of both. Once that happened…

Headlights appeared up ahead across the field, one of the lights having been damaged, the muted glow within doing little to brighten anything.

Not a police car.

Or was it?

Would they try to trick her with a car that looked all busted up?

If so, how would they know where to send it?

They wouldn't.

They couldn't.

"Bitsy," she said.

Bitsy didn't respond.

"Bitsy!"

Nothing.

"Bitsy!"

This time the girl looked up at her, and though her eyes were a bit glazed, there was enough life in them for Misty to know that she was still there and would do what was needed to try to get away.

"Come on, we're going to go get those people in that car to help us," Misty said.

Bitsy looked in the direction she was motioning, eyes now

squinting to see through the wire mesh. "That's where the graveyard is."

"Oh?"

"That's near where I was picked up earlier. I thought they were going to help me."

"Maybe these people will. Come on, we need to hurry."

"Do you like my dress?"

"What?"

"My dress. Lindsey let me borrow it. I wanted to look nice when I found you."

"It's very nice, and I want to see more of it once we're in the light, but to do that we have to get moving, so come on."

Bitsy nodded and scooted over toward the door.

Misty stepped out of her own and then shut it behind her.

Bitsy was still in the car.

What was she waiting for?

Voices.

Way off in the distance, but still too close for comfort.

And more emergency lights.

They were heading down the road off to her left, toward the farm.

"Bitsy! Come on!"

Bitsy knocked on the window with her elbow.

What was she doing?

Bitsy knocked again and shouted something.

Misty reached down and opened the door.

"What is wrong with you?" she demanded.

"It doesn't have a door handle."

"Oh," Misty said, stepping back so Bitsy could scoot out, her injured hand held out before her. "Sorry."

Bitsy cocked an eyebrow at her.

"Come on, let's go."

TWELVE

"I think it was a dome light," Tess said.

"A dome light?" Ramsey asked. "In the middle of the field?"

"Yeah."

He shook his head, disappointment growing. "Come on, you were wrong. Nothing's happening here." He pointed toward another set of police lights off in the distance. "We should follow those."

"It's too far south. We picked the girl up out that way." She pointed toward the east with her free hand, the camera in the other. "And that girl said they were going to the cemetery."

"Tess!" he said, voice stern. "No one is here. And if they were, they have moved on, probably out toward where all those police cars are heading. We're too late."

Tess considered this for several seconds and then gave a nod. "Okay, maybe you're—"

"Help us!" a female voice cried.

They both froze, eyes back on the field.

Nothing else was said, but then two figures stumbled from the darkness, one a tiny female police officer, the other a young girl in a dress.

"Where's your car?" the police officer asked.

"My car?" Ramsey asked.

"Yes!" the officer snapped. "I need you to take us to the nearest precinct. I have a girl here that is—"

"Bitsy?" Tess asked.

The girl in the red and white dress looked up.

Shit! It was Bitsy.

Ramsey eyed the police officer, who stared back at him.

"You're not the police," Tess said.

"What? Of course I am, and I need you to"—she aimed a gun at them—"drive us away from here."

"Misty," Bitsy said, one hand holding her other. "These are the storm chasers from earlier, the ones that brought me to the police."

"Are they now?" Misty asked. "Well, this time I think we'll just have them take us as far from here as possible." She eyed the young man. "How does that sound?"

"You can't get away," the girl said. "There are police everywhere."

"Which is why we should hurry," Misty said. She motioned with the gun. "Now move!"

"No."

"Tess!" the young man hissed.

"I will shoot you," Misty warned.

"No, you won't," the girl said.

"I will!"

Misty pulled the trigger, and though she was aiming at the girl, the bullet missed her, the sound of it pinging off a tombstone somewhere between the two echoing.

"Okay, okay," the young man snapped, hands held high. "We'll drive you wherever you want to go."

This time the girl did not protest, the bullet having likely scared her to the point of realizing that Misty was serious. It was either do what she instructed or die.

"The car is this way."

They started walking, the two storm chasers in front, Misty and Bitsy behind, Misty's gun aimed at their backs, a sudden question on how many bullets there were inside of it coming to mind.

"This is where Lindsey's mom is buried," Bitsy said.

"What?" Misty asked.

"The schoolgirl you shot, the one that tricked me."

"Oh."

Up ahead, one of the storm chasers said something, the other shaking his head.

"No talking!" Misty snapped.

Neither said anything else, the only sound that of their feet on the gravel that wormed its way through the graveyard, which Misty hoped would end soon so they could get into the car she had seen pulling in from the field.

In the distance, more emergency lights appeared, one turning onto the road the graveyard was on.

No, no, no.

It stopped about half a mile away and just waited.

They're setting up a perimeter.

Just like on TV.

"Now!" the girl up ahead shouted and then darted to the left while ducking down and disappearing behind a row of tombstones, all while the young man stood frozen in place, body turning toward Misty, a plea for her not to shoot leaving his lips.

Misty fired toward where the girl had bolted, one of the bullets hitting a tombstone, the other simply flying off into the night.

"Misty," Bitsy said, her good hand pointing toward where more emergency lights had appeared, these ones to the left. "They might hear."

Fuck!

They were running out of time.

She turned toward the young man, gun aimed at him.

"Please no!" he said. "Don't shoot me!"

Rather than shoot, she hurried forward and grabbed him by his shirt, hand twisting him around so that he would continue forward with the gun pressed into his back. "Take us to the car, now!"

"O-okay!"

Misty glanced toward where the girl had disappeared, her eyes unable to spot her anywhere among the dark tombstones. It didn't matter though. As long as this one could drive, they would be fine. But only if they could get onto the road and away from the area before the police closed off everything.

Waving her flashlight in a slow but steady arc over her head, Katie signaled the first patrol vehicle that neared the scene, one that took several seconds to find the gravel driveway that led up to the farmhouse and turned toward them.

Two minutes later, a part-time officer named Kevin Carter was on the scene, his eyes wide, face pale at the sight of Abigail. No doubt about it, this was his first-ever gunshot wound.

"Carter!" Katie said, voice calm but firm. "Get your kit."

He blinked twice and then nodded, hurrying around to the trunk of his cruiser.

"She has a bullet wound to the lower back, no exit wound, which means the round either fragmented within or got lodged into a bone somewhere, possibly a pelvic one if it was fired at a downward angle. The blood is clean, but moving her too much without a board could rip something that is just hanging together by a thread, so make sure she stays still until the paramedics get here."

"What're you going to do?" he asked, panic returning.

"They headed off into the field, which means they will bog down." Katie was certain of this. "I'm going after them."

"No, no, you need to stay here and help me with them, and wait for backup."

"Backup?" she asked. "We'll be lucky if we get enough manpower out here to simply block off all the roads, which won't do diddly-squat if they're on foot and simply leave the field."

"But—"

"Help them," Katie said and then, without another word, turned and headed into the field.

Tess's frustration toward her older brother for not bolting when she had shouted to do so was at a level that was difficult to shift her focus from. But shift it she did, her eyes trying to keep the three in sight as they headed toward where the car was, all while not alerting them to the fact that she was following, her hope being that they thought she was simply running for dear life, brother forgotten.

It's what you should have done.

Probably what Ramsey would have done, the spineless prick.

No.

He would not have left her behind with these two.

And she would not leave him behind.

And once they reach the car?

She had no idea.

Right now the important thing was to keep after them, so that when they did reach the car she could hopefully act, the camera that she still carried ready to be brought down on the girl's head, the weight enough that one solid blow would likely end things.

If she got close enough.

And if the gun was not pointed at Ramsey's back.

She wants him to drive.

That means him getting in the front seat.

The girl would have no choice but to step away at that point, likely getting in the back seat, gun momentarily away from his back.

That would be the moment.

The only moment.

She would have to make it count.

"Gary, they're on foot," Katie said, lungs heaving from her run, eyes searching the ground with her flashlight to see if she could spot any tracks that showed which direction they had headed in once they left the car.

"Where?" Gary asked, voice heavy with static.

"In the middle of the field between 7 and Harris, with Old Grove to the north and the Sanders farm to the south." She found the tracks. They were headed northeast, toward the cemetery. "We need eyes on these roads now. Crossroad checkpoints are no good if they emerge from the middle of a field."

"We're getting people there as fast as we can," Gary said.

It's not fast enough! she shouted to herself. Aloud, "I know. What's the ETA on the paramedics for Abigail and Lindsey?"

"Ten minutes."

Shit! "Okay." Nothing she could say or do would make them get there any sooner. "I'll let you know when I have them."

"Katie," Gary said. "Be careful. This girl is…" He simply let his voice fade.

Katie didn't reply, her hand hooking the radio back onto her chest so that she could hold her flashlight in one hand and her pistol in another.

· · ·

Ramsey was scared shitless, the barrel opening that was pressed into his back feeling as if it were as wide as a cannon and ready to blow his insides all over the place.

Making things worse, police were descending upon the area from all directions, their lights and sirens everywhere. Normally that would be a good thing, but when a gun was pressed into one's back, perspectives changed. If the police blocked them in, what would stop the girl from shooting him? She would likely get shot in return, but in her mind that might be better than any of the other options.

And then there was Tess.

She was out there somewhere, and while he hoped she was simply running as fast as she could toward one of the sets of flashing lights, he was pretty sure she was doing just the opposite.

He was fucked.

Either the police would get him killed, or his little sister would.

It was as simple as that.

Bitsy was worried. And in pain. But it was the worry that dominated her thoughts, all because she could tell that Misty was scared and didn't know what to do. How she knew this, she didn't know, but know it she did and because of that, she too was scared.

But maybe everything would end up okay.

The storm chaser guy could drive, so that was good, and once they were in his car, they could leave.

But where?

Could Misty really find them a new place to live?

The Daddy-man could. He was an adult and knew how to do things like that. Misty didn't. She wasn't an adult. And neither was Bitsy. She was just a doll, one that had boy parts.

But maybe the storm chaser would know how to find a house for them.

It seemed like he was an adult.

Not as old of an adult as the Daddy-man was, but still an adult, which meant he probably knew how to do many things that they didn't.

"No, no," Misty said.

Bitsy turned and followed Misty's gaze to the left.

A new police car had appeared on the horizon, one that was nearing the graveyard.

Would it pass it and join the other that had parked itself off to the right, or turn into the tiny lot?

It turned into the tiny lot, passing beneath the stone entrance that Bitsy had passed through earlier in the day.

"Where's your car?" Misty demanded.

"It's—it's—"

"*Where?*"

A spotlight came on before he could answer, one that speared the red car with its brightness.

"Is that it?" Misty asked, voice sounding off.

"Y-y-yes," he said.

The spotlight shifted, the beam now coming their way.

"Down!" Misty snapped.

They all went down, the beam passing over them.

"Misty?" Bitsy asked. "What're we going to do?"

Misty didn't answer.

The police car that had appeared up ahead changed things.

For better or worse, Tess didn't know, but one thing was now clear: if that police car stayed where it was, Ramsey would not be driving the two away in his battered Kia, which meant he might now be considered useless.

Tess had to do something.

But what?

No answer appeared.

It all depended on what the girl did.

If she simply shot him and ran, there would be nothing Tess could do, not at ten feet, not at five feet. Nothing. Not with the gun pressed into his back.

But if she tried to get away on foot, sneaking away from the police in the darkness, Tess could keep following.

It would likely be one thing or the other.

Wrong.

"Bitsy!" Misty hissed as Bitsy stood up. "What are you doing?"

"I'm going to distract them for you."

"What? No."

"It's the only way. They will take me into the police car and leave, and then you can get away in his."

"No."

"Yes. I have to."

"Please. Don't leave me again."

Bitsy stopped, crouching back down, and looked at her.

"I need you," Misty added.

"What?" Bitsy asked.

"You're all I have left." Tears appeared. "Please!"

"You really still want me?" Bitsy asked.

"Of course I do," Misty said. She wiped away her tears.

"Even after I acted like a boy?"

"That wasn't your fault," Misty said. "I made you do it."

"I liked it."

Misty smiled. "I did too."

"But then you got mad at me."

"I know. I'm sorry."

Bitsy stared at her.

"That won't happen again," Misty said. "I promise."

Bitsy smiled and then put her arms around Misty. "I love you."

"I love you too."

Ramsey felt the gun move away from his back and though he wasn't positive that it was no longer aiming at him, he decided to take a chance and thrust himself backward against the two, his right foot pushing off against a tombstone.

A cry of surprise echoed as they all toppled backward.

A gunshot followed.

His leg burned.

A second gunshot echoed, this one bouncing off a tombstone.

Bitsy screamed.

The third gunshot went off somewhere into the darkness.

Katie heard the gunshots and instinctively hunched over while moving along the tombstones, her eyes able to see the flashing lights of a police cruiser near the entrance of the cemetery, its spotlight swinging around to find the gunshots.

On the radio, a voice called for help.

It was Officer Nick Harris.

He urged everyone to come to the cemetery, his lips actually using the word "haste" in his plea.

Katie lifted the radio to her lips and advised that she was on the south side of the cemetery, making her way toward the gunshots.

Once that was stated, she turned off the radio so that its cackle would not give her away as she approached.

Ears ringing and leg burning where it had been hit, Ramsey went for the gun, his hands finding it right away and taking hold, the barrel singeing the fingers of his left hand as they closed upon it, while his right found Misty's wrist and squeezed.

Screams echoed.

Some were his, some were hers, the words "Let go!" clearly audible.

And then an arm was around his throat, choking him.

Bitsy!

She had grabbed him from behind.

Teeth sank into his jaw.

Jesus!

He tried hitting Bitsy with his elbow but couldn't, her body clinging to him as he swung back and forth, his hands trying to keep a grip on the gun while also dislodging her.

A knee smashed into his groin.

All thought but the pain left him, his fingers falling from the gun as he lost his balance.

Another screamed erupted, this one different than all the rest.

The spotlight speared them.

In it, Ramsey saw a figure looming over Misty, something in hand over her head, just as Misty brought the gun around toward his face.

The object came down with a nasty crunch.

The gun went off.

He felt the bullet singe his arm and then hit something behind him.

Bitsy gasped, her arm loosening from his throat, teeth gone.

Another beam of light appeared, this one from a flashlight.

It blinded him for a moment and then shifted over to where Misty was kneeling against a tombstone, forehead on it, blood oozing from beneath her hair.

Tess stepped up behind her, something raised over her head.

"Tess, no!" Ramsey cried, his voice doing little to penetrate the air.

Tess didn't hit her again, her hands lowering the object after a few seconds.

Ramsey sighed.

And then froze as he felt the gun barrel pressed into his temple.

"Bitsy," Katie said. "It's all over. Put the gun down."

Bitsy did not reply, anxiety and terror dominating her face, her body encircled by light from both the patrol vehicle spotlight and Katie's flashlight.

"Please," Katie continued. "We can help you. And Misty."

"You're lying!" Bitsy spat, voice quivering.

"No, Bitsy. No one is lying to you. We will help you. We want to help you. But first you need to put the gun down."

"You killed Misty!"

"Bitsy, she's not dead. But she is hurt and needs help, and we can't help her until you put that gun down."

Bitsy looked around, eyes frantic.

A second police car arrived at the cemetery, a third nearing, lights flashing, sirens echoing.

Katie considered her chances of hitting Bitsy if she fired, but then quickly dismissed the option. She was adequate with a pistol, but nowhere near the level of a Hollywood hero who could simply take out a hostage taker in such a situation as if it were second nature. Shit, even if allowed to take several seconds to aim, she might still miss.

Plus, she didn't want to kill Bitsy.

Or Misty.

The two were victims.

They might not see themselves that way, but that didn't change the fact that they were. The only one who she wanted to kill had already been taken out by the storm.

"Bitsy," a calm voice said. "Please let him go."

Katie did not turn to see the source, but knew it was Tess.

"No!" Bitsy cried. "You hurt her!"

"I had to," Tess said, voice still calm. "She was going to kill my brother."

Bitsy's face scrunched up as she tried to process this.

She also shifted herself a bit, the spotlight from the patrol vehicle revealing that the left sleeve of her dress was covered in blood.

"Bitsy, your arm is bleeding," Katie said.

"I'm fine," Bitsy said.

"It looks bad. And painful. And Misty is hurt too. We need to get you both to the hospital."

"Just let us go."

"We can't."

"Please! We need to leave."

"Where?" Katie asked.

"We're going to find a new house."

"How? You can't drive and you have no money to buy one."

"The Daddy-man has money. And Misty has gift cards. We can use those."

"That Daddy-man is dead," Katie said. "And Misty won't be able to use any of his money until things are settled, so you might as well let us help you until then."

Bitsy didn't reply.

"Bitsy, I know your arm hurts. I have been shot before. We can make it feel better."

"I'm fine!" Bitsy spat.

"I know you're tough. I've seen the pictures of what has been done to you. But if you don't let us help you, this will only get worse and then you'll get sick and die. If that happens, Misty will be all alone once she gets better. And she will get better. We can help her."

Bitsy's face changed.

"But she'll need your help to do that. Your strength."

"You'll really help her?" Bitsy asked.

"Yes."

"You promise?"

"Yes."

Bitsy thought about this.

"We'll help both of you, but first you have to set the gun down."

Bitsy didn't reply, nor did she set the gun down.

Katie didn't know how much longer they could keep this up, not with Misty having been struck senseless with a blow to the head and Bitsy bleeding.

And if she accidentally squeezed the trigger…

Or purposely.

"Bitsy," Katie said. "I'm going to put my gun away, okay."

Bitsy didn't reply.

Katie put her gun in her holster.

"Now I'm going to step forward and you're going to hand me that gun."

"No."

"Yes."

"No."

"Yes." She stepped forward. First just one step and then another and another.

Bitsy backed up, but only by one step.

"Bitsy, please, it's getting late. The Daddy-man is dead, Misty is hurt, and you're bleeding. It's time we put everything away."

No response.

"If you don't, Misty will die."

Bitsy shifted her gaze toward where Misty was prone on the ground.

"Earlier you wanted us to help her, and now that we want to help, you're not letting us. If she dies, it will be your fault."

Tears started to well in Bitsy's eyes.

"Please. Let us help her." Katie took another step. "Let us help you." Another step. "And then once you're both better, you can be together again." Her final step. "All you have to do is hand me that gun." She held out her hand.

Bitsy shifted her eyes from Katie's to the open palm.

Ramsey, obviously terrified, stared at it as well, the smell of piss from his wetting himself strong.

"Give me the gun," Katie repeated.

Bitsy hesitated for another second and then said, "You promise to help her?"

"I promise."

Bitsy handed her the gun.

Katie vomited all over a tombstone, the furious screams as Bitsy was put into a police car echoing within her mind as she leaned over it.

Bitsy thought Katie had lied to her, likely because she was being taken to the hospital in the back of a patrol vehicle, while Misty went in one of the ambulances that had finally arrived from Smith's Grove, strapped to a gurney. Truth was, Bitsy was right. The idea that she and Misty were simply going to be patched up and allowed to live out the rest of their lives together was far-fetched, especially if the DA decided to file charges. And even if the DA didn't file charges, they most likely wouldn't find themselves sharing some sort of home and living out their days together. No. Years and years of therapy and time spent in special wards, support groups, and then, depending on their ages and progress, and whether or not family could be found, foster homes. Today had ended one journey and started them on the path of another, one that would be long and trying.

And the man responsible would never be held responsible.

She shook her head, a lack of satisfaction present.

"Sorry about your camera," Tess said.

Ramsey looked at her for a moment and let out a small laugh.

Tess grinned.

"I forgive you on account of you having saved my life," he said.

"Okay, good, so that means you won't make me pay for it then?"

"Well, I wouldn't go that far…"

His smile faded, his eyes going toward the window of the hospital room.

"You okay?" she asked, more serious.

"I don't know."

Tess didn't reply to that, mostly because she didn't know how.

"You talk to Mom?" he asked.

"Yeah, she's completely confused. I don't think I was able to *articulate* the situation very well."

Ramsey let out another small laugh, though the smile did not return, his eyes still on the window.

"She hasn't woken up yet," Tess said.

"Who?" Ramsey asked, turning back toward her.

"That girl, Misty."

"Oh."

"At the time I wanted to kill her, so I hit her as hard as I could, but now…" She shook her head, unsure how she felt.

"Tess, you did what you had to do."

Tess scrunched up her face, trying to keep the emotion at bay.

"You need to understand that," Ramsey added.

"I know, I do. But still…"

Ramsey didn't say anything else.

"Pretty fucked up, isn't it?"

This time a smile accompanied Ramsey's chuckle. "Yeah."

"You were right," Lindsey said, an image of Liz's body on the ground, smoking, refusing to leave her mind. "We should have simply called the police."

Gloria didn't reply to that.

"All I managed to do was get her killed, that kidnapped schoolgirl shot in the back, and myself shot in the shoulder."

Gloria simply nodded.

"I didn't even get a shot off."

"You did what you thought you had to do," Gloria said.

This time it was Lindsey who didn't respond, mostly because she knew what Gloria said wasn't true. Several times while driving toward the cemetery and then beyond it, and while crossing the field, she had told herself she was being an idiot, yet for some reason she had persisted.

"And now there's nothing you can do to fix it," Gloria added. She then stood up and left.

Lindsey didn't ask where she was going. She knew the visit wasn't one of offering support and comfort. Gloria had simply wanted to see that she was okay, acknowledge it, give condolences about her father, and leave. Lindsey's statements on how she knew she had made a mistake wouldn't change anything. If Liz had still been alive, maybe they would, but with her dead, they wouldn't.

Katie's mother suggested she come home and get some rest,

but Katie said she still had work to do. It was the truth, though none of it would get done. Not that night. Not while she sat in the waiting area in the hospital, trying to drum up the courage to try to talk to Bitsy. She wanted to tell her that Misty would be joining her in the room she was in, but she knew Bitsy wouldn't believe her. It was true though. Misty would be joining her once she could be moved from the ICU, not out of any sort of compassion for the two but simply because they didn't have many rooms available at the hospital, what with all the injuries from the storm, and even fewer rooms for those who needed to be guarded.

"Hey," a voice said.

Katie looked up. It was Tess.

"How's Ramsey doing?" Katie asked.

"He fell asleep. I helped. Told the nurse he was having some pain but wouldn't admit it and that he needed to be calmed down. Was hoping they'd give him the Demerol in pill form so I could swipe it, but it was a shot of something, so…" She shrugged.

Katie smiled.

"That was pretty amazing, you talking her into giving up the gun," Tess said.

Katie gave her a second smile and then sighed.

"You want a soda? I want one. Let's go see what they have."

"I'm good," Katie said.

Tess frowned.

"But I'll come with you to get one."

The frown disappeared. "Thanks."

They headed to the end of the hall to the stairwell and started down it.

"So what happens now?" Tess asked somewhere between the second and first floors.

"I have no idea," Katie admitted.

"Do you think they'll be okay? Bitsy and Misty. I mean, how does one recover from shit like that?"

"I don't know."

"It's fucked up."

"That it is."

Nothing else was said, the two eventually finding the cafeteria, which was closed but had a row of vending machines.

HEADLINES

From the Champaign-Urbana *Online Journal*, April 22, 2017

Ninth Body Found Buried on College Professor's Property

From the *Daily Happenings: A Local Girl's Thoughts* blog, April 24, 2017

No Charges Yet—DA Needs to Get Off Her Ass!

From the *Daily Happenings: A Local Girl's Thoughts* blog, April 25, 2017

DA Feels Psychotic Daughter of Psychotic Serial Killer Is a Victim!

. . .

From the *Daily Happenings: A Local Girl's Thoughts* Facebook
page, April 26, 2017

Share If You Feel Misty *Last Name Censored by FB Guide-
lines* Should Be in Jail

SUMMER 2017

"*Honey, wake up.*"

Misty opened her eyes, confused.

"We have to go," Crystal said, right hand shaking her awake.

"Go?" Misty asked, rubbing at her eyes.

"Downstairs," Crystal said. "We have another test they want to do."

"*Nooo*," Misty whined, hand gently covering her inner arm, which had turned yellow from the repeated needle pricks the other day. "They promised they were all done."

"It's okay. Today there will be no needles. They're just going to put some gel on your tummy and then rub it."

"Oh?"

"And then afterwards we can get you some yummy soup and some juice, and then if you're feeling up to it, you can go back to the children's home. I think I overheard someone say that tonight there was going to be a movie in the activity room."

Misty shook her head.

She didn't like the activity room.

The others were mean to her.

Especially Nancy.

She was the worst.

But Barb was bad too.

And Chris.

And Britney.

And Suzi.

They all were.

She wanted Bitsy.

But Bitsy wasn't here.

She had been at the hospital after Misty had woken up. They had even been in the same room together. But then one day some people had taken Bitsy to meet some other people, and she had never come back. Misty hadn't even been able to say goodbye.

"Speaking of your tummy, how does it feel this morning?" Crystal asked.

"It's okay," Misty said, caressing it.

"No more throwing up?"

"No."

"That's good," Crystal said with a smile and then guided her from the bed toward the wheelchair that was waiting.

"Can I walk?"

"If you feel up to it."

"I do."

"Okay."

Not much else was said as they headed down the hallway toward the elevator.

Crystal held her hand during this.

It was not a friendly grip, its firmness contradicting the rosy smile she always presented when taking Misty to the various rooms where they did the tests. The nurse with the needle the other day had been the same way, and Misty had a feeling all the pricks had been on purpose rather than misses. Crystal had told her that was nonsense and it was sometimes difficult to get at a vein to draw blood, especially when someone had skinny arms like hers, but Misty didn't believe her.

"Can I see?" Misty asked.

The two ignored her.

"Please?" Misty asked.

One looked at her for a moment and then went back to looking at the screen.

The other didn't acknowledge her at all, simply kept holding the device against her tummy, the gooey gel they had put down cold but not painful like the needles had been.

The soup was cold by the time they brought it to her and didn't have any crackers, but the juice was good. She drank that while considering what to do with the soup. A part of her wanted to throw it on Crystal when she came back, but then she realized that since it was cold, it wouldn't hurt her, just make her messy. That wasn't worth whatever punishment they would deliver. Instead, she drank it quickly because it was gross when cold and then moved her tray away and looked for the TV clicker.

They didn't have Netflix or Amazon here, but sometimes there were other things to watch, which was good.

Today there wasn't.

And she didn't have a book to read.

She had asked for one, but no one would bring any. They didn't come out and say no, but they gave answers that made her realize it wouldn't happen.

Seconds ticked by.

She put a hand on her belly, fingers trying to see if she could feel the baby kicking.

She couldn't.

She would ask Dr. Samantha how long it would take

before she could feel such things. Dr. Samantha was nice and would tell her, though then she would also likely start asking about her daddy and if he had touched her down there.

He hadn't, but it seemed like Dr. Samantha never believed her.

None of them did.

The only one that ever touched her down there was Bitsy.

But could the baby really be hers?

They had only been pretending that she was a daddy. It hadn't been real. But maybe that didn't matter.

She would have to ask Dr. Samantha about that as well.

HEADLINES

From the *East River Times*, August 26, 2017

Parents of 2002 Kidnapping Victim Seek Custody of Granddaughter

From the *Smith's Grove Post*, September 2, 2017

Pregnant? Unnamed Staff Worker's Shocking Claim

From the *LGBT Online*, September 27, 2017

Opinion: Parents of "Bitsy Cole" Are Exploiting Daughter on Talk Show Circuit

From the *St. Louis Chronicle*, September 30, 2017

. . .

Online Harassment of Kidnapping Victim Following Talk Show Appearances Continues Amid Gender Identity Confusion

From the *Daily Happenings: A Local Girl's Thoughts* blog, October 1, 2017

Put Some Pants on HIM!

CPSIA information can be obtained
at www.ICGtesting.com
Printed in the USA
LVHW031039300121
677871LV00005B/32